P9-DVO-184

HIGH PRAISE FOR COTTON SMITH!

"Cotton Smith is one of the finest of a new breed of writers of the American West."

—Don Coldsmith

"Cotton Smith's is a significant voice in the development of the American Western."

—Loren D. Estleman

"In just a few years on the scene, Cotton Smith has made a strong mark as a Western writer of the new breed, telling it like it was."
—Elmer Kelton, Seven-time Spur Award–winning author of *The Day It Never Rained*

"Cotton Smith is another modern writer with cinematic potential. Grand themes, moral conflicts and courage are characteristic of his fiction."

—*True West Magazine*

"These days, the traditional Western doesn't get much better than Cotton Smith."

—*Roundup Magazine*

"Fans of the Western genre will find much to enjoy."
—*Longmont Times-Call*

"Acclaimed novelist Cotton Smith is a Western legend."

—*Recorded Books Direct*

MORE PRAISE FOR COTTON SMITH!

"Hats off to Cotton Smith for keeping the spirit of the West alive in today's fiction. His plots are as twisted as a gnarled juniper, his prose as solid as granite, and his characters ring as true as jinglebobs on a cowboy's spurs."

—Johnny D. Boggs, Wrangler and
Spur Award–winning author of *Camp Ford*

"When it came to literature, middle-age had only three good things to show me: Patrick O'Brian, Larry McMurtry and Cotton Smith."

—Jay Wolpert, screenwriter of
The Count of Monte Cristo
and *Pirates of the Caribbean*

"From his vivid descriptions of a prairie night to his hoof-pounding action scenes, Cotton Smith captures the look and feel of the real West."

—Mike Blakley, Spur Award–winning
author of *Summer of Pearls*

"Cotton Smith turns in a terrific story every time."

—*Roundup Magazine*

TWO AGAINST ONE

As he strode onto the sidewalk, an anxious Jeremiah came forward with the Ranger's wolf-dog, Chance, at his side.

The boy started to say something, but Ranger Time Carlow saw a reflection from a dark figure across the street beside the general store. A gun!

"Jeremiah, get inside. Now!" Carlow drew his hand-carbine. "Down, Chance. Down, boy!"

The boy hesitated and Carlow shoved him down, and stepped in front of him. Chance dove on top of the boy.

Orange flame spat from the figure—and from a second-story window to his left.

Both shots missed; one splintered the sidewalk; the other slammed into Mrs. Jacobs's store front. Carlow leaped off the sidewalk and to his left, to direct the gunfire away from the boy. He held his gun butt against his thigh with both hands and fired, levered and fired again, then again and again.

Other *Leisure* books by Cotton Smith:

RETURN OF THE SPIRIT RIDER
THE WAY OF THE WEST (Anthology)
BLOOD OF BASS TILLMAN
BLOOD BROTHERS
STANDS A RANGER
DEATH RIDES A RED HORSE
DARK TRAIL TO DODGE
PRAY FOR TEXAS
BEHOLD A RED HORSE
BROTHERS OF THE GUN
SPIRIT RIDER
SONS OF THUNDER
WINTER KILL

DEATH MASK

Cotton Smith

LEISURE BOOKS NEW YORK CITY

To Don Coldsmith for his friendship and guidance

A LEISURE BOOK®

July 2009

Published by

Dorchester Publishing Co., Inc.
200 Madison Avenue
New York, NY 10016

Copyright © 2009 by Cotton Smith

All rights reserved. No part of this book may be reproduced or transmitted in any form or by any electronic or mechanical means, including photocopying, recording or by any information storage and retrieval system, without the written permission of the publisher, except where permitted by law.

ISBN 10: 0-8439-6200-3
ISBN 13: 978-0-8439-6200-0
E-ISBN: 978-1-4285-0703-6

The name "Leisure Books" and the stylized "L" with design are trademarks of Dorchester Publishing Co., Inc.

Printed in the United States of America.

10 9 8 7 6 5 4 3 2 1

If you purchased this book without a cover you should be aware that this book is stolen property. It was reported as "unsold and destroyed" to the publisher and neither the author nor the publisher has received any payment for this "stripped book."

Visit us on the web at www.dorchesterpub.com.

DEATH MASK

Chapter One

Texas Ranger Aaron "Thunder" Kileen rose in one smooth motion, belying his huge size. "Here they be comin'. Beards they be wearin' to mask their treacherous souls. Aye, an' fine hosses they be ridin'. Like always."

He pointed from the second-story window of the San Antonio hotel where he and his Ranger nephew had been waiting.

"Where?" Ranger Time Carlow scrambled to his feet, pushing aside the fuzziness of rereading his last letter from Ellie Beckham. He'd read it at least ten times.

He had met the young widow three years ago in his hometown. The rest of her letters were carefully folded in his saddlebags. He hadn't written as often; the last had been six months ago, he thought. Another unsent letter was still in his gear. Somewhere.

"Pulling up in front of the bank, they be. Do ye see?"

"Yeah, I see them. Let's get the bastards."

Sweet thoughts of Ellie were pushed into the corner of Carlow's mind for later. He shoved his chair away and yanked on the permanently pushed-up brim of his Stetson in the same motion. Long dark hair danced along his shoulders. A trim mustache and expressive eyebrows reinforced his combative appearance—and nature. Smaller than his uncle, the young Ranger was deceptively strong, with a solidly built chest, arms heavy with hard-earned muscle, and a natural inclination to fight.

The superstitious Kileen grabbed his Henry rifle and headed for the door. He glanced at the lone candle on the dresser. It had gone out. That meant someone would die.

Shaking off his shiver, he said, "Be rememberin', me son. Captain wants them alive. 'Tis the best chance of gettin' back the money they be stealin'."

"Let's hope they got the same report." Carlow grinned, a step behind him. "Shall we put on our badges?"

"Aye. There might be more, so be keepin' your attention. Some be sayin' there be a gang." The big Irish Ranger waved his huge paw of a right hand, scarred from many past fistfights.

His ruddy face was weary from waiting. A former bare-knuckle prizefighter, the highly superstitious lawman was dressed, as usual, in a well-worn three-piece tweed suit. He thought it made him look like a gentleman; no Ranger dared comment otherwise. The material and buttons had fought a long and losing battle with his thick chest and arms. He looked even bigger in his dust-laden, high-crowned black hat. An old bullet hole in the upper crease had long since been forgotten. Across his coat was a heavy bullet belt with holstered Colt and sheathed bowie knife.

As he moved, the big Irishman felt in his coat pocket for his own badge, reaching past an acorn and a tiny pouch of dirt from Ireland itself, a small token of the green isle that his late sister—Carlow's mother—had brought with her to the new land. It, too, held great powers, he had decided. Carlow had a smilar pouch, but he kept it in his saddlebags. At least, it had been there the last time Kileen had looked.

Stopping, Kileen yanked free his badge and pushed it onto his coat lapel as he moved.

Hurrying from the room, Carlow reached into one vest pocket, then the other, to find the star placed there among extra cartridges, pieces of hard candy, a silver watch and chain, an acorn given to him by Kileen for luck, and two tiny flat stones, darkly stained with long-ago blood, a memory possession. He pinned the badge on his coat lapel without slowing down.

His hand dropped to the guns at his waist. From his right hip, he drew a special cut-down Winchester, shortened in stock and barrel, and cocked it easily with the enlarged circular lever. It was worn as a handgun in an unusual holster of rawhide bands and thick leather backing tied to his leg. The weapon provided the quick handling of a revolver with the impact of a rifle. On the shortened walnut stock was carved a Celtic marking, an ancient war symbol for victory.

He carried a short-barreled Colt on the left side of his gunbelt; its walnut handle tilted forward for a right-handed draw.

At the doorway, Kileen tapped the wood frame three times with his rifle. For luck. Carlow smiled; he didn't agree with his uncle's superstitions. Carlow turned toward the far wall where his wolf-dog companion, Chance, waited for direction. Carlow had sneaked him in and out of the hotel.

"Come on, Chance, we've got work to do."

The great beast barked and was beside him in an instant.

Together, the threesome charged down the stairs of the Gleason Hotel, across the street from the First

National Bank. In the restaurant next to the bank waited two more Rangers, Julian Mirabile and Pig Deconer. The younger of the two lawmen, Pig Deconer, had insisted on eating while they waited. Food was his great passion.

Carlow took the lead, bounding down two steps at a time. Two eagle pinfeathers, dangling from the top of his Kiowa leggings, responded to the movement and fluttered their understanding. Large-roweled Mexican spurs sang their own reaction. Jiggling in rhythm was the bone handle of a Comanche war knife, barely visible above the right legging.

At the base of the stairway, a startled businessman watched them advance, unsure of what he should do.

"Step aside, like a good fellow. 'Tis Ranger business ye be watchin','" Kileen bellowed. His thick mustache was graying, but the rest of him spoke of a massive fighting man. His nose had been broken twice and his ears were definitely cauliflowered.

The businessman gladly moved away, bringing his hand to his mouth in fascination.

The Rangers had been in town for two days, posing as cattlemen so no townsman would inadvertently warn the bank robbers or do something foolish. It was an unusual assignment and an unusually high number of Rangers were involved. Fellow Rangers—Tanneman Rose and his younger brother, Hillis—were expected to make an attempt to rob the bank, as they had apparently held up five others over the past two years.

Kileen had been reluctant to accept the responsibility. Tanneman was certain he had lived a previous life as a gifted shaman in Persia many centuries ago. That made the superstitious Irishman uneasy.

"Come on, Chance. We've got a Persian shaman to

arrest," Carlow called over his shoulder and grinned again. It was an easy, confident smile that said everything was going to be all right. It was a smile Kileen loved to see, even when he knew it wasn't always so.

"Be ye rememberin' Tanneman Rose be a dreamer," Kileen cautioned as he stutter-stepped and almost lost his balance. "He be seein' the future, he be." Kileen steadied himself with his outstretched left arm against the wall. His rifle remained in his right fist at his side. To himself, he muttered, " 'Tis the comin' again to this earth that does it. Friend of the black spider he be." The grizzly bear of a man who was Kileen studied the young man he had raised into a fine Ranger.

The discovery of criminals in their special ranks had the four state lawmen on edge. Especially Kileen. Reincarnation was something mystical, something beyond the mind's ability to comprehend. He wished this confrontation could be avoided. Still, an order was an order and he intended to follow out the captain's wishes.

Carlow had no problem with the task. First, he didn't believe in reincarnation. Second, he had never liked the Rose brothers. Never trusted them. He couldn't tell why he felt that way, only that he did. Now his feelings were about to be proven correct. He was also worried about how the brothers would react to being arrested. Tanneman Rose was cruel as well as accurate with any weapon. Carlow had seen him shoot down surrendered outlaws, simply because he didn't want to be troubled with taking them to the nearest settlement. His younger brother tried too hard to make Tanneman proud of him. That, too often, meant similar violence.

The Rangers and the wolf-dog hit the lobby floor

and became aware, for the first time, that a handful of people in the lobby were watching them. The customers' faces were a mixture of fascination and fear.

"Everything will be fine, folks," Carlow said. "Just stay inside."

A woman saw Chance and whimpered, "My God, that's a wolf, Jacob! A wolf."

Acting like he hadn't heard, Carlow headed for the hotel front door.

The frightened woman's husband shushed her and guided her toward the far end of the lobby.

"How do you want to play this, Thunder?" Carlow asked, already knowing the answer. He always referred to his uncle by his nickname, earned years ago as a bare-knuckle prizefighter back east. His fellow Rangers called him "Old Thunder," but not to his face.

"Wait. We must let them do the dastardly deed, then we arrest the blaggards. Be lookin' for their gang." Kileen was breathing hard from their rapid descent. "I be hopin' Tanneman has not dreamed of our plan."

Ignoring the comment, Carlow opened the door a crack, enough so they could see the street and the two riders pulling alongside the bank's hitching rack.

Kileen couldn't help worrying about his young nephew. He shouldn't have, though; Time Carlow could handle himself as few could. But he worried anyway. The big Irishman was uneasy.

"What about Pig and Mirabile?" Carlow asked.

"Be waiting for us, they be." The big Irishman spoke with more confidence than he felt.

That was the plan, but Pig Deconer was young, like Carlow, and might choose to adance too soon. Captain McNelly had sent the four of them because he wasn't certain whether or not there were additional gang members. Rumors were that there was a whole gang.

Kileen was distracted by a young woman carrying a baby and walking along the planked sidewalk in front of them. Silently he hoped the child had been lifted high on a chair after its birth, or carried upstairs, to assure success in this world. His nephew had. For a moment, he considered going outside to ask the woman. He told himself to concentrate, but found himself wondering if Tanneman could transform himself into another creature. Hadn't he read somewhere that some ancient shamans had such abilities?

Across the street, Tanneman Rose, wearing a fake beard, went into the bank. He nodded at the exiting businessman and quietly took his place at the teller window, behind a tall woman and a short man making a deposit. Hillis Rose, also wearing a fake beard, remained mounted, holding the reins of his brother's horse. Their other two brothers, Portland and Barnabas, had come to town earlier; they were out of sight and would stay that way, unless necessary. They, too, carried fake beards in their pockets.

The brothers had done this five times already. Successfully. Only once had the other two brothers needed to join in, shooting down a marshal and wounding some townsmen. The trick was to do it calmly. Not give anyone a reason to panic—or do something foolish. Just as importantly, Tanneman had kept the money hidden. None of them knew where. Of course, he had doled out spending money, but that was it.

Tanneman chuckled to himself; it had been a perfect system. As usual, he would ride back into town without his brother, present himself as a Ranger and offer to help find the bank robbers. Of course, he would shed his beard and long coat and change hats before doing so. The other step was to arrest some poor bastard for the deed. It was so easy. It was theater, his one great love.

All four of the Rose brothers were tall and a little on the thin side. Tanneman and Hillis were clean-shaven with thick, light brown hair pouring out from under their hats. Hillis wore long sideburns that covered too much of his face. Tanneman was definitely fiercer and far smarter; his catlike face was a permanent scowl. Ice blue eyes looked at others from somewhere beyond eternity.

At times, it seemed Hillis simply went along to please his older brother. Tanneman had told him that Hillis had also lived a previous life, as a Roman soldier. So had the other two brothers; Tanneman thought Portland had been a Navajo chief and Barnabas had been a Chinese trader. Only Barnabas ever talked about Tanneman's ideas. Tanneman tugged on the brim of his hat and lowered his eyes. Never look a teller in the eyes, he reminded himself. He couldn't help letting the remnants of last night's dream creep into his mind. Dreams were important messages. Advance looks at the future, if one heeded them well. In last night's dream Ranger Kileen had led a hundred Rangers into Tanneman's house. They came from every direction, through windows, through closed doors, even through the ceiling itself.

He shook his head and the dream fragments rattled away. Maybe it meant they were on to him. That was the difficult part about dreams, he knew. Interpreting them correctly could be difficult. He had watched the town for signs of Rangers when they came in. He shook his head to clear it; now was not the time. Later, he would assemble a proper ceremony and learn from the other world. As he had done hundreds of years before.

For now, he touched the necklace of jaguar teeth he wore under his shirt. It was a necklace, from a Mexican peddler, to remind him of his earlier life. He decided the necklace was the symbol of his genius, an ability to plan no one could match. Tanneman's initial plan was to rob ten banks in three years, then quit forever. It was a good plan, not too greedy. Maybe the dream meant the Rangers would soon discover his actions. Maybe.

The short man finished and turned around, mumbling to himself. He almost ran into Tanneman.

"Sorry, I'm in the way," Tanneman said, stepping to the side.

"Sure. Sure," the smaller man said, and left the bank.

Ahead of Tanneman, the woman completed her transaction, spun and headed out. He half turned to watch her leave. It gave him the opportunity to flip back his coat and draw his weapon.

"May I help you, sir?" Without looking up, the teller's voice was reedy and laced with self-importance and a continuous sniffing.

"I'd say you can." Tanneman spun around, a long-barreled revolver in his right hand and empty saddlebags in the other. "I need all your money, and I need it now. My gang's outside. Hidden. If there's a shot, they'll come shooting."

The teller turned white and held up his hands. His nose honked and snorted.

From the corner of his eyes, Tanneman Rose saw the bank's vice president stiffen at his desk.

"Don't be a fool, mister." Tanneman waved his gun at the officer.

Minutes later, Tanneman exited the bank with filled saddlebags over his shoulder and saw four Rangers running toward them. A few feet behind was what appeared to be a wolf. Deconer had a fried chicken drumstick in his left hand and a Colt revolver in his right.

Hillis was as surprised by their sudden appearance as Tanneman was. He spun in the saddle and fired his Winchester. Ranger Deconer groaned and stumbled. Both his drumstick and gun plopped onto the street. Only a few steps behind, Mirabile swung his Sharps in the direction of Hillis, and the big gun roared.

From the middle of the street, Kileen fired at almost the same moment. The younger Rose brother jerked sideways and toppled over. His rifle slid across the uneven street.

Holding his hand carbine in his right fist, Carlow never took his eyes off of Tanneman while the other Rangers fired at Hillis.

Tanneman sneered, but didn't want to test the young Ranger. He'd seen him in action. He lowered his gun, but held it at his side.

"Glad you're here, boys. We were told the bank was being robbed," he said. "I've got the bank money here." He patted the saddlebags. "For safekeeping." He looked around. "I'm guessing we were given a false alarm. Haven't seen any robbers. But it pays to be careful." He tugged at the false beard, pulling it from his face. "That's why we put these on."

"Drop the gun, Tanneman," Carlow pointed with his hand carbine. "You're under arrest."

"I don't understand."

"Of course you do. Drop it now."

Slowly, Tanneman knelt and laid his gun, beard and the saddlebags on the ground. As he leaned over, a necklace made of jaguar teeth dangled from his shirt. He stood and held up his hands. But as his arms moved upward, he made a hand movement like he was pushing something away. A message? To someone across the street? The young Ranger wheeled to look. He saw only three frightened townsmen.

"That's a good lad, Tanneman," Kileen said. "No time we be havin' for the wafflin'."

"Wait a minute, boys." Tanneman glanced at Hillis, who wasn't moving. "You've got this wrong, boys. We thought the bank was being robbed."

"It was. By you." Carlow stepped closer.

"What? That's silly." Tanneman looked at Kileen. "Thunder, tell your nephew here we're Rangers, not crooks."

"Mirabile, check on Pig." Kileen motioned with his gun. "Be hopin' the lad's not hurt bad, Tanneman."

"I-I'm hit, Th-Thunder. I-I'm b-bleeding bad. My leg."

Mirabile knelt beside Deconer, trying to calm him, using his kerchief to stop the blood oozing from the man's thigh.

Tanneman motioned toward the downed Ranger. "Hillis thought you were the robbers. We were told the bank was being robbed."

Not interested in pursuing Tanneman's alibi further, Carlow started to say something, but deferred to the big Irishman. Kileen's missing-teeth smile was like a jack-o'-lantern's, but Carlow had long ago overlooked that image. This man was more like a father, a battle-savvy warrior of a father.

Shaking his head, the big Irishman laughed out loud. "Well, 'tis a grand day for blarney, it be. As thick as meself can ever recall."

Carlow was proud of him for making a stand against Tanneman. He knew it wasn't easy.

Tanneman Rose turned toward Kileen, his eyes flashing. "I thought you were my friend. We shared dreams. And things of the past. But you've killed my brother. You'll be sorry about this."

"Aye. All who wear the proud badge of a Texas Ranger be sorry. About ye and Hillis," Kileen said. "Ye have disgraced the fine brotherhood we be." The big Irishman looked around the street. "An' where be your fellow outlaws, Tanneman? Go easier on ye, it will, if ye be cooperatin'."

Tanneman bit his lower lip and took several steps forward. His voice was barely a whisper. "Look. I'll make a deal with you. Let me ride out of here. One of you can take the saddlebags and all of you can follow after me. Shooting and hollering. This piss-ant town is too scared to know the difference. Once we get away from here, I'll keep going and you can split the money. There's a lot in there."

Without waiting for his uncle's response, Carlow took three quick steps toward Tanneman, who was smiling. With his hand carbine at his side, Carlow's left fist exploded into the evil Ranger's face and blood burst in all directions. Tanneman staggered backward and Carlow hit him again, this time in the stomach.

Groaning, Tanneman grabbed for the hot pain with both hands.

"How dare you suggest we're on your level, Rose, you bastard." Carlow pulled back his fist for another blow.

Behind him, Kileen said gently, "No, me son. That not be the way."

Carlow dropped his fist and stepped away.

Kileen rushed past him, muttering, "This be the way." His own right fist slammed against Tanneman's chin and the man flew into the air. The huge man stood over the unconscious outlaw Ranger and shook his fist.

"Be sendin' ye back to Persia, I be. Ye have blackened the fine name o' the Rangers. Blast ye, Tanneman Rose."

Chapter Two

A week later, a special guard of two Rangers, Mirabile and Kileen, led a subdued Tanneman Rose into the courtroom for trial. Actually, it was a warehouse not being used at the moment. The building was packed with interested townspeople, sitting on hastily brought-in logs or standing. A reporter had come from as far away as Dallas.

Circuit Court Judge Wilcox Cline was presiding, having arrived by stage the previous day and staying at the Gleason, where he had a regular room.

Outside, Carlow was in charge of making certain no one entered the makeshift courtroom carrying a weapon. For an hour before the trial, men stepped up and laid their weapons on the table set up for the purpose. Asleep at the Ranger's feet, Chance made most of the approaching men wary. Carlow guessed several men disclosed weapons they might not have otherwise, because of the wolf-dog's presence. At least, that was what he told the other Rangers later.

Galloping hooves grabbed his attention as two riders whirled into view. They reined their horses hard, jumped down and hitched them to the rack in front of the warehouse. As soon as he saw their faces, Carlow knew they must be Tanneman's brothers, even though he had never seen them before. Both were tall and thin with ice blue eyes, like Tanneman and Hillis.

A thought raced through Carlow's mind: Could they have been in town during the attempted bank robbery and had Tanneman's hand movement sent them away? Rumors of a gang were plentiful, but so far there had been only one holdup where more than two were definitely involved. A lawman had been killed then. By ambush. Carlow turned his attention to the advancing men. Were they here to watch—or to attempt to break their brother out? He needed to assume the latter.

The older man had a face that reminded Carlow of a panther. A raw-boned panther. Somewhat the same as Tanneman, only older, and thicker in his jaw and cheeks. A long scar on the man's right cheek spoke of violence in his past. Powerful arms reinforced that idea. He was dressed roughly, wearing clothes of the range and a wide-brimmed hat that had seen much weather.

The youngest Rose, Barnabas, was eighteen. He, too, looked like his brothers, only his appearance didn't seem quite right. It was something in his eyes, combined with the way his body occasionally jerked uncontrollably. His shirt and pants were too small and well-worn; an odd-shaped fedora was cocked on his head. He wore a pistol attached to a lanyard around his neck. Under his worn shirt was a jaguar tooth necklace just like Tanneman's. It was visible where his shirt lay open, its top buttons missing.

Stepping up to the gun table, Portland sneered and laid two short-barreled Webley Bulldog revolvers on the table. One from each coat pocket. Carlow had seen British handguns like them before and knew they were double-action weapons.

"I take it you two are related to Tanneman. Brothers, I suspect."

"Damn proud of it, too, Ranger. I'm Portland. This here fool's Barnabas," Portland said, staring at the Ranger.

He motioned for his younger brother to come up and leave his gun. Barnabas shook his head, then placed his fists on his hips defiantly. His shoulders and head shuddered.

"Get your ass over here and leave that damn gun," Portland growled. "Or I'll rip it off your scrawny neck."

Blinking his eyes wildly, Barnabas hurried toward the table, lifted the gun lanyard over his head and laid it on the table. He patted the gun affectionately, then looked up at Carlow. The corner of the youngest Rose's mouth twitched.

"You the one who killed Hillis?"

"No. But your brother tried to gun down a Ranger. He made the decision. To die instead of surrendering."

"W-what do you m-mean? Decision?"

Nonchalantly, Carlow looked at Portland and said, "You tell him. You were there. I'm busy."

Portland's eyes flashed hatred for an instant. Then he grabbed Barnabas by the arm and pushed him toward the door. Barnabas asked his bigger brother what Carlow had meant and Portland told him to shut up.

"Tell your little brother not to try goin' in until he gets rid of that gun in his boot," Carlow barked, and reinforced his command by drawing his hand carbine.

Portland jerked his brother to a stop. The big man's face was crimson. He let go of Barnabas and turned around, glaring at Carlow.

The young Ranger's eyes connected in heat with Portland's. The big man blinked and looked away.

"Barnabas, get that damn pistol outta your boot."

The youngest Rose frowned and rolled his shoulders.

"Do it now, you damn fool."

Licking his lips, Barnabas laughed and pulled up his pants to reveal another Webley Bulldog revolver stuck down in his boot. He pulled it out, laughed and held the gun.

"Either drop it or bring it back to the table. Make your decision now," Carlow said.

Barnabas mouthed the word "decision" and slowly let the gun drop from his hand. His head and shoulders quivered again. He laughed again and Portland shoved him again toward the door.

A step away, he turned toward Carlow. "We were at our ranch that day, Ranger. It's a long ride from here."

Carlow knew he had guessed right: the two brothers had been in town on the day of the robbery. It had to be. Tanneman's motion was for them to stay hidden. There was no proof of that, of course.

The two continued inside and took seats on the back row. Tables were set up, one each for the defense, the prosecution and the judge. The judge's table had two chairs—one for him and one for witnesses. District Attorney Waddell Johnson had been brought in to handle the prosecution; Tanneman had decided to be his own attorney. He had refused to tell where earlier bank robbery money was hidden—or if he had a gang.

Time Carlow joined Kileen and Mirabile on the first row of logs. Chance stayed outside as he had been told. Next to them were the town marshal and the bank's president and owner. Ranger Pig Deconer was too weak to attend. Seated to the right of the rows was a jury of twelve men, all townsmen.

"This is the worst part of it." Hump-shouldered from too many years in the saddle, Mirabile shook his head and checked his pocket watch. It was the sixth time he had done so.

Marshal Timble looked at Mirabile and smiled. "Know what you mean, Ranger." His pockmarked face received the lines cracking from around his eyes.

Mirabile's sunburned face showed the tension of the entire effort. He withdrew the makings from his shirt pocket and methodically rolled a cigarette. Kileen was glad to see him occupied for the moment and not talking. Snapping a match to flame on his belt buckle, Mirabile let the new smoke drift casually around his face and asked about something that had been on his mind ever since they learned of this assignment.

"Captain never told us how he knew the Rose boys would be coming here," he said. "Do you know? You being with the captain the longest an' all."

Together, the four Rangers—and the two Rose brothers—were part of the Special Force of Rangers led by Captain Leander McNelly. The other unit was the Frontier Battalion, led by Major John B. Jones. Kileen had served with the legendary captain since the Rangers had finally been reinstated after the war.

Kileen rubbed his unshaved chin, stood and stretched. He looked bigger than his six foot two frame and 220 pounds. "Hillis, he be a wee bit o' a talker. After sippin' a mite o' whiskey."

He ran his hand across his mouth, wishing he could have a drink from the flask in his coat pocket. He was worried Tanneman might suddenly change himself into some animal and escape. That was what the evil Ranger said he had been capable of, in his previous life.

A drink would sure help. Kileen thought about getting up and going outside for a quick swig or two. Of course, it was against Ranger rules to drink on duty. It was a rule the big Irishman consistently ignored—and

Captain McNelly consistently ignored his breaking of it. Kileen was too valuable not to do so.

"So, Tanneman's little brother spouted off, eh?" Mirabile said, studying his cigarette.

"Aye."

Kileen stretched again, trying to decide what he should do.

"But how could they do it—and none of us know?"

Kileen shifted his weight and glanced at Tanneman Rose seated at the defense table, apparently deep in concentration. Kileen growled, "Rangers be doin' their fine an' sacred duties. Aye, busy we be. Meself, I suppose a smart man be able to do such robbin' without our knowin'."

He wanted to say the man had probably transformed himself into something else, or someone else, but decided it would only upset Mirabile. He explained that Ranger Manuel Ramos had overheard Hillis Rose bragging about how rich he and his brothers had become. Hillis had whispered to the man next to him that they were headed to San Antonio and winked.

"Manuel's a good man, even if he is Mex. Surprised the captain trusted the Rose boys so long." Mirabile drew on his cigarette and let a white finger of smoke dance around his battered hat and disappear. "You know, I'm too old for this. Bertha wants me to quit. Spend all my time workin' our ranch. When this is over, I'm gonna do it." He checked his watch again.

After telling his wolf-dog to remain outside, Carlow had taken a seat beside Kileen and asked him if he knew Tanneman had two brothers. The big Irishman indicated he knew, explaining that Tanneman had said they had a small cattle ranch not far from Bennett.

"Think they're part of this?" Carlow asked, glancing back at the two Rose brothers.

"Me not be knowin'. Findin' out soon, we'll be doin', me thinks."

"Yeah."

Judge Wilcox Cline entered the packed courtroom. He was young for the job and eager to please his constituents, especially Captain McNelly. His hair was thinning fast and the baldness gave him, he thought, a certain look of authority, and of age. Seated behind the table and chair brought in for the purpose, he still looked more like a college student than a judge.

After announcing the purpose of the gathering, Judge Cline turned to Johnson and asked him to present the state's position. Enjoying the attention, Johnson stood and paced the creaking floor as he delivered a blistering attack on Tanneman and Hillis Rose. Most of the jury actually nodded when he finished.

"What does the accused have to say on his behalf?" Judge Cline asked, without really caring about the answer.

Tanneman stood, drawing himself to his full height. He was dressed in a dark suit with a new boiled shirt and fresh collar; his cravat was a dark crimson. The clothes were actually from his travel gear and had been properly pressed for the occasion. Around his neck, outside his clothes, he wore his jaguar necklace. He looked impressive—more so than the wrinkled district attorney—and a bit strange.

Carlow whispered this observation to Kileen. The big Irishman dismissed the concern as inconsequential, but his eyes didn't leave the necklace. Tanneman had told him of its significance.

The young Ranger couldn't help recalling how fascinated with the theater Tanneman was. He reminded Kileen, whose only response was to mumble something about beards. Whenever they were in a town where theater was going on, Tanneman had always taken time to see the performance. There was no doubt that Tanneman was acting now. This was his stage. It bothered Carlow. He didn't think Johnson was ready for the recital.

"Gentlemen, this is a most unfortunate day—and yet it is a bright one for San Antonio," Tanneman declared, motioning toward the jury. "First, your money is safe. Thanks to the Texas Rangers. Second, none of your townspeople were harmed in this incident. And thirdly, you have the opportunity to deliver true justice today—for I am an innocent man, as well as a proud and decorated Ranger. So was my brother."

He stepped around the table and headed toward the seated jurymen.

Carlow looked at Kileen; the old Irishman shrugged his shoulders and mouthed "shaman."

"For you see, the reality is, my brother and I went to the bank because we heard it was being robbed. It is our sworn duty to protect you. To protect Texas." He paused to let the words sink in.

"My fellow Rangers, as you will hear, were also in wait," Tanneman continued, making a motion toward the seated Rangers. "There have been a spate of bank robberies lately—and the Rangers were trying to catch the men involved." He straightened his cravat. "My brother and I were not on that assignment. And did not know of it." He stared at the closest juryman, a thick-faced man with uneven teeth. "That is common, of course. Each Ranger has his own assignment. My brother and I were en route to El Paso to help stop cattle rustling there. A nasty problem involving border crossings." He shook his head to emphasize the seriousness of the situation. "We stopped in your fine town to get a bite to eat. Trail food can be mighty poor sometimes. Especially when neither of us cook well."

Several jurors chuckled.

His continuing tale was fascinating as he strutted back and forth. The Rose brothers had just come to town when someone ran by, telling them of the bank being robbed. They had hurried to the bank. He said they had taken the money as assurance it wouldn't be stolen. He left out the beards covering their faces.

Without a pause, he went into a full explanation of how the Special Forces of the Rangers worked. Under McNelly's command, most of his forty-Ranger unit worked the border region. Mexican and Indian raiders hit and ran across the Rio Grande with some regularity. Friction between ranchers—and between ranchers and farmers—occupied Ranger time as well. Bank robbery and even upheavals of local citizenry would bring state law enforcement. McNelly's objective was to stabilize the region in two years. Rose's presentation had nothing to do with the case, but it served to bring the jury into seeing him as one of the noble lawmen in the state.

He went on to explain the other Rangers thought he and his brother were the bank robbers, adding that the jury should understand that lawmen, like himself, were especially concerned about dishonesty in their own ranks.

"All in all, it was a terrible mistake, costing the life of my brother, a fine Ranger. This lack of communication may tell all of us of the need to inform all Rangers of what and where their brethren are involved. It is my great wish that you will see through this terrible mishap and grant my innocence so that I may again serve the great state of Texas—and my dear brother be honored in death," he concluded as he walked back to the defense table and sat. His fingers danced along the individual jaguar teeth.

"Amen to that," Portland Rose yelled.

"Cockle-doodle-doo!" Barnabas howled.

Judge Cline hammered his gavel for quiet.

Tanneman looked straight ahead, knowing several jurymen were talking with each other. Two looked frightened.

Rattled by the impression made by Tanneman, Judge Cline cleared his throat and asked the district attorney to proceed with his case. Immediately, Johnson called Kileen to the stand and the big Irishman told about the Rangers suspecting the Rose brothers and setting in wait for them. His testimony was littered with Irish phrases. His eyes rarely left Tanneman's unreadable face. Kileen explained to the jury that the four Rangers had been waiting at two locations, watching the bank.

Smiling confidently, Johnson asked Ranger Kileen why the four Rangers were in town.

"Aye. Orders, it be," Kileen growled. "Orders from himself, Captain Leander McNelly."

"And who this Captain McNelly?"

Folding his arms, the big Irishman proudly described their Ranger leader. Carlow grinned at his uncle's enthusiastic description.

"What were these orders?"

"Wait for Tanneman and Hillis Rose, the blaggards, to come to town an' try to rob the bank o' these fine citizens. We be lookin', too, for their gang, but the blaggards never were seen." Kileen went on to explain what had happened. He finished, smiled at Carlow and folded his arms in self-satisfaction.

"Any cross examination, Mr. Rose?" Judge Cline pointed with his gavel.

Chapter Three

Tanneman stood behind the desk. He was silent for a long moment, looking down at the table. As he looked up, his right hand fingered his necklace briefly and then dropped to his side.

"I thought we were friends, Ranger Kileen. Sharing many of the same interests. The same duties," he said softly.

"Aye, that be so. Before ye misused the trust of this fine Ranger badge. I not be likin' any man who does so." Kileen held out his coat lapel where the badge was pinned.

"I think you were deceiving me—about your friendship. You were eager to do this to us, weren't you? In fact, you volunteered."

Kileen twisted his face to match the snarl in his voice. "Nay. Me did not. Captain McNelly hisself gave me the orders."

"I see. Tell me, just how did you come to think Hillis and I were coming here—to rob the bank of these fine citizens?"

Kileen told the story about a Ranger overhearing Hillis.

"As a lawman, you realize, of course, this is hearsay—and not admissible in a court of law," Tanneman said.

"Besides that, my brother is not here to defend himself. Please advise him of this, Judge."

Nodding his head, Judge Cline told the jury that they should disregard that statement, as it was inadmissible. Carlow realized Tanneman was making the jurors think about something that didn't matter. It was a fascinating spin of secondary information that had nothing to do with the actual robbery.

Kileen's face reddened and his mouth became a thin, tight line.

"What did you see when you came toward the bank?"

"I be seeing ye with your pistols out, and fine, thick beards be coverin' your faces." Kileen snorted and nodded to himself. "An' full saddlebags o' the town's money be on your shoulders." He leaned forward, putting his elbows on his legs. "Your late brother, bless his miserable soul, be holdin' your hoss for a quick getaway. That's what I be seein'. Yessir."

"That's interesting." Tanneman smiled and looked at the jury again. "You saw two Rangers with their guns out. Like they would be if they were expecting trouble, is that right?"

"Aye."

"Would that be the way we would come out of the bank if we thought there were robbers near? Would you have one Ranger standing guard outside while you went in to check the situation?"

Kileen frowned. This wasn't what he had expected.

"Would you think wearing a beard might be helpful so the robbers wouldn't realize you were a Ranger—until it was too late?"

Tanneman cocked his head to the side and went on, not waiting for Kileen's response. "Of course that makes sense." He spun toward Kileen. "Tell me, Ranger Kileen, has Captain McNelly ever been wrong?"

Kileen started to blurt his assurance that his leader had never been wrong, saw Carlow shaking his head, and said softly, "Aye, be sure that he has. Rare that it be." He felt as if he had spoken blasphemy.

"I see. Did he ever cross the Rio Grande illegally and create a problem between our government and Mexico's?"

"Aye, but . . ."

"Did McNelly hang three men in the center of El Paso—without trials?"

"There be a reason for . . ."

"Did McNelly ever use torture to make a man confess?"

"When it be necessary."

"So, would you agree there is reason to think Captain McNelly could be wrong about me and my brother?" Tanneman said, nodding toward the jury, then spun back to the rattled Kileen.

The big Irishman glanced at Carlow, then back to the cold-eyed Tanneman. Kileen wondered if the man would begin to chant some ancient Persian incantation. He muttered something under his breath and stammered that it wasn't possible.

Tanneman folded his arms and sat down. "Thank you, Mr. Kileen. I am finished."

Johnson was clearly relieved to have Kileen off the stand and Time Carlow in his place. In response to Johnson's opening question, the young Ranger explained the situation.

The district attorney stepped back, pleased. "Your witness, Mr. Rose."

Tanneman was not as confident as he had been earlier, but he knew discrediting Carlow was crucial. He remained in his chair, leaning forward on the table.

"Ranger Carlow, how many so-called bank robberies have you broken up?"

"This is my first."

"I see."

"No, you don't," Carlow snapped. "Because it was my first, I wanted to make absolutely sure of what was going on. I don't want Rangers involved in crimes, so I was hoping you and your brother wouldn't try to rob the bank. But you did—and we stopped you."

"Ranger Carlow, your fellow Ranger . . . your uncle, I believe . . . mentioned something about other bank robberies my brother and I were supposed to have been involved in." Tanneman cocked his head to the side. "Forget for the moment that it is irrelevant to this case, and answer this, please. Do you know if any of those supposed robberies have gone unsolved?" He folded his arms. "That is, Ranger, were the robbers— or some of them—or any one of them—arrested?"

Carlow grinned back. "You already know that. In each case, you arrested an innocent man for the crime."

Tanneman was stunned by the statement. He rubbed his chin, trying to think of what to say next. He had to make the young Ranger appear rash. Careless. Too eager.

"Interesting statement, young man," Tanneman said. "So my brother and I robbed those banks—and then arrested somebody totally innocent of the crime."

"That about sums it up."

"Why didn't the folks in those various towns recognize us?"

"That's why you were wearing beards—and those long coats. Makes it hard that way. Just like you were wearing when you came out of the bank here," Carlow said. "You want to show the good folks by putting that beard on again?" He motioned toward the beards on the table.

Judge Cline hammered his gavel to rid the room of laughter.

"I appreciate your comment, Ranger. It's a fascinating theory," Tanneman said, running his fingers along a scratch on the defense table's surface. "Maybe you should be writing for one of those penny dreadfuls, instead of being a Ranger."

Dramatically, he stood again and walked around to the front of the table. Leaning against it, he gripped the table and asked, "Tell me the names of these towns where my brother and I were supposed to have robbed banks."

Without hesitation, Carlow rattled off the five towns.

Grinning evilly, Tanneman reached inside his coat pocket and retrieved a folded sheet of paper.

"Tell me, Ranger Carlow, what do you think of this?" Slowly and dramatically, he unfolded the paper. "This is a wire from Marshal Tipin of Paris. It reads: 'In response to your query, the city of Paris is thankful for your help in arresting the bank robbers.' I can wire the other cities you mentioned if that will help."

Shaking his head, Carlow straightened his back. "Nice try, Tanneman, but it won't wash. Why don't you tell us how you and your brother just happened to be in town during each of those robberies?" He paused and added, "And tell us how you managed to catch the robber each time—but never recovered a cent. Not one."

Portland guffawed and Barnabas giggled. Tanneman glanced at them, frowning.

Instead of answering the young Ranger, Tanneman

waved his arms and asked, "If you were my brother and me, and you rode into town and heard the bank was being robbed, what would you have done?" Tanneman looked up slowly.

Carlow cocked his head to the side. "I would've waited outside, so no one in the bank got hurt. Like we did." He leaned forward. "You didn't answer my question, Tanneman."

"Judge, please inform the witness that he is to respond only to my questions. Not make speeches."

Looking toward the end of the table, Judge Cline said quietly, "He's right, Ranger."

Smiling victoriously, Tanneman continued, "Now, answer this, please. Wouldn't you be worried that the robbers would shoot the people inside—and leave one of your fellow Rangers on guard outside?"

"You asked me what I would have done, Rose. I told you." Carlow stared at the accused Ranger with a look Tanneman had seen before, but never directed at him. It was a look that tore into a man and challenged his manhood. He didn't like it.

"I have no more questions of this witness, Judge." Tanneman looked away.

Carlow turned to the judge. "Your Honor, I have written testimony from Ranger Deconer. He was wounded by Hillis Rose and is recovering. Should I read it?"

Tanneman winced, but didn't look up. The judge directed Johnson to ask Carlow about the wounded lawman's testimony. Carlow read the simply written text and looked up at the arrested Ranger again.

"Now, Mr. Rose, do you have any questions for this witness related to this written testimony?"

Tanneman Rose licked his lips. A dream last night had him enjoying revenge against all of them.

"Yes, I do," he said without raising his head.

"Ranger Carlow, if you entered a bank thinking it was being robbed and came out looking for the robbers, what would you have done if someone came at you, shooting?"

Carlow looked down at the hilt of the war knife barely visible above his Kiowa leggings. He flashed a wide smile as he looked up.

"Well, Rose, if I had on a fake beard and was holding a bag full of the bank's money, I would figure the town had discovered what I was doing—and either surrender or start shooting. Kinda separates the wheat from the chaff."

The same jurors who had chuckled earlier laughed.

"You didn't answer my question."

"Yeah, I did. You and your brother wanted the town's hard-earned money," Carlow said, his voice showing glimpses of temper. "But we were waiting for you. Your brother tried to kill us. You decided it wouldn't happen to you."

He started to add that the other two brothers had been waiting to help, but didn't. There was no proof of that, only his hunch. It might muddy the case against Tanneman, giving him the opportunity to point out they weren't there and that this was a personal vendetta against them—with no real evidence.

Somewhere in the packed audience, a man cheered. Portland stood to see who it was until Judge Cline told him to sit down.

Tanneman again said he was finished with the witness and Johnson called the bank teller to the stand. Carlow returned to his seat beside Kileen. As the skinny teller walked to the designated witness chair, he glanced in Tanneman's direction, then sat down, blowing his nose into a handkerchief,

Carlow realized something was wrong. Terribly

wrong. He whispered his concern to Kileen and asked if anyone had visited the prisoner while he had been taking his turn helping with guard duty, as the Rangers had done. Nodding, Kileen indicated that Tanneman had asked to see the teller and the vice president, stating as his own counsel he had a right to interview key witnesses. Both had met with him for a few minutes, at different times, then left. So had Tanneman's other brothers. Kileen didn't think anything untoward had occurred.

"Aye, fooled, we may have been," Kileen growled.

Judge Cline turned toward him briefly. His scowl indicated he wanted silence.

Turning back toward the now seated witness, Johnson crossed his arms. "Mr. Branson, would you please tell us what happened in the First National Bank on the morning in question."

"Well, there was a lot of confusion, I can tell you that," the man said, rubbing his hands together as if the motion would relieve his nervousness. His nose made even more noises than usual, almost a symphony.

"Yes, go on." Johnson liked the sound of his voice.

"Ah, it's my opinion that Mr. Rose—and his brother—came to our bank thinking we were being robbed. They're Rangers, you know. They were trying to disguise themselves so the robbers wouldn't realize what was going on."

The courtroom erupted with questions, assertions and shouts. Portland yelled his agreement. Barnabas giggled loudly. Carlow glanced their way; the big man glared back and the teenager giggled again.

Judge Cline pounded on the table for silence. Not sure of what to do, he pointed toward the district attorney and told him to continue, if he wanted to.

"Ah . . . yes, Your Honor," Johnson said and faced

the teller who was blowing his nose again. "I don't think I heard you correctly, Mr. Branson. Will you state that again?"

"Ah, I said I thought Tanneman, ah, Mr. Rose, came to the bank thinking we were being robbed. It was all a big mistake in . . . ah, knowing what was going on. Between the Rangers and all." He blew his nose and looked at his feet.

Carlow jumped to his feet and blurted, "Rose, how much did you pay him?"

Johnson spun around, half angry and half relieved that someone else was getting involved.

"That's enough, Ranger. This is a courtroom," Judge Cline ordered, but without much conviction.

"Then make it one," Carlow snarled. "This man is under oath—and he's lying."

"We don't know that, Ranger," Judge Cline responded, wishing he hadn't.

Without waiting to be asked, Tanneman reinforced the teller's dramatic statement with a few questions.

Stunned but unable to adjust, Johnson then called the bank's vice president William Debo to the stand. The stocky man in a three-piece suit glanced at Tanneman as he approached the witness chair.

"Be steppin' aside, Johnson, me be handlin' this." Kileen put a hand on Carlow's shoulder and moved toward the bank officer, pushing Johnson away.

"What is this? Your Honor, I object," Tanneman said loudly.

Carlow looked at him. "I bet you do, Rose. I just bet you do."

"Beggin' your pardon, Your Honor," Kileen said, rather quietly, "but this teller fella an' this bank officer boy has to know they be headin' for trouble by not tellin' the truth. I'll be doin' the askin' for now."

Tanneman stood and pounded his fist on the table. "This is not right, Your Honor."

Judge Cline looked at Tanneman, then back at the huge Irishman, took a deep breath and said, "If the district attorney agrees, I see no problem with the change."

Kileen marched to where the vice president sat, not even waiting for Johnson's timid agreement. All color was vacating the bank officer's face. He looked at Tanneman, frowned and tried not to look at the advancing Irishman.

"Look at me, boy," Kileen charged. "Ye be close to makin' a big mistake—with your life." He glanced at Tanneman, who was fuming. "An' all for a few pieces o' gold."

"This is ridiculous, Judge," Tanneman yelled. "He's trying to badger the witness."

From the back, Portland yelled, "Yeah, tell him to stop." Barnabas looked at both brothers and giggled.

Nodding his head, Kileen said, "Aye, that I be." He turned back to the terrified vice president. "But only to be savin' ye, lad, from an awful mistake." He folded his massive arms. "Yah see, if ye stay with this made-up story, he will go free. Two things will happen then. One, he will kill ye before ye can change your minds an' talk. Two, we will be comin' after ye for helpin' one o' the worst kind o' bandits to get away. The judge has a word for it. Perjury 'tis the word." His big shoulders rose and fell.

Standing as he pounded his fist on the table, Tanneman blurted, "This is not justice, Your Honor. This is a lynching."

The judge looked at Kileen, who nodded, glanced at Tanneman and said, "Oh, an' by the sweetness o' the day, ye should be knowin' . . . Tanneman Rose has no money to pay you." His eyes bore into the frightened man's face. "Now, me lad, do ye want to try your story again?"

The jury made its decision quickly after the bank vice president, followed by the teller, reconfirmed what everyone knew, that Tanneman and Hillis Rose were attempting to rob the town's bank. Guilty. The two bribed bank employees were not charged, but they were soon dismissed from the bank and left town immediately.

Barnabas was stunned by the verdict, unable to accept the reality of the decision. His brother—the one he adored—was going to prison! His entire body trembled and he didn't seem able to move for an instant.

Finally, he stood and yelled, "No! No! No! Tanneman!" He grabbed his necklace with both hands and pulled it out of his shirt.

Carlow watched him carefully, half expecting the odd teenager to try to use a gun he had hidden somewhere.

Scowling, Portland caught his eye, then grabbed Barnabas by the shirt collar. "Let's go, Barnabas. Come on."

"B-but . . . b-but . . . m-my brother . . . Tanneman . . . my brother . . ."

Carlow turned to Kileen. "I'm going out. To the guns. Just in case."

"Aye." Kileen drew his pistol from his gun belt. "Takin' care o' the prisoner, I'll be. Me an' Julian."

Outside, Carlow watched people leave the courtroom, quietly retrieving their weapons from the table set up for that purpose. Most looked at the Ranger and nodded. In his hand was the sawed-off Winchester. Cocked. At his side, Chance was alert and watching. The town marshal left, engaged in a conversation with the bank president.

Portland half dragged his youngest brother from the courtroom and glared at Carlow. "You bastard! You'll rue this day, you an' that big Irishman. I swear it. My brother's innocent. He's a Ranger, dammit."

"And you need to know hiding stolen money makes you as guilty as the robbers. So is helping with some of the holdups," Carlow said, cocking his head to the side. "And shooting down a lawman makes you a murderer."

The look on Portland's face confirmed what the Ranger had suspected. The other two brothers *were* involved.

Pushing out his lower lip in an exaggerated pout, Barnabas stepped toward the table and laid his hands on his pistols. He looked up at Carlow and grinned. "What are ya thinkin', law dog? Wonderin' if I'm gonna shoot ya?"

"I think you're smarter than that, Barnabas," Carlow said.

"What would ya do—if I did?"

"This isn't a game. Take your weapons and leave."

"Which one o' ya killed Hillis?" Barnabas asked, his eyes widening and his head twitching.

"Why don't you just tell us where all that stolen money is—and we'll give you a reward." Carlow wasn't certain Captain McNelly would like the offer, but it seemed logical to him.

Barnabas grinned with half of his mouth.

Portland moved up beside his brother. His expression was taut with anger, his pale eyes cold and narrowed.

"Don't know nothin' about any stolen money, Ranger. No murdered lawman either. An' we ain't no bank robbers. Just poor cowmen, understand?" Portland said, almost offhandedly.

"Whatever you say."

"Gonna kill my brother on the way to Huntsville?" Portland reached for his two Webley pistols.

Carlow tensed.

"Don't worry, Ranger," Portland said, shoving them into his coat pockets. "Ain't no fool, like Barnabas here. I'm headin' back to my cattle."

"Let's go to the ice cream parlor first. I like chocolate," Barnabas said. He swung the gun lanyard over his neck and shoved the other gun back into his boot. His eyes twinkled.

"Not today. We've got a long ride back to the ranch."

"You promised. After it was over, you said," Barnabas whined.

Wheeling toward his younger brother, Portland pushed Barnabas to their horses and they rode off, spurring their mounts.

A loud "cockle-doodle-doo" popped through the day from a waving Barnabas.

As Carlow watched the brothers leave, Mirabile came from the courtroom, announcing that Kileen was bringing Tanneman. Carlow asked him to stay with the gun table so he could assist Kileen.

"Sure thing, Time."

An older couple came up to them. Removing his hat to expose a shock of white hair, the man said, "I want to thank you for what you did, Rangers. We had all our savings in that bank."

"Yes, thank you," his wife responded, adding a short curtsy.

"You are most welcome, folks," Carlow said, smiling. "Just sorry it had to be Rangers who tried to rob the bank."

The old man took a deep breath, finding the courage to say what was on his mind. "Yes, we were, too.

Doesn't anyone check on you fellows—to make sure you're . . . ah, honest?"

Mirabile swallowed. Red creeped around his neck as Carlow sought words.

"The rest of us are, sir. We ride for Texas."

"I know you do, son. I know you do."

Chapter Four

It was a long walk back to the jail. Kileen and Carlow flanked the handcuffed Tanneman, staying to the side of the street itself, to keep away from passersby on the boardwalks. They moved along easily, in spite of the constant string of wagons, freighters, carriages and riders pushing through town. Chance trotted proudly at Carlow's side.

Everywhere people were busy, the interest of the trial already behind them. The boardwalks were thick with merchants and clerks, aristocratic women and dance-hall ladies, ranchers and farmers, Mexican peasants and immigrants, mostly German. In the distance, Carlow saw the clock tower of the *cabildo*, the old town hall building, and was impressed with it all. San Antonio was definitely bigger than where he had grown up.

"Ever see anything like that network of ditches?" Tanneman suddenly said, motioning with his head. "Built by Franciscan priests. A long time ago. *Acequias*, they call it. Goes through the whole town. Really something."

"Aye. Not be smellin' so fine," Kileen observed as they walked.

"Well, it brings water for gardens around town." Tanneman smiled. "Afraid it's also a sewer. Sort of."

"Aye."

As they walked, Tanneman looked over at Carlow. "See that old mission? East of the river. Down there." He pointed with handcuffed hands.

Carlow listened without speaking.

"That's the Mission San Antonio de Valero."

Carlow's eyebrows arched in puzzlement.

"The Alamo. Where our boys fought all those Mex. A long time ago," Tanneman explained. "Think it's an army quartermaster depot now."

Carlow wanted to ask how it became the Alamo, instead of the long mission name, but decided he didn't want to give Tanneman any sign of interest.

As if he had read the Ranger's mind, Tanneman said the mission had become a fort in the early 1800s, when a company of Spanish colonial mounted lancers arrived to support the existing garrison. They were known as *Alamo de Parras*, from a Mexican town of El Alamo, near Parras in Nueva Vizcaya. The name, Alamo, had taken hold because of their decades-long presence.

Tanneman looked again, but Carlow didn't appear to be listening. He was watching a cowboy shuffle from a saloon.

"Afraid my gang's going break me out, Carlow?"

Carlow's responding glare was enough to silence him.

Near the jail, Kileen told Tanneman a prison wagon was coming to take him to Huntsville prison.

"Looks like you boys aren't talking any chances with me." Tanneman snorted.

"A patrol o' fine soldiers be ridin' with ye. Keep ye company. They be here in a few days," Kileen said as they eased along a full hitching rack.

"Damn. That sounds like McNelly's doing."

Kileen smiled and pushed him along the street.

"You boys are going to feel the wrath of my gang. You shouldn't have done this," Tanneman warned.

"Would that be Portland and Barnabas?" Carlow asked.

Tanneman's face became a dark snarl. "You keep them outta this, you hear? They had nothing to with Hillis and me. Nothing."

Tanneman glanced behind them, then turned to Kileen. "You know, when I was a shaman in Persia, hundreds of years ago . . ." He stopped and looked around again. "I was imprisoned. Back then. For doing black magic." He shook his head. "I escaped—and was killed."

" 'Tis a good idea for ye to be careful in the prison."

Tanneman smiled. "I think you really mean that."

From an alley thirty yards behind them, two riders came and wheeled in their direction, leading a third saddled horse. Tanneman was droning on loudly about the importance of dreams, reincarnation and his former life as a Persian shaman. Kileen was riveted to the words; Carlow was watching the boardwalks ahead for any signs of trouble. He wished they had sent someone to follow the remaining Rose brothers to ensure they left town.

Chance half twisted around and growled, his ears flat against his head.

Turning to determine the reason for the sudden anger, Carlow saw the terror headed right for them. At a gallop.

Portland and Barnabas!

Both had knotted their reins and looped them over their saddle horns to free their hands. Portland raised his Winchester. Leading the third horse by its reins, Barnabas leveled his lanyard pistol with his other hand. His body was completely still and focused.

"Thunder, look out!" Carlow yelled. He crouched and spun toward the charging horsemen, drawing his hand carbine in one movement.

Chance, growling and snapping, charged the oncoming horses. The mounts swerved to the right, seeing the oncoming frenzy. The sudden move was enough to cause both brothers to miss. Bullets ripped through the space where Carlow had been moments earlier. One burned the side of his face.

Holding his gun with both hands, Carlow levered and fired rapidly five times. A long burp of lead. Four at Portland, one at the screaming Barnabas. The oldest Rose brother straightened, dropped his rifle and collapsed against his horse's neck. An unseeing Portland bounced against the horse and slid from the running animal, leaving a streak of red on the saddle. His left foot remained in the stirrup and the trapped body thudded along the street like a large doll, until sheer weight pulled his foot free.

At the same time, Kileen drew his long-barreled Colt and laid it across Tanneman's head. The outlaw crumpled to the street. The big Irishman turned, aimed at the wild-firing Barnabas and fired twice. The youngest Rose brother flipped backward. His freed gun spun on the lanyard around his neck like some distraught windmill. He hit the ground headfirst and lay without moving. The three snorting horses rushed past on Carlow's left, their stirrups flapping like big birds unable to lift off.

Then it was over.

A woman sobbed. A man groaned, hit by one of Barnabas's bullets. Hushed voices began to fill the awful void. The acrid smell of gunsmoke took over the street, then vanished with the first breeze.

Mirabile came running from the courthouse, the

marshal and his deputies from the jail. Kileen leaned over to check on Tanneman. At the far end of the street, the three Rose horses slowed and finally discovered a watering trough more interesting than running. Chance studied each dead man, then trotted back to Carlow.

Marshal Timble arrived first, holding a shotgun. Gasping for breath, he stared at the two bodies in the street. "Who are they?"

Two deputies and Mirabile joined the gathering a few strides later. Immediately, the older Ranger went to Carlow and Kileen to see if they were hurt.

"You've been hit, Time." Mirabile pointed at Carlow's cheek.

"I'm all right." Wiping the blood with his sleeve, Carlow answered the marshal's question. The adrenaline of battle was quickly leaving him, making him weary. "That's Portland Rose. That's Barnabas Rose. They were in court. Thought they rode out. One of us should've followed them. I should've guessed they would try something."

He knelt beside his wolf-dog and massaged his ears. His eyes stayed on Chance, not wanting to look at anyone. He had killed a man. It was an awful experience that no one should have to know. Even if the person was evil and trying to kill you. It was awful. One moment, the other person was vibrant with dreams and hopes. The next, he was a mound of dust.

"Would've worked, too, if it hadn't been for Chance. He heard them coming and charged them." Carlow shook his head. It helped some to talk. "Can you believe that? He charged three galloping horses coming at us. Made them swerve. Made the Rose brothers miss."

"Damn. Tanneman's brothers. Fools." Marshal

Timble tugged on his hat brim. His pockmarked face was pale. "Wilson, go get the undertaker. Tell him the state of Texas will be paying." He looked at Carlow and grinned.

"Guess so. Unless San Antonio thinks it should be paying for the funerals of the men who tried to rob their bank." The young Ranger stood and shoved new cartridges into his hand carbine before returning it to its special holster.

Marshal Timble frowned. "Never thought about it that way."

On the boardwalks, cords of silent townspeople watched the scene. A smattering of hushed comments barely cleared the air. Outside the saloon, the same drunken cowboy tried to clap, slamming his free hand against his glass of beer. Foam and liquid spilled over his shirt. He studied the wetness, unable to connect it to his own action.

Kileen helped the dazed Tanneman to his feet. His scalp was bleeding from the blow, but he appeared all right, just dazed. He stood, breathing deeply, unsure of what had happened or where he was.

Tanneman stared at the big Irishman, then at Carlow, and then his eyes found the two dead bodies. His face crumpled in agony and he screamed a long unintelligible cry.

"My God! My God! Why did you do this? My brothers!" he choked.

Kileen let him run to his downed brothers. Tanneman flung himself over his oldest brother. "Oh, Portland . . . Portland. This is so wrong. So wrong." He touched the stiff face and closed his eyes. "I will see you again. I will know it's you."

He half stood, half crawled to Barnabas. "Oh, sweet Barnabas. You never had a chance. Your first life was better than this, I know. Your next will be fine. Yes, fine." He patted his brother's head and stood, glaring defiantly at the two Rangers.

"You will pay for this. All of you," he snarled.

Carlow jumped to his feet and pushed past the marshal, his deputies and Mirabile. "Wasn't what you expected, was it, Tanneman? You thought we wouldn't hear them coming—with all your loud jabbering." He motioned toward Chance, now sitting quietly. "Only you forgot about him. He's a Ranger, too."

Biting his lip, Kileen wanted to say the wolf-dog carried the spirit of Carlow's best friend. Shannon Dornan had been a Ranger and died in the awful Silver Mallow Gang battle in Bennett. He didn't say it, though; Carlow would have been angered by the thought. Tanneman would have appreciated it.

Tanneman's lower lip quivered and he mumbled some jibberish that only he understood.

From the boardwalk behind them, the same older couple hurried to Carlow. They stood near him. The white-haired man said, "Are you all right, son? That was awful. Awful." His gentle wife patted Carlow on the shoulder. "You need the doctor to look at that. My goodness! That was close, wasn't it?"

Mirabile and the local lawmen led the distraught Tanneman away.

"This is the last straw for me, Tanneman. Never thought I'd have to lead a fellow Ranger away to prison," Mirabile declared. "That's it. I'm retiring. Going to my ranch. Get away from all this."

Tanneman screamed a mixture of obscenities, threats about his brothers coming back and strange phrases that sounded like ancient chants.

Chapter Five

Once inside the jail cell, Tanneman Rose was left handcuffed and would stay there until a cavalry escort arrived with a prison wagon to take him to Huntsville. He settled down somewhat, chanting softly in a language no one understood.

Kileen said it was Persian; Carlow said it was gibberish intended to make people think it was Persian. The Rangers left him in Marshal Timble's care and went to the telegraph office to report in.

Carlow outlined Tanneman's guilty sentence and the resulting gunfight with his two brothers.

Mirabile sent a separate wire, resigning.

" 'Tis time for a retirement lunch, me lads," Kileen boomed as they left the telegraph office. "A proper way to see our friend off to his new ways." He pointed at the restaurant across the street.

"You know, I'd like that," Mirabile said, checking his pocket watch. "Then I'd best be riding. It's a ways to the ranch. I'll camp somewhere along the way."

Nodding, Carlow glanced across the street, where the undertaker's assistants were already moving the bodies. He grimaced and looked away. It was like his uncle to talk about eating at such a moment. However, he didn't have a better idea and it would be good to sit down with Mirabile before he left. The three of them had been good friends, and for a long time, in the case of Kileen and Mirabile.

At the restaurant, Kileen grandly ordered for them: a bottle of whiskey, rare steaks, potatoes and apple pie. In that order. As soon as the bottle and three glasses arrived, Kileen poured a generous glass, passed one to each Ranger and raised his own.

"A toast to you, Julian," Kileen announced, holding up his glass of whiskey. "May you live as long as you want, and never want as long as you live."

Both Carlow and Mirabile laughed and all three clinked their glasses. More toasts followed, from all three. Soon, their meals were served and eating took the place of talking and toasting. In spite of what he had expected, Carlow ate well, enjoying their get-together. On finishing a second piece of pie, Mirabile looked at his watch, shook his head and declared he needed to be going.

As they strolled out onto the sidewalk, the telegraph operator came running across the street, waving a piece of paper.

"Ranger Kileen! Ranger Carlow! A wire from Captain McNelly."

Striding up to them, the lanky operator ran his free hand through his slicked-back hair and held out the paper with the other. His right eye blinked, as it often did without his knowing.

"Well, that be fast. Let's be readin' the fine captain's orders."

Mirabile excused himself and headed for the livery to get his horse. He rolled a cigarette as he walked. His horse was already packed for the trip home.

Carlow took a look at the note and yelled out, "Julian! Wait. Looks like we'll be riding out with you."

The slump-shouldered Ranger stopped and turned,

pulling the lit cigarette from his mouth. It was obvious he was happy to have the company.

"Sure thing. What's up?"

"Captain wants us to go to Portland's ranch. Now," Carlow declared. "We'll need to tell the marshal . . . and the judge."

"Aye." Kileen slapped him on the back.

Their orders were to ride to Portland Rose's ranch immediately and look for the bank money taken from previous holdups. A search warrant was to be obtained from Judge Cline. Afterward, they were to check in by wire with McNelly in Bennett and get their next assignment. He was en route with a force of Rangers to stop a gang of Mexican rustlers working the border. If the stolen money was found, Kileen and Carlow would arrange for its return. If they weren't successful, they would join him. They were also to advise Deconer that he wasn't on the Ranger payroll until he was ready to ride. Ranger policy. Actually state policy, to save money.

"Rather be riding with the captain," Carlow said. "We aren't going to find anything at Portland's. Tanneman's too smart for that."

" 'Tis our duty to find that money, me lad. 'Twas Rangers who stole it," Kileen said, motioning toward the marshal's office. "Hisself the captain be worryin' Tanneman's gang might get there before we do."

"Thunder, the only gang Tanneman had is dead. All three of them." Carlow stepped off the boardwalk. "Anyway Tanneman's not going to let boneheads like Portland and Barnabas handle that kind of money."

" 'Tis the captain's orders."

At the marshal's office, Kileen and Carlow advised the marshal they were leaving, but didn't tell him where they were going. Carlow had suggested to his uncle that it would be wise not to share that specific detail.

From the cell, Tanneman held on to the bars and said, "Heading to Portland's, are you, boys?"

"No," Carlow snapped. "Heading for the border. The captain wants to stop all the rustling down there. Got Mexican gangs using the border for safety."

Tanneman smiled evilly. "Looks like one of my brothers got pretty close, Time."

"Not as close as I got."

"You bastard!" Tanneman screamed.

Marshal Timble pledged to keep a two-man watch until the wagon came in the next couple of days, rotating his deputies and himself. One deputy would be stationed inside the jail and one outside, at all times.

Satisfied, Carlow turned to go to the door. Kileen walked over to Tanneman's cell.

" 'Tis sorry I am that this is the way it must be," he said. "Ye will see your brothers' burials, I promise."

"Well, ain't you a real sweetheart, Kileen," Tanneman said. "You ride on. One of these days I will kill you. You an' that smart-ass nephew of yours." He spat at Kileen between the bars.

Kileen let the spittle slide down his cheek. He turned away, then spun back and spat into Tanneman's laughing face. After leaving the jail, Kileen and Carlow got supplies from the general store and left with Mirabile. They checked again on Deconer, who was resting in a hacienda; his thigh wound was slow in healing and he wasn't yet able to walk. He didn't take his removal from the Ranger payroll well and wanted to go with them, but knew he wasn't ready. None of the three Rangers talked after leaving Deconer and getting their horses. Leaving a fellow Ranger—and a friend—behind was never easy.

"Thunder, we don't know exactly where their ranch is," Carlow said as the town disappeared behind them and they slowed their horses to a walk.

"Aye, not so. Tanneman told me about it. Some months back, it be. Not far from Bennett, it be. A wee north."

"Why didn't you say so before?"

Winking at Mirabile, Kileen looked over at his nephew and said, "Ye not be askin'." His jack-o'-lantern grin followed. "Some time seein' Angel an' Ellie we be takin', too."

"There's a lot of land . . . 'a wee north,' " Carlow said and grinned back. "Julian's ranch, for example."

"Aye. We'll be askin' folks as we go."

Changing the subject, Kileen asked, "Do ye be thinkin' Tanneman be put away for the good?"

Carlow took so long to respond that Kileen asked again, "Would ye be thinkin' his previous life—as a Persian mystic—be helpin' him?" Kileen crossed himself.

"No. I was thinking he would try to escape," Carlow said. "I was wondering if we should've stayed until the army came."

"Turn hisself into a small animal, he might," the big Irishman declared. "That necklace he wears—of jaguar teeth—that be from a time he was a big cat."

It was Mirabile's turn to look at him. "Come on, Thunder. You know that's not possible."

Kileen's face indicated he thought it was.

The threesome rode silently, Kileen and Carlow thinking ahead to how close to Bennett they would be after checking out the Rose ranch. Mirabile looked forward to seeing his wife again—and this time, staying at the ranch for good. Kileen was already savoring the idea of a reunion with Angel Balta, the infamous

Mexican woman bandit. Carlow was thinking of Ellie Beckham. He glanced back at his bulging saddlebags. Among his supplies were a special brooch for her and a beaded sheath knife for her son, Jeremiah. They had been purchased in San Antonio.

"Oh, tell me 'tis not so," Kileen blurted and reined his horse to a stop.

"What?" Carlow said, drawing his hand carbine.

Mirabile was in the middle of rolling a cigarette and dropped the makings in surprise.

The big Irishman pointed to a dead crow almost in the center of the trail.

"It's a dead crow, Thunder," Carlow said, reholstering his weapon.

Mirabile shook his head in relief, brushing off the tobacco shreds.

"Aye. 'Tis bad luck. A sign of death, me lad."

With that, he made his nephew get down to pluck a feather from the crow's tail and stick it in the ground.

"Good, me son. Now ridin' around it we go. All o' us. Three times."

Carlow cocked his head. He might have been Irish, but he had none of their superstitious nature—or their lyrical brogue, thanks to his late mother, Kileen's sister.

"We've got riding to do, Thunder."

Mirabile frowned, but said nothing.

"Three times around, me lads. Three times around."

Carlow griped all the way through the little ceremony, but Kileen only smiled, as did Mirabile. The land ahead looked flat, but was broken by hills, canyons and sudden arroyos. White rock decorated most of the ridges. Prickly pear and mesquite added their own touches. In the distance, an occasional ranch house disturbed the wildness.

Dusk found the three lawmen camping near a half-dead pond that badly needed rain to restore it to glory. But the remaining water was clear, not brackish like so many small pools and springs in the region. The appearance of mesquite had alerted them to its presence. Mesquite usually meant water. Two downed cottonwood trees, a wobbly pecan tree and a few lonely willows were solemn testament to high winds and the lack of consistent water. A batch of buffalo grass thrived near the pond. Around them the prairie was highlighted with mesquite, prickly pear, catclaw and alkali. If it was grazing land, there wasn't much for cattle to work with.

The Rangers stayed far enough away from the pond that animals seeking water wouldn't be scared away. That was Carlow's idea.

Kileen rolled his shoulders to relieve the fatigue and took a swig from his flask. He offered it to Mirabile, who enjoyed a long pull and returned it. Carlow declined. After returning the flask to his pocket, Kileen yanked the saddle from his tall horse and studied the rising moon.

" 'Tis a wanin' moon. Matters of importance should nay be done durin' a waning moon. Nay, should not. Should be waitin' for a new moon." He rubbed his chin. "Vegetables are to be gathered while the moon is on the wane. Wood be cut best when the moon finds herself below the horizon."

"Any problem with us gathering mesquite? For a fire?" Carlow teased and nudged Mirabile with his elbow. "Or rubbing down our horses?"

"Nay. 'Tis no problem."

"I'll help get us some wood," Mirabile said.

Soon a small fire cut into the growing dark. They built it in a narrow hollow where the glow was not

likely to clear the land. After cooking, the men doused
the fire. This was Indian country. Small bands of Comanches and Kiowas mostly. No use taking unnecessary risks. At night a fire could be spotted a long way
away.

Bitter hot coffee washed down a pan of salt pork
and beans with a little hardtack. Chance shared Carlow's meal, enjoying the meaty morsels tossed his way.
With so little grazing about, they gave their horses
grain from the small sacks each Ranger carried. Afterward, they walked the horses to the side of the pond
where the water appeared to be clearest, then tied
them up for the night to sturdy branches of the downed
trees. Carlow knelt beside the pond and rubbed the
bullet burn on his cheek with the cool water. It felt
good.

Weary from the riding, the Rangers stretched out,
using their saddles for pillows. Only their boots and
gunbelts were removed. Their weapons were cleaned
and reloaded, including their saddle guns. Of course,
Kileen reminded his nephew not to use the thirteenth
bullet when reloading his hand carbine. Carlow licked
his lips and didn't respond. Mirabile lit a cigarette,
then decided the tiny light could be seen a long way
off and rubbed it out on the ground.

Settling into bed, Carlow reread one of Ellie's letters,
using a small candle for light. He cupped his hat
around it so the tiny flame wouldn't be seen from any
distance. Chance nestled next to him, his head resting
on Carlow's stomach.

Kileen watched and said, "Even if we not be findin'
the money, we must be making a ride to Bennett afterward. The captain be wantin' to know. Aye?"

"I'd like that," Carlow replied. He blew out the candle and made certain his hand carbine was next to him and cocked.

A weary Mirabile said, "Hell, why don't you boys wander up my way afterward? Bertha'd be glad to see you. She's a helluva cook, you know."

"Sounds good to me. How 'bout you, Thunder?" Carlow asked.

"Aye. Bertha be a most wonderful cook. We be doin' it."

Carlow shifted to get more comfortable. The silver crest he wore on a silver necklace slid outside his shirt. It was the only material thing remaining of his mother. She had told him it had belonged to his father. Kileen had told him it was the symbol of a Celtic warrior. He stuffed it back inside his shirt and shut his eyes. No image of his father ever came and now images of his mother were blurred. His solid chest and well-muscled arms were well hidden within his coat. They had helped him win many fistfights as a lad and some as a Ranger. Not as many as his uncle, of course. Few could match that.

Minutes passed.

Carlow was almost asleep when Kileen said, "Me lads, do ye be thinkin' there be a Rose gang still about? Some be sayin' 'tis so."

"Don't know, Thunder," Carlow said, and yawned to reinforce his disinterest in talking more. "Don't know. Could be. Might find them at Portland's ranch, but I doubt it. Let's get some sleep."

"Not my problem anymore," Mirabile said and rolled over to sleep.

"Aye. Don't be starin' at the moon. She not be likin' it."

"I won't. Got my eyes closed."

Carlow was up first and had coffee on and bacon frying when Kileen awoke. Mirabile was still sleeping. Chance's growl jolted the young Ranger from his morning reverie of cooking.

"What's the matter, boy? Coyote wanting water?"

He looked up to see eight mounted Comanches on the ridge twenty yards to the west. They seemed as surprised as he was to see others. It was definitely a war party, with their painted faces, thick chests, arms and legs. Plucked eyebrows added to their fierce appearance. Although short and stout, they were most graceful on horseback. Magnificent horsemen, Carlow thought, and fierce fighters.

"Thunder, Julian, we've got visitors."

"Aye," Kileen responded, already moving beside their horses; his rifle, cocked and ready. "Next to our hosses, I be. They'll be takin' a likin' to 'em, me thinks."

"I'm ready," Mirabile said, stretched out where he had slept, his Spencer rifle cocked. His revolver lay next to him, along with his bullet belt.

The apparent war leader carried a Henry rifle; its stock was decorated with studs and feathers. His face was painted in vertical stripes, alternating between red and yellow. His right arm was similarly painted. So were his leggings. He wore a wolf's head as a headdress, its skin draped down his back.

The others carried bows and arrows and lances shortened for horseback warfare. A warrior with his entire face painted black had a long-barreled revolver resting in his stud belt. Another carried a Springfield rifle, adorned with eagle feathers. Two of the lances held fresh scalps. Silver conchos, tied feathers and strings of cloth decorated their long black hair. One wore a white woman's dress and a white man's fedora, obviously the spoils of a recent raid.

"Stay, Chance. Stay," Carlow said as he grabbed his hand carbine, levered it into readiness and said to Kileen, "I'm going to motion for them to water their horses. Keep your rifle down. Maybe we can keep this from being a shooting affair."

"Aye. 'Tis a good idea. But if 'tis a fight the lads be wantin', ye take the striped lad first. I'll be takin' the fine lad with the black face. Julian, you take the boy with the fine Springfield there. After that, I'll go to the boys on the left. You two take the right. An' we'll meet in the middle." Kileen chuckled, in spite of the situation.

Carlow took a deep breath to ease the tension. He lowered his gun and waved toward the water.

"Paa."

It was the Comanche word for "water." It was also the only Comanche word he knew that would help. He couldn't think of "friend" so he made the sign for it, then gave the sign for "drinking water."

The war leader eased his horse forward two steps, halted and raised his rifle in one hand. He shouted something Carlow didn't understand, but he repeated his words and the sign.

"What's that boy a'jabberin'?" Kileen asked, not taking his eyes off the warriors.

"Don't know. Hope it was 'good morning.'" Carlow looked down at Chance, who was hunched, his teeth bared. "Steady, boy. Maybe they'll water and go."

Mirabile frowned. "That's a big risk."

The war leader spoke again to the other warriors and they began to descend one at a time to the pond to water their horses. He remained where he was, watching Carlow.

"They might try something after they water. Think they've come a long way. Our horses must look mighty good," Carlow said.

"Sweet Jaysus. So do our guns, me son."

"You call it, Time," Mirabile squinted down the barrel of his gun.

After the seven horsemen had watered their horses and returned to the ridge, the leader nudged his pony toward the pond. He looked up at Carlow and smiled.

Smiled! Carlow didn't know at first how to react. He nodded and forced a smile. Was it a trick to make him think they wouldn't attack? His fingers tightened around the hand carbine.

Suddenly, the warrior in the dress screamed a throaty cry and charged his horse toward Carlow. The others held their mounts, watching; the war leader looked up from watering his horse. His face was unreadable.

From his position by their tied horses, Kileen yelled, "Switch. I'll take the lead bastard hisself. Ye dispatch the lady a'comin'."

"Wait."

Carlow didn't move as the warrior galloped down the ridge toward him, waving his lance and screaming.

"Not long, me son." Kileen aimed his rifle at the headman. "Not long."

Holding the cocked hand carbine at his side, the young Ranger's eyes locked onto the rapidly advancing Comanche.

Chance growled.

"No, Chance."

From the pond, the war leader yelled and the warrior reined his horse to a skidding stop. The pony's hooves slammed into the hard earth; the warrior shoved his legs forward to maintain his balance and waved his lance over his head. Grinning, he came to a complete stop five feet from Carlow. Raising his gun, Carlow touched the brim of his hat with the weapon, in a salute, and returned it to his side.

The other warriors grunted their approval. The warrior nudged his horse closer and slowly raised his lance. Carlow knew what was coming. Counting of a coup. The bravest act a warrior could do: touch an armed enemy and return.

"Naugh," Carlow barked, shaking his head and pointing his gun at the warrior.

The move might be a mistake on his part, but he didn't like the idea of the warrior forcing some kind of ritual submission on him. The warrior glanced over at his leader, who motioned with his head for him to return to the others.

"Aiieee!" the warrior shouted, wheeled his pony and galloped back up the ridge.

Minutes later, the eight disappeared as quickly as they had come. Carlow told Kileen to keep watch while he and Mirabile saddled the horses.

"We'll eat while we ride. They might change their minds and come back," Carlow said, grabbing a piece of bacon and pushing it into his mouth. He took another and held it to let it cool before giving it to Chance.

"I'll be havin' me coffee first, lad. No damn redmen be stoppin' me from it," Kileen said as he filled his tin cup, added some whiskey from his flask and savored it.

"That sounds good to me," Mirabile said, holding out his own cup. His hand was shaking. "Maybe I won't ride off by myself until we get closer."

"Pour me one, then the rest on the fire. The coffee, not the whiskey." Carlow grinned.

Chapter Six

Late that evening, Tanneman Rose selected the deputy who would help him escape. Peter Gaggratte didn't know it. Yet. It was one o'clock in the morning. Gaggratte was alone, sitting at the marshal's desk, his boots propped on its scratched top. He was examining an itch on his forearm. Another deputy, Henry Stevenson, sat outside on a bench. The two men would be relieved early in the morning.

Tanneman said, "Got three thousand dollars waiting for you. A day from here. All you have to do is ride with me there. It'll look like I broke out and you chased me. You'll be a hero . . . for trying so hard."

He didn't expect anything to happen right away. It was best to let the idea seduce the guard. Three thousand dollars would go a long way for a man with a wife and four kids. A long way.

That morning before leaving his post, Deputy Gaggratte strutted over to the cell. "You think I'm some kinda fool? You ain't got no money. None close anyway."

Tanneman said, "That's where you—an' the Rangers—are dead wrong." He stood and looked around to make certain no one was listening. His voice lowered. "An hour's ride. South." He looked around again, like a deer at a stream. "It's the money from our first bank job."

"How do I know you're not makin' this up?"

"Look, we ride out at night, you behind me all the way. With your gun. If it's there, we split it. If not, you bring me back. And you're a hero. Either way, it's good—for you." Tanneman folded his arms. "No one will know. I'll tell you how."

"I'll think on it."

"Well, you'd better make up your mind quick. When those soldiers get here, there won't be a chance."

"I don't see how I get away . . . with it." The guard's voice was little more than a breath. "And what about Henry? He's outside whenever I'm on duty."

"It's easy," Tanneman said. "You give Henry a bottle of whiskey. Take the money for it from my stuff in the drawer. You know where it is. In fact, keep the rest of it for yourself. I'm sure your family could use it."

Trying to keep from smiling, he continued, "When Henry's asleep from the whiskey, we walk out. To- gether. Tomorrow night. Easy as that. You'll need horses waiting. In the back." He paused and contin- ued, "If you don't want to do it, I understand. I'll find someone else. Just thought your family could benefit from some extra money."

The next day Tanneman was taken to the burials of his three brothers. Marshal Timble told him it was something Kileen had asked them to do. The ex-Ranger chuckled and chanted softly at the grave site. Gripping his hands together in front of him, he let his mind be- come the shaman he had been in another life. It was something he had developed over the years. None of his brothers had ever understood its meaning. Barna- bas had said he did, but he had been a fool. Of course, the chant was something he made up. Rather, he told himself that it was a ritual coming through, hidden in his brain. The ritual would guide him toward making his escape, guide his words and actions.

"That's enough, Tanneman. We'll head back now," Marshal Timble said, adjusting the shotgun in his arms.

Tanneman hated the raw-faced man. The ex-Ranger took a deep breath and said, "Of course, Marshal."

"What the hell are you doing anyway? Praying?"

"You wouldn't understand."

That evening Gaggratte took his post and the marshal left. Near midnight, Peter Gaggratte opened Tanneman's cell. They walked into a dark night with only a handful of stars watching, passed the drunken deputy and made their way silently to the back, where two horses were already saddled and waiting. A filled canteen dangled from the saddle horn of Tanneman's horse.

"We did it! We did it!" Gaggratte said, barely able to contain his excitement. "Aggie will be so happy. We're going to buy some land. Raise some beef."

Tanneman hushed him as they rode out.

"How far is it to my money again?" Gaggratte asked with a huge smile.

"This way."

An hour outside of town, and a half mile off the main road, Tanneman Rose dismounted near a rather large cave overlooking a creek that showed little interest in keeping its water moving. Three cottonwood trees stood as sentries. He remembered the place as one that he and Hillis had used to hide from a posse.

Gaggratte pulled alongside him.

"There it is, my friend." Tanneman pointed.

"In that cave? There?"

"Right. You'll need a candle and matches. Like I said," Tanneman said, dismounting and tying his reins to a branch.

"Got 'em." Gaggratte jumped from his saddle, tied the reins to another branch and immediately went to his saddlebags. It was awkward holding his rifle and looking for the materials at the same time.

"Let me help." Tanneman smiled. "Step back."

"Sure. Sure. They should be right there," Gaggratte said, so excited he couldn't keep from jumping. "Oh, my, will Aggie be happy. She's the one who told me to do this, you know."

Tanneman's face darkened. "No, I didn't know. I told you not to tell anyone."

"Well, Aggie's not going to tell anybody. She's my wife."

Finding the candle and matches, Tanneman turned from the saddlebags and held them out. "Here you go. Maybe I should go in there first."

Gaggratte frowned. "No. I don't think so. You just might not bring it all out."

"Now why would I do that?" Tanneman held back a smile and motioned for the guard to enter the cave. "Better light the candle out here. It's dark in there. You'll need to go in . . . oh, about twenty feet. Off to your left. Saddlebags are under some rocks. You can't miss it." He paused and added, "Remember now, we're going to split it. Might be more'n six thousand in there."

Gaggratte propped his rifle against his leg and popped a match against his belt buckle. His too-eager movement took away the flame. A second match produced a better result. After lighting the candle, the excited guard disappeared into the dark fissure. Immediately, Tanneman looked around, found a sizeable rock at the edge of the creek and climbed above the cave entrance.

After a few minutes, Gaggratte came to the cave's entrance. "I got it! I got it!"

Tanneman slammed the rock into his head and the guard crumpled. The dust-covered saddlebags flew toward the creek.

"Stupid fool," Tanneman said, pulling the rifle from Gaggratte's body. Blood was working its way down to the creek bed. Tanneman retrieved the saddlebags and left them near the waiting horses.

A shot from Gaggratte's gun to the guard's head made certain he was dead. As if nothing had happened, Tanneman sat beside the body and repeated the chant that was becoming his own ritual, grasping his jaguar necklace. He stood and looked around. If he could find a crow, he would kill it and drink some of its blood. He had decided this was a tradition of his previous life. To kill a crow would grant him success over his enemies.

The shaman's great gift was the ability to transform himself into an animal, he had decided. The gift had been passed on to him in his ability to transform himself as necessary. It was too dark to see much of anything, especially a crow, he decided. More important, for now, was to complete the rest of his plan.

After a drink from the stream, Tanneman mounted his horse and took the reins of Gaggratte's. He laughed. The next thing to do was to "kill" himself. The ultimate transformation. But he had to do it quickly, before anyone came to the jail and realized there had been an escape.

Quickly, he returned to the main road, riding his horse and leading Gaggratte's. He reined up beside a long gully snuggled parallel to the well-traveled path. It was the first of a line of slopes and arroyos that stretched out for a half mile, broken by several clusters of trees. This was a good place for an ambush. He needed someone to become *him* in death. If not, he would ride on until someone suitable was found. He didn't expect any posse until after the morning shift of lawmen arrived.

He tied the two horses well off the trail in a shallow ravine that was two over, so they wouldn't give away their presence and alert anyone. Lack of sleep was pushing its way into his mind, but he couldn't let that deter him. The next step in his plan was the one that would stop any Rangers from seeking him. He would stage his own death.

" 'When devils will the blackest sins put on, They do suggest at first with heavenly shows.' " Tanneman muttered one of his favorite passages from the second act of Shakespeare's *Othello*, letting both of his hands swing dramatically toward an imagined audience. His shrill laugh turned the horses' heads toward him, their ears cocked for understanding.

Discovery of his escape would not be too far away. Still, it was vital to be patient.

"Patience, ah, the wondrous virtue," he said. "Something I learned centuries ago." He laughed, then heard something.

Yes, someone was riding on the road. Probably headed for town. He crouched behind the rocky incline. Good. The rider was alone. But even in the dark he could tell the horseman had light-colored hair. That wouldn't do. Patience. Two more riders passed and he was beginning to wonder if he should ride on and stage his "death" later.

A half hour slid by and he almost dozed. The noise of a rider brought him alert.

From his concealed position, Tanneman fired. The

horse reared in fright as the man threw his hands in the air and fell from the saddle. Tanneman quickly fired a second shot. The startled horse stutter-stepped and stopped, its ears alert. Speaking softly, Tanneman gathered the reins. Faint blushes of rose lined the dark sky.

He carried the body back to where Gaggratte had died and tied the three horses to nearby trees. Without wasting motion, he stripped off the body's clothes and put them on. The dead man was slightly taller than Tanneman, but the clothes would do until he could buy some. A bonus was discovering the man was carrying a small wad of gold certificates and a short-barreled Colt, but no extra bullets. The gun was more important than the money—for his special presentation.

False dawn was strutting across the sky as Tanneman dressed the body in his own shirt and pants, then built a small fire. The light of a new day took away any real concern about it being seen. Reluctantly, he placed the jaguar necklace around the dead rider's neck. The spirits would understand. He dragged the body onto the flames, pushing the dead man's face into the hot flames. The crackling sound made him queasy, but it was necessary. That was the final touch. No one would be able to identify the body. Tanneman left it as if *he* had died and fallen there.

Even though Tanneman didn't want to do so, the guard's rifle had to be left at the scene, placed carefully near Gaggratte. Tanneman left the guard's handgun in the man's hand. He fired both guns three times each, with the noses next to the ground to muffle the sound. His boot covered the holes with new dirt.

To the posse eventually coming, it would appear that the guard and Tanneman had killed each other in a wild fight. No one would examine the body of "Tanneman" closely; it would be enough that the breakout had been solved. Gaggratte would be treated as a dead hero. He laughed. It was the ultimate in theater. After removing the saddlebags, he turned his horse and Gaggratte's loose and encouraged them to run. They would return to town—or be found by the posse. He strapped both sets of saddlebags and the canteen onto the third horse, mounted and rode away, giggling.

His next projects would be to kill the men who had brought him to this: Judge Wilcox Cline; District Attorney Waddell Johnson; Marshal Timble and all the Rangers who had been involved, including Captain McNelly. All would die. It was time to bring his previous self into full bloom; the Persian shaman had been known for his transformations and his masks.

His shrill laugh echoed through the quiet land.

Chapter Seven

After riding for two hours toward the fast-rising sun, Tanneman Rose passed a lone shack off to his left. His tired mind took a few seconds to let it register in his thoughts. He reined up and looked back at the small building resting in a shallow ravine, almost like the place had grown from the land. It definitely looked abandoned. Probably had been a line cabin at one time. He swung the horse around and headed back.

"Aho, the cabin!" he yelled, holding his pistol at his side as he neared the building.

If anyone were here, Tanneman would kill him. Immediately. There was no reason to take any chances now. He was too close. He yelled again, but no one answered. Assuring himself that it was, indeed, abandoned, Tanneman rode his horse up to the structure and swung down. His empty canteen bounced.

A small corral, probably big enough for six horses, adjoined the shack. Unsaddling his horse, he turned the animal loose in the enclosure. The bay went to a low water trough half-filled with old rainwater. It was enough to quench its thirst and leave enough for later. Tanneman found an old bucket filled with grain shoved against the edge of the house and away from the rain. After smelling and verifying it still had food value, he brought it to the center of the corral for his horse to enjoy.

Drawing his pistol again, Tanneman went to the closed door and shoved it open. It didn't like the idea of moving and groaned a sad reaction. He stepped inside. The one-room building danced with shadows, disturbed by his intrusion. Thick cobwebs and layers of dust confirmed a long absence. A quick inspection brought only a nearly empty sack of coffee, a dented coffeepot and two china cups, both chipped. No food. A cot lay against one wall. Across the way was a fireplace that hadn't been used in a long time. He guessed at least a year. Didn't matter. Heat wasn't a concern. Sleep was—and after that, something to eat. Unfortunately, he would have to ride on for food.

He was asleep almost as soon as he hit the cot, not even getting his boots off. His dreams were wild and unsettling. The Rangers, who had arrested him, rode on fiery horses through his body. Kileen and Carlow pointed their fingers at him and laughed. Laughs that turned into curling snakes. Running through the dream was a strange wagon that ran over the snakes.

He awoke with a start three hours later. Sweat glistened on his face and arms. Listening intently, he could just hear the snorting of his horse outside. His stomach was growling with the need of food. The only water he knew of was in the horse trough. He grabbed his canteen, filled it from the trough and drank deeply, letting ribbons of water run down his chin and the front of his shirt. At first, he had thought this would be the right time to prepare himself ceremonially for his strategy of revenge. A Persian shaman would do such.

A stronger desire, however, was the demand for food. The ceremony of revenge could wait. Even in his hungered state, he studied the shack, noting it was made mostly from long planks of wood.

A few minutes later, he was traveling again. He knew of no large towns nearby, but it seemed to him there were several small communities. Clearing a long bluff, he saw a settlement and his mind jumped with a tired joy. Twelve buildings straddled the short main street. He had no idea of its name, nor did he care.

Tying his horse to the hitching rack in front of the restaurant, he went inside. Instinct made him study the restaurant's inhabitants as the door closed behind him. There were no Rangers, at least none he knew. The five men eating looked up out of curiosity, then returned to their food.

He tried not to overeat, but his stomach cried out and he was glad to oblige. A pot of hot coffee chased down two bowls of beef stew and large chunks of cornbread. Sipping a last cup, he asked the waiter for the name of the town.

"Some are callin' it Prairie Village," the bucktoothed waiter replied. "Most folks around hyar jes' call it 'town', though."

Tanneman nodded to keep from smiling. "Haven't looked around. What all's here?"

"Not from hyar, are ya?" the waiter said. "Knew it ri't off. Know'd ever'body 'round."

"Good for you."

The waiter proudly explained that besides the restaurant, Prairie Village boasted a general store, livery, two saloons, a whorehouse, gun shop, boardinghouse, surveyor's office and bank, drugstore and a barbershop and bathhouse.

Tanneman paid him and headed for the barbershop. An hour later, a cleaned and shaved Tanneman Rose entered the small house on the far corner of town. A woman, plain of face with weary eyes and long dark hair resting along her shoulders, gave a lifeless smile and invited him in. She brought practiced enjoyment, faster than he wished, but he wasn't in a mood to complain.

Afterward, he paid her, opened the door and studied the surroundings. An old habit.

A one-armed peddler riding an enclosed wagon bounced along the street. The side panels proclaimed: hard goods . . . knives . . . shirts . . . books . . . clothing . . . medicines . . . horseshoes.

Tanneman was fascinated. He turned back toward the whore. "Who's that?"

Licking her lips, she said, "Oh, that's just the peddler. Comes around every now and then. Selling stuff. Always moving. Lost his arm in the war, I heard. Usually stopping at farms and ranches, you know. Don't know his name. Usually comes here when he's in town."

She flipped her head to move and resettle her long hair. Her hand rested on her extended hip; it was her best provocative pose.

He didn't notice and left without another word.

"Need to get a fresh horse," Tanneman said, strolling into the livery stable. "What can you offer? I'll trade mine." He motioned toward the bay he was leading.

The short, bowlegged livery stable manager studied Tanneman, then his horse. "How sound is it?"

"Been good for me," Tanneman said, "but it needs rest. I'm riding dispatch for the Rangers and I need to get to them soon as I can."

"Rangers, huh?" the liveryman said, scratching his chin. "Thought maybe yah was runnin' from them."

Tanneman laughed deeply and said, "No. Just trying

to help them. I'd show you the dispatch, but I'm not supposed to." He motioned toward his saddlebags.

"Say, how come they ain't usin' the telegraph?"

Biting the inside of his cheeks to keep from saying something angry, Tanneman said simply, "Where they are, it isn't."

"Oh sure," the liveryman said. "Kinda like here, I reckon."

"Yeah."

The liveryman waved his arms. "Oh, didn't mean nothin'. Just we don't get many strangers ridin' through here." He rubbed his chin. "I hear tell we might get the wire next year. Been here all my life, ya know."

"Well, good for you."

The livery operator beamed. "Ya know if you're stayin' around, there's gonna be a bunch o' races tomorrow. Hoss races an' footraces." He straightened his back. "Figure on enterin' the footrace myself. Took third last year."

Proudly, he explained the town would be celebrating its founding, an annual event. "Do it every year, ya know. Well, two years ago, we didn't. Too much rain. But I think that's the only time."

"Sounds like fun, but I've got to be moving on."

Looking genuinely disappointed, the livery operator added that a cake contest and a spelling bee were also planned. Tanneman nodded and brought the conversation back to horses.

Tanneman rode out of the livery on a long-legged buckskin horse, then stopped at the gun shop and bought a Winchester, two boxes of ammunition, a pistol belt and holster for his Colt, and a large sheath knife. An idea was forming in his head. He remembered the distinctive mask of theater, combining tragedy and comedy. A mask would be perfect. In its own way, it would be a death mask. For the men who had betrayed him.

Another stop, at the general store, took longer. He entered the cluttered store and let its smells of fresh coffee, bacon, tobacco, spices, vinegar and leather surround him. Like most such stores, it carried a little of everything. Walking around barrels and kegs of grocery staples, he examined the supplies displayed on rough-planked shelves. With a basket, he gathered a shirt, pants, canteen, leather strips, a small sack of coffee, another of beans, one of flour, a wrapped package of beef jerky, another of salt pork, eight cans of peaches, a glass jar of preserves, two pencils and several sheets of paper.

Satisfied with his selections, he moved to the lumber-and-hardware section of the store. He selected a sack of nails, hammer, chisel and twenty thin pieces of wood. Each was about eight inches wide and a foot long. After choosing the wood Tanneman grabbed a can of white paint and a brush.

"Those'll work good for shingles," the clerk exclaimed as he checked out. "If you've got roof problems." He smiled, revealing two missing teeth, and slid his hand along the side of his head, caressing his combed-back hair.

Irritated, Tanneman caught his anger before responding. "Well, my wife, you know, she got real unhappy when the roof leaked. After that last rain." He shook his head. "Got to keep on their good side, you know."

"Sure do. Looks like she's got you doin' some painting, too." The clerk winked and then asked, "Haven't seen you in here before, have I?"

Tanneman didn't like the innocent curiosity, but tried not to show it. "No. We live over yonder. Only been there a short while." He motioned toward the east, hoping the vagueness would suffice. "Thought I'd give the town a try."

"Good. Glad to have you here," the clerk said and started to ask another question.

"Thanks now. I'll be seeing you next time," Tanneman said and turned toward the door with most of his purchases juggled in his arms.

"Hey, you might want to bring your wife in tomorrow," the clerk said.

Tanneman stopped without turning.

"It's our big day. Celebrates the founding of the town," the clerk declared. "All kinds of things goin' on. Contests an' races. Everybody around will be here. Good time to meet folks."

Turning toward the counter slowly, Tanneman thanked him and went outside to pack his purchases in his saddlebags and return for the wood. The clerk was busy helping a woman with a bolt of cloth, so the ex-Ranger didn't have to talk with him any longer. He tied the shingles onto the back of the saddle and headed out.

By dusk, he had returned to the shack and begun creating a mask from one of the wooden pieces. He gouged eye and mouth holes into the narrow wood, and carved an indentation in the wood to allow his nose some room.

A small circle with a cross in its center was painted in white where a nose would have been. It was a symbol of the Persian shaman he had been. He had seen the mark often in his dreams. He laid the new mask on the floor to dry. He studied the hand-painted design and smiled. A circle was the symbol of reincarnation. Of completion. Of accomplishment. The lines extending from it, like a sun's rays, represented the men he would kill. The mask itself was a symbol of death. Like a funeral mask of ancient tribes. Whenever he was conducting one of his planned revenges, he would wear the wooden mask to disguise himself. That would allow him to direct the law to someone else. Someone innocent. Someone who would pay with his own life.

He worked for hours before taking a break. Hot coffee and a can of peaches tasted good. Four hours later, he was exhausted and went to sleep on the floor in the middle of his mask making. Next to him were ten finished masks.

When he awoke, he continued to work on the masks, stopping only to relieve himself, drink coffee and eat something, usually more peaches. Finally, twenty masks were finished. Nails held rawhide strips that would hold the mask to his face; another strip came from the top of the mask and would be tied to the cross pieces. This would keep the mask steady and less likely to slip down.

Before a yellow half moon, a naked Tanneman sat before a small fire fifty yards from the shack. He chanted, waved each mask over the smoke of his fire and raised it toward the silent moon. When he was finished, he straddled the small fire and let the smoke plumes crawl up his nude body.

Holding up a mask with both outstretched hands, he yelled into the dark night. "Aaron Kileen, you will die."

Laying the mask aside, he picked up a second and repeated his ceremonial commitment. "Time Carlow, you will die."

With each mask, he screamed the name of one of his intended victims. "Julian Mirabile, you will die. Pig Deconer, you will die. Waddell Johnson, you will die.

Wilcox Cline, you will die. Marshal Timble, you will die. Leander McNelly, you will die."

Stepping away from the smoking fire, his shoulders rose and fell. He felt like the shaman he had been so many years before. Yes, he was the same man. He could sense it throughout his entire body. He had reconnected with his soul. From a distant tree, an owl saluted his determination. Tanneman smiled; the owl was definitely a reincarnated being. He was certain it was his late brother Hillis. The large bird's feathers reflected gold and red from Tanneman's fire.

"Hillis, it is good to have you here." Tanneman saluted. "Do you know where Portland and Barnabas are?"

He was ready. Revenge would be his. Sweet revenge. All it would take was time—and his own brilliance. Carefully, he prepared, on a sheet of paper, the list of men who would be killed.

Chapter Eight

Morning brought the sounds of a creaking wagon outside. Tanneman Rose jumped from the cot and grabbed his new Winchester. My God, has the law already figured out my escape? he asked himself as he hurried to the door.

He peeked through the barely opened door and saw the peddler's wagon outside. In its seat was the one-armed peddler from yesterday. He was a heavyset man in an old suit and barely shaped fedora. His age was difficult to gauge, probably in his forties. A chestnut horse with two white stockings and a bay pulled the wagon and appeared happy to stop.

From what the prostitute had told him, the man traveled from town to town, ranch to ranch, farm to farm, selling goods. Why was he here?

"How may I help you?" Tanneman opened the door. His rifle was clearly visible.

"Wal, I am certainly sor-ry, suh," the peddler responded in a high-pitched Missouri drawl. "Didn't think nobody was hyar. No suh, I didn't." He waved his right arm. "I, uh, have stayed hyar. Before. I'm sorry."

In that moment, Tanneman Rose made a decision. Becoming a peddler would be a perfect way to move about the region without raising suspicion. The perfect transformation. The perfect theater. The wagon had been sent to him for the fulfillment of his plan. He had dreamed it.

"I'm just doing the same. Come in and I'll get us some coffee on," Tanneman invited.

Eagerly, the peddler lashed his reins around the brake stick and climbed down.

Tanneman fired twice and the Missouri peddler coughed and collapsed next to the right front wheel. The two horses were too tired to get excited and instead looked around for something to graze on. Calmly, Tanneman walked to the wagon and fired again into the unmoving body.

His inspection of the covered vehicle revealed that every inch was packed with goods, from ready-to-wears to sewing patterns, from boxes of needles to thread and thimbles. Even pairs of black silk gloves and green gauze veils were shoved into a box. Three pillows and two worn blankets occupied a small corner. Several loose books sat on top—two on poetry, one of Shakespeare's plays and three old school editions. A large box contained a wide assortment of bottled medicines, mostly home remedies of Epsom salts, cod-liver oil, opium, paregoric, camphor and snakeroot. Other items included folded linens, small mirrors, coils of rope, bridles and two saddles, pots and pans, boxes of tobacco, horseshoes and bullets, a heavy knife-sharpening wheel, a box of knives and a few revolvers from the War of Northern Aggression.

Laughing at his luck, he decided to develop the disguise he would wear as the peddler, using the dead man as a model. The spirits wanted him to prepare his transformation. A pillow from the wagon became stomach padding, held in place around his waist with long leather strings, also from the peddler's wares.

What to wear? He decided on the peddler's own

worn suit coat of gray woolen heritage, a wrinkled string tie and his battered hat. There was no need to change his pants or boots; both would work. His own shirt, taken from the earlier road traveler, would also be fine. Besides, the peddler's was bloody and sported bullet holes. Everything fit well enough for his purpose, especially when he wore the pillow.

He walked around the small room, working on a limp he decided would add to his new persona. A cane from the wagon would help the presentation. As he practiced, he imitated the Missouri accent and high voice of the peddler. He wouldn't attempt to be the man literally, but the transformation required mannerisms, and it was easy to imitate something he had already seen or experienced.

Then Tanneman inserted tiny rolls of paper from his paper pad between his lower jaw and cheeks on the inside of his mouth. With one of the mirrors from the wagon, he checked his idea. The effect made his face more full, but wasn't particularly comfortable. Strips torn from a towel, also taken from the wagon, would work much better. He shoved them into his coat pocket.

" 'When devils will the blackest sins put on, They do suggest at first with heavenly shows.' " He again muttered one of his favorite Shakespeare passages. His shrill laugh bounced around the room.

After testing the approach, he decided it made sense to present himself as one-armed as well. The coat sleeve was already pinned in place; he only had to work with his arm to decide the best way to conceal it. Keeping it curled inside his shirt, under his coat, worked well. It would be an easy way to hide a handy gun.

Looking into the mirror, he rubbed his unshaven chin and decided growing a beard would be a good way to hide his face. He smiled at the idea of such a transformation. This was more of the wonder of theater.

The man who had raised him and his brothers—Highland Griffin—instilled this love of the stage, of make-believe, in him. Neither Hillis nor Portland cared anything about performing. Barnabas had tried, from time to time. This gift of becoming someone else had carried the ex-Ranger to considerable wealth—and he had tried to make his siblings wealthy, too. Until they were foolish enough to get killed.

Certainly he had accumulated far more riches than anyone could ever earn prancing about in some threadbare costume on a makeshift stage, constantly moving from one forgotten town to the next, as their foster parent had done all his sad life.

Far more wealth than wearing a Ranger badge, for that matter. Actually, he had seen being a Ranger as a role to play, between bank robberies.

The idea of a beard simmered in his mind. It was limiting. He needed to be able to change disguises, to transform. A fake beard would be necessary. Stopping at a theater in one of the bigger towns would be a priority. He smiled. Of course. The theater.

He had never known his mother, but suspected she had been one of the dancers in the traveling troupe. He had also deduced that Highland Griffin was their real father, although the gentle man had never admitted it.

Definitely, black hair would enhance his transformation. It would make things easier if he wore it that way all the time. He would have to find some black hair dye.

Satisfied with himself and the next steps he must take, he walked toward the doorway. A spider meandered across the floor. His first instinct was to step on it, but then he reminded himself that he had been a spider in another life. After his life as a Persian shaman.

"Go along, fellow," Tanneman said. "I know what it's like. I was there, too."

He straightened and the thought that this might be Portland occurred to him. Or was it was too soon? His own past-life recall on that point was sketchy. Some of it, he admitted to himself, was painful. Most, though, was quite pleasant. But he had no sense of how quickly he had returned. He scooped the spider into one of the empty peach cans, with the help of the brim of his hat.

A mask served as a temporary lid while he looked for something bigger and better to hold the spider. Finally, he chose to dump the preserves into another empty peach can. A handful of grass and one of dirt were added to the jar, so the spider would have a nice place to stay. Then he moved the spider from the peach can to the jar. Small holes in the lid ensured air. He carefully carried the jar outside and placed it on the wagon. He was certain it was Portland, reincarnated.

After placing his masks inside the wagon, he dragged the dead peddler into a ditch that worked its way across the land, aided by a sometimes creek. He wrapped the bloody scalp in a towel for later disposal. Whoever found the body would blame Indians. Minutes later, he rode away on his buckskin toward Prairie Village. He would return for the wagon after he robbed the settlement's bank. With the excitement of the celebration at hand, no one would pay attention to the bank. The trick was to get there before it closed for the day.

Chapter Nine

Tanneman Rose went directly to a vibrant town southwest of San Antonio. He had been there once before—as a Ranger. And as a bank robber. All of his brothers had been involved. He smiled when he thought of his first bank robbery since escaping; the townspeople of Prairie Village never sent a posse, at least not one that came his way. Too busy with their day of races and cake contests, he supposed, and chuckled again.

Everything about the town was appealing to Tanneman Rose—and little had changed since his last visit. Saloons. Brothels. Gambling. A nice, fat bank. And most importantly right now, a theater. Even though the Brass Robin Theater had definitely seen its better days.

He rode past the building. According to the framed notice, *King Richard III* was appearing nightly. A traveling company, of course. Fifty cents was the price for a seat. The added stripe across the lower part of the poster declared: sold out.

Elsewhere, morning activity was taking over the main part of town. Freighters and wagons of all sizes attacked the streets while townspeople focused on their daily chores. No one noticed him. For that he was appreciative. The peddler's wagon and horses had been left in a nicely shaded basin a mile from town.

He liked riding the buckskin far more than being in

the wagon. He glanced back at his saddlebags, empty except for one mask. Soon, though, he would have to let the animal go. People would be suspicious of a peddler with a fine horse.

Rumors were everywhere that a large group of Rangers were moving toward the border to try to stop Mexican rustlers using the border as their safety. But the right Rangers would definitely come after he started his pattern of revenge. He would go first to San Antonio. If Judge Cline and District Attorney Johnson weren't there, he would wait for them, probably getting rid of Marshal Timble while he did so. Then he would head north to kill Mirabile. The former Ranger had a small ranch just outside of Strickland, two days' ride from San Antonio and a day from Bennett.

On the way he planned to retrieve all of the stolen money. How brilliant he had been to keep it—and its location—from his brothers. After killing Mirabile, he would again wait, this time for Kileen and Carlow to come. He knew they would and was certain they had gone to his brother's ranch to search. The fools. Mc-Nelly would definitely have to be tracked down. That would be the sweetest of them all. Then he would simply ride away to New Orleans. It was a fine plan.

Reining up beside the theater, he studied its aging frame with appreciation. He dismounted and led the horse to the back of the building. He expected to find the back door locked, but that wouldn't deter him. What he wanted from inside wouldn't take long, he expected. A fake full beard, mustaches and eyebrows. Hair dye. And a lotion to provide darker skin if necessary for a disguise. Other elements of disguise, if possible. He took a canvas sack from his saddlebags and shook out its wrinkles.

It only took a minute to break open the hanging lock

with the butt of his revolver, and he slipped inside.
The place smelled musty and shadows played everywhere. It seemed like home. He walked past three
small dressing rooms and out onto the stage itself.
Painted sets were positioned for the evening's performance. Additional sets lay in the corner.

A creak accompanied his steps to the center of the
stage. He jumped at the sound and laughed, then
bowed and took in the silent seating for at least four
hundred, counting the double-decked boxes in a semi-
circle above the main floor.

He presented the nonexistent audience with, " 'True
hope is swift, and flies with swallows wings; Kings it
makes gods and meaner creatures kings,' " then bowed
again. The sack flopped against his body. It was the
only line from *King Richard III* he could recall.

How appropriate, he thought. His first killing had
actually been the man who had broken his foster father's will and taken most of his money, in a theater
production gone bad. For a moment, he considered
staying in town and watching the evening's performance. That idea vanished as he reminded himself of
the need to rob the bank. His money from the Prairie
Village Bank was getting low. He spun and returned
to the first dressing room. What he sought should be
there.

The first room was a disappointment. Obviously, it
was earmarked for a lead actress. Only dresses occupied the large trunk; many more hung from a rope
across the entire side.

The second dressing room contained what he
wanted. Among the costumes, stage pistols and swords
was a flat box containing every manner of fake facial
hair, from wigs to beards and mustaches. He opened
the box, examined its contents and set them aside to

take. A pile of wigs and beards, even sets of fake heavy eyebrows. He added two pairs of fake eyeglasses. On the dressing room table, he found the rest of his needs: black hair dye and a large bottle of tan makeup. In the bottom of the trunk, he found a weathered and cheap imitation of an Indian headdress, yanked free three feathers and placed them in the sack as well. He might not need them, but the tan lotion and the feathers would give him a good start on an Indian disguise if he wanted it. He slipped them into his canvas sack and headed out.

A few steps from the back door, a loud voice interrupted his escape.

"Hold it right there!"

Tanneman couldn't see the person clearly and decided it was wiser to stop than to risk a hurried escape. He slipped his Colt into the sack and waited.

Within a few seconds, a stagehand with a pronounced limp appeared from the shadows. He wore worn Confederate pants, suspenders and a kepi hat. His extended belly was barely contained by his filthy shirt and stretched waistband.

"What do you think you're doing in here?" he demanded.

Tanneman smiled. "Hoping to buy a ticket. The back door was unlocked so I came in. Perhaps you can help me."

"Don't give me that crap. You busted the lock," the stagehand growled. "What you got in that sack?"

"Oh. Let me show you."

Tanneman reached into the sack with his right hand, withdrew the gun and fired. The surprised stagehand gasped and the ex-Ranger fired again. The shots rang through the quiet building, but Tanneman hoped they wouldn't reach the street. Stepping over the dying man, Tanneman reached the door, opened it and listened.

No sounds of alarm reached him.

He closed the door and decided to see if the show's receipts were kept somewhere. A few minutes later, he found a fat sack of certificates and coins, lying in plain sight on what must have been the stage manager's desk. He emptied a large cup of cigars into his sack, along with the money and disguise props. Retreating to his horse, he fixed the lock to appear unbroken from a distance.

After tying the sack to his saddle horn, he removed the mask from his saddlebags, tied it in place around his face, then pushed it onto the top of his head until it was needed. To the casual observer, it would appear to be a hat. He held his actual hat in his left hand at his side. He had practiced this move many times while riding.

The key was to move slowly to keep from attracting attention. Tanneman reined up at a hitching rack one building away from the bank. He dismounted and wrapped the reins around the pole for a quick release, then pulled empty saddlebags from the back of his saddle. He paused, a step before entering the bank, and yanked the mask into place and put on his hat. Pulling his Colt, Tanneman strolled inside. He didn't lock the door. It was better for someone to come in while he was robbing the bank than to realize the bank was locked and go for help.

Inside, customers and bank employees were stunned by the appearance of the wood-masked robber with a gun. He loved their reaction. It was grand theater.

"This is a holdup. Fill these saddlebags. Fast. My gang's outside, waiting," Tanneman growled. "Two of them will stay on the roofs across the street for five minutes. With Winchesters. Anyone coming out of the bank before then will be shot down. Understand?"

Outside the bank, Tanneman Rose kept his head down to avoid anyone noticing the mask, then pulled it off, returned his hat to his head, mounted and rode slowly away, holding the mask at his side. He rode through town without looking back. Again, slowly. His warning to the bank patrons had definitely worked. He slowed alongside a string of horses tied to a saloon hitching rack. Dismounting, he looked around to make certain no one was watching, then shoved the mask into the closest saddlebag and remounted.

A mile from town, he pulled up alongside his peddler's wagon. The two hobbled wagon horses, already hitched, barely looked up before returning to their grazing. He unsaddled the buckskin, threw the saddle gear into the back of the wagon and slapped the horse into a run. He hated to let the fine horse go, but it was necessary.

This time he expected a posse.

He added the filled saddlebags to the back of the wagon. Quickly, he put on the new fake beard and old fedora, hiding the rest of his new masquerade materials in a corner of the wagon, under some pots and pans. Unbuckling his gunbelt, he drew the Colt and shoved it into his waistband so his hidden hand could control it. He wouldn't take the time to add the stomach padding or special clothes, but he shoved the mouth rolls into place as he clucked the horses into a walk. He made certain the wagon wheels and horses covered the tracks of the buckskin being stopped and unsaddled. Appearing to be headed for town would further dismiss him from any suspicion. He shook his head and chuckled.

" 'When devils will the blackest sins put on, They do

suggest at first with heavenly shows.'" He again savored the favored Shakespeare passage.

His shrill laugh turned the horses' heads toward him, their ears cocked for understanding.

The creaky buckboard bounced and leaned one way, then the other, as they eased onto the road to town. Rattling and clanking, things slid behind him as he rode back along the road from which he had just come. He hadn't gone a quarter mile before a posse of a dozen armed men cleared the closest hill. He waved and the men reined up.

"Seen a man riding hard?" the red-faced marshal asked.

Tanneman answered in his practiced Missouri drawl. "Yah, I sur did. Yessuh. Ridin' a buckskin. Had a wood . . . ah, mask over his face. Scary as all git out." He wiped his mouth with his hand. "I feared he might shoot me an' I got off the road so's he could pass. What's he done?"

"Robbed our bank," the marshal declared and waved his arm. "Come on, men, he's not far ahead of us!"

Tanneman chuckled and headed on. The mask was left behind for someone to explain. San Antonio was next. He couldn't help wondering if he had been this brilliant when he was a Persian shaman.

Chapter Ten

The two Irish lawmen rode toward a familiar hacienda less than a day's ride from Bennett. Their long coats fluttered around their stirrups and against the flanks of their horses. Chance was a few feet behind. Mirabile had left them earlier to head to his ranch. Their search of Portland Rose's ranch had been fruitless. The only thing of interest they had found was a strange-looking shrine in one bedroom they thought Tanneman had built.

As they rode, Carlow had talked about the merits of settling down, marrying and raising a family. Kileen planned to stay with Angel Balta while Carlow rode on to Bennett to send the message to McNelly that no money had been found and wait for their next orders. Carlow couldn't wait to see Ellie Beckham; he could already see the surprised look in her eyes.

Pulling up, Carlow noted how the weather had turned the sun-dried alluvial clay and straw house into a rainbow of dull browns and grays. Kileen only grunted. To the west, the crop fields hadn't seen a plow in years, nor would they. Angel Balta, the one-time outlaw queen, wasn't interested. She preferred other pastimes.

"Angel, me darlin', do ye be there?" Kileen yelled out as they reined up.

"*Si*. You two geet yourselves down and in here," came an unseen, but hardy, female voice.

Before they had dismounted, Angel came hurrying from her house. She was a formidable woman even now. In her waist belt were two pearl-handled revolvers. An old sombrero bounced on her back. Long, mostly gray hair matched the rhythm along her shoulders. Her massive bosom jiggled and threatened to break through the strained buttons trying to hold their places on her blouse. Even though she no longer rode, her large Mexican spurs added their own music as she rushed to greet them.

Once a stunning beauty, she was reported to have bedded a hundred men. And shot at least fifty others. Heavy boots covered her calves and nearly reached her knees. The inset design of green, red and gold was mostly worn to bare horsehide and the remaining colors had faded to gray. But growing older had taken away none of her sensuous charm.

A wide grin took control of her wrinkled brown face. It forced the old scar across her high cheekbones and wide nose to move up and down. The scar was a reminder of a long-ago battle between the United States Army and a band of Mexican guerrillas near the border.

"*Buenas tardes*, *Senor* Beeg Thunder and *mi hijo Senor* Time," she exclaimed. "Angel ees *mucho* lucky. *Adelante!* Come in! Come in!"

Her dark eyes sparkled and her long lashes batted their welcome to Kileen. A stained tan leather skirt, accented with a row of tiny bells sewn around the bottom edge, flared wide at her knees. Carlow was certain it was the same outfit she had worn when they had stayed three years ago.

She wrapped her arms around the big Irishman and gave him a warm kiss on the mouth. He returned it with the same enthusiasm.

Talking quietly to Chance, Carlow tried not to look at their special moment. He privately hoped to be greeted the same way by Ellie Beckham.

"And *mi hijo*, you have come back to me," Angel declared and gave Carlow an enthusiastic hug and a kiss on the cheek. She stepped back from him, her hands still holding his shoulders. "Et ees so *bueno*. You ees strong, *mi hijo*. You ees warrior."

Carlow told her that she, too, looked wonderful, knowing that "*mi hijo*" was Spanish for "my son." He was the same age as her oldest son, Miguel, who had died years ago. She had helped heal Carlow after an awful battle in Bennett when the Rangers had fought the infamous Silver Mallow Gang. Kileen had brought him to her house, more dead than alive, a safe haven, he hoped, from the Mallow gang. Carlow's best friend and fellow Ranger, Shannon Dornan, had been killed in that same fight.

"Me lass, some fine Irish whiskey, I be bringing," Kileen declared. "An' pipe tobacco. An' some other surprises an' such. Good things to eat, they be."

Carlow retreated to his own saddlebags and retrieved a package wrapped in brown paper and a sack.

"I never thanked you . . . for all you did," he said, holding the gifts toward her. "Fact is, I wasn't very nice, seems to me."

Her smile was gracious and warm as she accepted the gifts. "*De nada, mi hijo*, you ees a warrior. They no like not being in ze fight. Eet ees their way. I know."

In a moment, her brown hands revealed the contents of his gifts: a pad of drawing papers and a sack filled with pencils, ink pens and two bottles of ink. Her face became a wide smile once more. Her drawing skills were exceptional; Carlow knew that firsthand.

"Ah, you know what Angel wants," she exclaimed. "Thees ees wonderful! I have used up all that I had from Beeg Thunder's last trip." She looked past him momentarily. "You steel have the *bueno* hoss. Shadow, no?" She walked over to the black horse and stroked its nose. "*Si*, you ees like *mi* Cuchillo, run like ze wind and ask for more."

"Good memory, Angel." Carlow smiled back and added, "Now, if you will excuse me, I'll be riding on. Got to go to Bennett and wire the captain. There's a certain young woman there I hope will remember me, too."

"If she not, she ees not a woman worthy of *mi hijo*." She grinned wickedly. "Then there be a house at the edge of town where a young man weel be treated well."

Carlow blushed.

She hugged him again and he returned to his black horse. He grinned to himself. So far she had made no attempt to ask him to stay. Good, he thought. *She will be good for my uncle.* He wondered if they would marry when his uncle was ready to settle down. Maybe they both should do that. Maybe retire to ranching like Mirabile had just done.

Leaping into the saddle, he said, "I'll be back in two days. Sooner if Ellie doesn't remember me." He made no mention of Angel's reference to visiting one of Bennett's cribs. He had been to a whorehouse once in El Paso, years ago, at Kileen's insistence. Never again.

"Come inside an' eat first. Angel insists." She smiled. "Angel has some *bueno* salve to heal that burn. A bullet came close, *mi hijo. Mucho* close." Without waiting for a response, she gave the big Irishman another kiss that made Carlow blush, and he headed inside.

After a big meal of tortillas, beans, eggs, bacon and coffee, complemented with toasts of whiskey, Carlow headed back to his horse, bringing pieces of bacon and tortilla for Chance.

Coming up behind him, Kileen said, "That double-yolk egg ye be eatin' this day, ye know what that be meanin'?"

"That it was twice as good?" Carlow teased as he checked the cinch.

Kileen frowned. "Nay, me lad. 'Tis a wedding it be tellin'."

"You and Angel getting hitched?"

"Me be thinkin' o' ye an' the fine Miss Beckham."

Carlow smiled. The thought had crossed his mind more than once. Other Rangers were married, some with families. Why not him? He patted his packed saddlebags. Among his gear was the silver locket and chain; the heart-shaped piece was engraved with intricate, floral designs. For Ellie. Even Kileen thought it was fine-looking. Next to it was his last letter to her. Unsent. He would deliver it personally. The young Ranger grinned. He also had the small knife in a beaded sheath for her son, Jeremiah, whom he cared for. The boy would be about twelve now. A time when Time Carlow had been running the streets of Bennett with his best friend, Shannon Dornan, looking for trouble and usually finding it.

Studying his nephew, Kileen proceeded to tell him of the wonders of a sprig of mint in a man's hand. It was to be held until it was moist and warm, and then the man could take the woman's hand. As long as their hands touched, she would follow him. However, they must be silent for ten minutes first for the charm to work.

Carlow was tempted to ask if his uncle thought he and Angel could be quiet that long, but decided it was better to just wave and ride on.

Without thinking about it, the young Ranger found himself heading toward the quiet place where his mother and best friend were buried. After several hours of letting his mind drift over the yesterdays, usually settling around Ellie Beckham, he saw the fat creek curled around a patrol of cottonwoods, signaling the quiet area. He cleared an uneven ridge and reined up.

A granite headstone had replaced the simple cross above Shannon Dornan's grave. It had been purchased by the two Irish Rangers some time ago and installed by the Bennett undertaker. White and yellow flowers similar to those around Carlow's mother's headstone caught his eye. Who had taken the time to plant them? He remembered his uncle telling him that if flowers grew around a grave it meant the person had lived a good life. It was a pretty story, he told himself.

Two other headstones had joined those of Carlow's friend and mother. The names of the deceased were vaguely familiar.

Looks like some other folks have joined them, Carlow noted to himself.

He didn't remember dismounting and leading Shadow closer. A huge tree overlooked Dornan's grave. The site had been selected by Kileen when Carlow had been lying, barely alive, in a wagon. The two boys had played often in that tree and Carlow found himself returning to those shadowed moments of yesterday.

A nudge at his Kiowa buckskin legging brought him back. Looking down, Carlow petted Chance. "We found each other, not far from here. Didn't we, boy? Do you remember?" He bit his lower lip. "Thunder thinks you're Shannon. Yeah, I know."

Tying his horse to a branch, he walked over to Dornan's grave, said a silent prayer and felt in his vest pocket for the two blood stones. One was his; the other had been his friend's. They were rock memories from a ceremony the two had held on Carlow's fourteenth birthday. From that day on, both carried stones with marks of each other's blood. It was their idea of an Indian blood-brother ceremony mixed with an ancient Gaelic rite, *Lia Fail*, or "the stone of destiny." Carlow had heard the story, from his mother, about how each king of Ireland had taken his oath upon this special stone.

Carlow's thoughts snapped to the Bennett jail three years ago, when the Silver Mallow Gang had attacked the four Rangers defending it, after some of the gang had already been arrested. Most of the town had turned against them, partly out of fear of Silver Mallow and partly because three of the Rangers were Irish.

His knees wobbled as he again saw Shannon Dornan cut down with bullets while he fought from the doorway of the jail. He vaguely remembered his uncle finding the two of them as Kileen and a few of the townspeople fought the gang into a retreat.

"Oh Shannon. Shannon. I know you are in Heaven and it is wonderful. I know that," he murmured. "Just wish you could have waited. For me."

He spun away and went to his mother's grave, with memories of their childhood friendship trailing him. Carlow reached inside his shirt and touched the silver Celtic cross hanging around his neck.

His name, Time, was the result of his mother thinking it meant "eternal." Time Lucent Carlow. Lucent had been his mother's maiden name. She hadn't known much English when he was born, but she had made sure her son did—and that his voice carried none of the Irishness about it and that he had no tendency to be superstitious. His uncle had enough of that for both of them. He chuckled. His uncle had taken care of his mother and her infant son when he was around, usually making money as a bare-knuckle prizefighter; Carlow didn't want to think about the times when he hadn't been.

That reminded him of the time when he first realized his uncle didn't have the last name he should have had. He should have been a Lucent, not a Kileen. Carlow was already a Ranger when the thought hit him. His uncle told him that he had changed his name because of an incident in New York, when Carlow was just a small child. Kileen had killed a man with his fists after the man refused to pay him for some hard work done. Money was sorely needed to buy groceries for his sister and her child. Kileen had put them both on a train and said he would follow as soon as he could. The name change was to help keep anyone from tracking him down. They never spoke of it again.

Touching the top of the gravestone, he said, "Mother, I know you are taking good care of Shannon. You remember he was a bit shy at times."

A soft smile reached his face. "He was almost as superstitious as Thunder, too." He paused and looked again at the gravestone. "*Mo mhíle grá.*"

The Celtic phrase meant "My thousand loves."

Returning to his black horse, he stuck a boot in the stirrup, but stopped his mount. He stared down at himself. Trail dust. Sweat. A tear in his shirtsleeve. Why in the world should he see the woman he loved, looking like this? Of course, he could take a bath in town unless the bathhouse had closed. But that didn't seem right. He wanted to go directly to where Ellie worked after his Ranger business was completed. He could see the appearance in his mind, strolling in and announcing he had a letter for a Miss Beckham.

His eyes took in the creek. Why not? He and Shannon had taken more than one bath there when they were young. No one was around.

It didn't take long for Carlow to be settling his naked body into the cool water, a bar of soap from his gear in hand. His stretched-out kerchief, in his other hand, would serve as a washcloth. It would serve to clean the kerchief at the same time. On the bank were his old clothes and next to them was another pile: his one clean shirt; fresh underwear and Levis. Even a clean pair of socks, although one had a major hole in it.

Right on top of the new clothing was his hand carbine. Cocked. Being prepared was the Ranger's way of life; Kileen had drilled that into him. Another pile held his Kiowa leggings with the warrior's knife, long coat, gunbelt, boots, vest and hat.

Chance wandered over to the creek, inspected his master's antics for a moment and dove in.

"Hey, bud! Welcome. Welcome." Carlow laughed and decided to give his wolf-dog a bath, too.

After both man and wolf-dog were cleaned, Carlow managed to shave, using a piece of cracked mirror and razor from his gear. Lather from his soap was the best he could do. An hour later, a refreshed and clean Time Carlow swung into the saddle and loped away. His wrung-out, still-damp kerchief bounced loosely at his neck. Chance followed, rejuvenated by his own bath.

Carlow cut off the shadows in his mind that wanted to remind him of the last time he had ridden from this place. He had thrown away his Ranger badge and their bloodstones, swearing to kill the town mayor. The mayor had arranged for the Silver Mallow Gang to slip into town. He shook his head to clear the awful memories.

Ahead, the trail looked familiar. Gray rock formations and low hills greeted him like old friends. Even the loose rock and silt on the trail sang a gentle song as his horse moved through them. In such places, it was easy to understand why his uncle believed in faeries, druids, banshees and leprechauns. Who really knew what lived in such a land? It was along here that Chance had joined him. A mystery, perhaps. Or just serendipity. He looked back at the shaggy beast working his way along behind him.

"Hey, bud! This is where we met. Remember?" he called out.

Chance's ears perked up and the wolf-dog cocked his head.

Spotting a small spoon of open land among the rocks and boulders, he said, "Let's take a breather, Chance."

It wasn't a question. He reined up and swung down. Shrugging his shoulders, Carlow told himself it was to let his horse—and Chance—have a breather before going on. The real reason was to regather his nerve before seeing Ellie again. What if she had forgotten him? What if . . .

He settled against a rock to relax. The reins remained gripped in his fists, leaving plenty of room for the animal to graze the few sprigs of grass and weeds that had found their way to life. Out came Ellie's last three letters. Communication between them hadn't been easy, as he was constantly on the move. Her letters would arrive at Ranger headquarters and wait until he either returned from an assignment or was in a town long enough for the letter to be forwarded. He had read them many times. His own responses were infrequent. He dared not read his latest unsent letter, afraid he would decide it wasn't worthy of presenting to her.

Carlow's eyes focused on her closing salutation, "Fondly," and wondered if that were really true. Didn't people often write things they didn't really believe? However, when he compared her last letter to one written two years ago, there was a marked difference. He hadn't seen it before. Or hadn't wanted to. Her last letter was more formal than the others and she made a reference to finding some friends in Bennett and that this was adding much to her days.

Friends? What kind of friends, he wondered. Hadn't she lived in Bennett a long time? She hadn't mentioned any such friends when he had last seen her. That had been well over a year ago, when he had taken some time to ride in. Oh well, she had probably just been looking for things to tell him.

Standing and brushing himself off, Carlow returned the letters to his saddlebags. He couldn't resist taking a look at the locket and unfolded the white cloth that held it. Next to it was the beaded sheath knife.

He whispered, "It's almost as pretty as she is."

A taut growl and Chance was running. Carlow's hand went to his hand carbine. Then he saw a large hare bounding across the trail with the wolf-dog in full pursuit. He chuckled and released his grip on the gun.

After returning the jewelry to its place in his saddlebags, Carlow smiled and called out to his animal, "Come on, Chance, leave that fella alone. We're going to Bennett." He swung into the saddle.

From somewhere behind a boulder, the wolf-dog yipped and followed. Carlow studied him and decided the hare had escaped.

"Next time, huh?"

The closer they got to his hometown, the more Carlow wondered what kind of welcome he would receive. Not from the townspeople, who had rejected all of them because they were Irish. He didn't expect much to have changed. His concern was about Ellie Beckham, the young widow he had met in Bennett. He could see her in his mind's eye. Feel her last kiss, the touch of her hand in his, and her eyes dancing with his.

Would she welcome him like Angel had welcomed his uncle? He hoped so. Would her son remember him?

Chapter Eleven

That night, a few miles from San Antonio, Tanneman Rose conducted the same ceremony he had performed at the line cabin, waving each mask over his small fire and chanting into the night. Each time, he made a circle in the dirt around the fire, then added lines in all directions coming from the fire. The moon. He had decided his earlier life had included worship of the moon. So he should, too. Each time, the spider in its jar was given a place of honor near the fire. Occasionally, he considered going to Portland's ranch and retrieving the shrine he had built. It had always comforted him. Barnabas had liked it, too.

So far, he had been able to secure several flies to add to the jar, for the spider to eat. Usually, he did it by leaving a dab of the preserves on the wagon seat, then grabbing some of them when they attempted to fly away. It became a game; he was quick with his hands and knew it.

Midday found Tanneman, disguised as a peddler, driving his wagon slowly down the main street of San Antonio. He was filled with arrogance. No one knew it was him. No one. Turning to the spider jar, he spoke of his feelings.

"Portland, I wish you were here—as yourself. You'd like this. Very much. It's the town where they killed you. Yeah. And tried to send me to prison." He looked over as he rode, noting the bank. "There's the bank. Across the street, yeah there, that's where those bastards waited for us. And there's where you and Barnabas hid." He snickered. "Don't you love it?" He looked again at the jar. "I'll kill that bastard judge, and that fool district attorney. Maybe I'll rob the bank. Maybe. We'll see. I don't need the money." He looked again at the street, watching a passing freighter.

He pulled up alongside the Duvall Livery and offered the filthy-haired livery operator a free square of tobacco. It was accepted eagerly.

"Looks like thar's a lot a'goin' on," Tanneman said in his Missouri drawl.

After biting off a large chunk of the tobacco, the operator told him a trial was taking place. Tanneman smiled. Just as the newspaper had said.

"Yas suh, got Judge Cline hyar—and that other fella, Johnson, he's hyar, too," Michigan Duvall declared, licking his front teeth with his tongue. "Big dispute ov'r some grazin' land. East o' hyar. Milo Henry—and sum other fella. A stranger. From Ohio, I think." He spat to the side, disappointed at the color and thickness.

Tanneman resisted the desire to explain who Waddell Johnson was. Duvall said the judge always stayed in the Gleason Hotel and Johnson always boarded at the Horman boardinghouse on Second Street. Warming to the conversation, Duvall said an ex-Ranger had escaped from jail last week. He explained about the posse finding him and the deputy dead, then said a wounded Ranger was recuperating in a hacienda near the edge of town. That would be Pig Deconer, Tanneman realized.

Tanneman thanked him and left. Duvall would be a good choice to take the fall for the crimes, he decided.

Tanneman rode through town, stopping once. A plain-dressed woman wanted to know if he had any books. She finally chose a poetry volume and two school-books. After settling his wagon and one of the horses outside of town, he returned, riding the brown. He had removed his beard and unpinned the coat sleeve. He had shoved one of the masks into his saddlebags and belted on a handgun, placing another in his waist-band.

In an alley a block from the boardinghouse, Tanneman waited as patiently as possible. His saddled horse stomped its feet and snorted anxiously. A hand-ful of grain from the ex-Ranger's pocket settled the animal into a quiet wait. Tanneman, too, was hungry and chewed on a piece of hardtack he had brought along. Under his coat was a wooden mask. He wasn't worried about his clothes giving him away, should any witnesses happen to see him. It was too dark and they were nondescript anyway.

He didn't have to wait long.

Waddell Johnson came strolling toward the boarding-house from a nearby saloon, after a nightcap to follow his meal at the next-door restaurant. He was in a happy mood, whistling to himself as he walked with his hands in his pockets, and greeting three couples cheer-ily as he passed.

Wearing the wooden mask, Tanneman stepped in front of the surprised attorney and fired his pistol three times. All three bullets hit Johnson's left shirt pocket. The district attorney grasped his heart, stum-bled and fell face forward.

As the three couples watched in horror, Tanneman fired in their direction. He wheeled and ran into the alley where his horse waited. Jumping into the saddle, he rode toward the end of town, turning into an alley between two long rows of buildings and disappeared into the night.

At the other end of town, Ranger Pig Deconer stepped out of a small restaurant, full and sleepy. He stretched his arms, holding a cane. His leg was improving, he told himself. A slow walk to the hacienda where he was staying would refresh him, he decided. Being sidelined like this was terribly boring. His fellow Rangers were on assignment somewhere. All except him. He rolled his shoulders to rid the tiredness within him as he limped along. Nodding to an older man and woman passing, Deconer stretched again and paused, hearing something next to the hacienda.

In the alley, a man in a black hat and long black coat and wearing a wooden mask emerged from the shadows and fired a double-barreled shotgun into the Ranger's stomach. Deconer half turned, trying to pull his pistol, then collapsed. The masked adversary disappeared into the alley as swiftly as he had appeared.

The man and woman, who had just passed Deconer, hurried back, frightened, but determined to help. Breathing hard, the woman excitedly said, "Is he . . . ?"

"He's dead," the squatty businessman said, kneeling beside Deconer. "According to this badge, he was a Ranger." He swallowed his fear. "The killer, he had a mask. A wooden mask."

Her face taut with worry, his wife placed her hands on her face. She closed her eyes. "It was dreadful. Will he come back? Oh, I think I'm going to faint."

Just outside the last row of small huts and old haciendas, Tanneman Rose howled his joy at these first two acts of revenge. It was as sweet as he had hoped. The only thing better would have been to kill Kileen and Carlow, but that would come. Patience. Patience. It was his destiny. He rode toward a series of rolling hills where he had left his wagon. Methodically, he crossed the names of Deconer and Johnson off his list. His dreams that night were about spiders wearing masks.

The murders were the talk of San Antonio the next day. Everyone knew the key detail: killers wearing wooden masks. Some thought it had to be wild Indians. Others were certain it was revenge by someone the district attorney and the Ranger had put in jail. No one could provide the peace officers with any additional details. None of the hoofprints in either alley were distinctive.

Dressed as a goateed businessman, Tanneman tied his horse to the rail and checked into the Gleason Hotel, presenting himself as J. William Jilles of the Indiana law firm of Jilles and Torkkle. He was in town to evaluate a possible real estate investment for a client. He declined the bellhop's offer to carry his valise.

"Where would be a good place to eat, my good fellow?" Tanneman asked the bucktoothed clerk.

"Oh, definitely the Colonial. Right across the street. Next to the bank," the clerk said, licking his tongue over his exposed front teeth. "Judge Cline eats there all the time."

"I see—and who is this Judge Cline? I'm not familiar with the name."

Eager to impress, the clerk explained that the judge was in town for a trial. That he always stayed in the hotel when he was in San Antonio, in the same room. Room 246. Shaking his head, he explained about the murder of the district attorney and said he supposed it would delay the trial, but he hadn't heard yet.

"I'm sure Judge Cline will let me know what his plans are." The clerk straightened his back, trying to look important, and ran his fingers through long, greasy hair. "Everybody is pretty upset about these killings. Weird. The guys had on wooden masks. Can you believe that? Jumped right out of the alley and shot Mr. Johnson. Dead. Then did the same to a Ranger."

"My goodness! Is it safe to walk the streets?" Tanneman asked, his false eyebrows arching.

The clerk quickly assured Tanneman that he thought the killings had something to do with the trial and were not random acts. After further conversation, the clerk told Tanneman that he would be on duty all night. He even showed him a long-barreled revolver he kept under the check-in desk. Whispering, he said he usually got some sleep in the first room off the lobby; management didn't mind as long as he was available for any guest service in the morning.

"I always keep it unlocked, you know, in case somebody needs something."

"That is comforting to know."

Taking the key to room 412, Tanneman climbed the stairs to his room, noting where the clerk said he slept. The ex-Ranger had changed his mind; the clerk would be the one arrested for the murders. He might still set up the livery boy if he could get an opportunity to kill Marshal Timble. Inside the room, he opened his valise, took out the spider jar and carefully placed it on the lone dresser.

"What a great day, Portland. Today the fool Judge Cline gets his just desserts. Vengeance is so sweet."

He pushed his valise, which contained a mask, a hunting knife in a weathered leather sheath and his peddler beard and hat, under the bed. At the cracked mirror, standing over the dresser, he rechecked his fake goatee and eyebrows. The pistols in his waistband and under his vest were not visible.

" 'He was ever precise in promise keeping.' " Tanneman recited a line from *The Merry Wives of Windsor*

and let his mind wander to the first time he had realized that he had lived other lives. It had happened in a
theater, of course. He had been fourteen and watching
a touring company rehearse that very Shakespearean
play. Hillis and his other brothers had been outside
playing, but he had wanted to watch the performance.

One of the ladies in the troupe had sat down behind
him; she was not in the act being rehearsed. In a handful of gloriously memorable statements, she had convinced him that he had lived before. In fact, she was
the one who had suggested he was once a shaman of
ancient Persia. That was also the day he had entered
into manhood under her gentle guidance in an unused
storage room.

He smiled and headed out. Still lost in sweet memories, mostly of the woman's lovemaking, Tanneman
marched onto the far sidewalk and bumped into a
townsman walking toward him. As the man stutter-
stepped backward, his fedora popped from his head
and spun to the boards.

"Oh, I'm sorry. Wasn't watching where I was going,"
the ex-Ranger declared, stepping back and leaning
over to pick up the hat.

The surprised man had been a juror in his trial. Tanneman recognized him immediately; the townsman
frowned and tried to place the stranger who had just
collided with him. "Don't I know you . . . from somewhere?" Terrace Allen, a watchsmith, asked as Tanneman returned his fedora.

"Sorry, I don't think so. I'm J. William Jilles of the
Indiana law firm of Jilles and Torkkle. Just came to
town to investigate a real estate opportunity for a client," Tanneman said in a tone that carried as much of
an Eastern accent as he could muster.

He didn't like the situation, but knew he had to play

it out. To do anything else was tantamount to admitting his identity and shooting his way out of town.

"Oh."

Tanneman patted him on the shoulder. "That happens to me often. Guess I just have a familiar face." He smiled. "Hope it's a friendly one."

"Of course. Of course. My mistake."

Watching the man walk on, Tanneman tried to quiet himself. He wished he hadn't used the name and occupation he had used earlier. Saying something about the law might trigger the man's memory. Why was he surprised at such an encounter? There were twelve jurors somewhere in town or close by. He watched the man enter a small watch repair shop; Allenburg Clock & Watch. That made it worse. Allen, or whatever his name was, would be a perfectionist. Keyed to tiny details.

Tanneman ate little of his lunch; his appetite was gone. In his mind was the growing thought that he must deal with the former juror before the man remembered where he had seen him. How? Where? The best idea was to wait until dusk, just before the store was closed, and kill him then. There would be plenty of time to kill Judge Cline afterward. He smiled, but his nervousness grew.

He spent the rest of the day in his room. It was the safest place to be. From the window, he could see the Allenburg shop with its tiny single window and finally decided not to wait until dusk. He could eliminate the man and be gone in minutes. The only trick was to enter without Allen realizing who it was. Ah, the challenge of the theater. Immediately, he was reenergized and pulled his valise from under the bed.

A half hour later, he left the hotel, crossed the street and slipped into the alley next to Allen's shop. There he put on the full beard and the old hat used for the peddler. A scarf around his neck covered his shirt and necktie. A limp would add to the transformation. He removed his pistol from his coat pocket; the barrel was now wrapped with a hotel towel, which was tied in place with a leather thong. Taking a deep breath, he pulled the silver watch from his vest and gripped it tightly in his left hand. His right held the gun behind him.

This part of the sidewalk was clear of people; most were usually on the other side of the street where the general store dominated. He decided the watchmaker had chosen this location because it would have been cheaper to rent because of the lower traffic.

"Guten Tag!" Tanneman said, shouting a German greeting and holding up the pocket watch with his left hand as he limped inside.

Terrace Allen adjusted his glasses and looked up. It had bothered him all day that he couldn't place where he had seen the fellow from this morning. He was sure that he had. Somewhere.

"Trouble with your watch, eh? Let me have a look," Allen said, smiling as best he could. Being friendly wasn't natural to him; working on watches was. It was a smile he had worked on.

The German-speaking stranger walked closer, swung the pistol forward from behind his back and fired. Twice. The muffled shots sounded louder to Tanneman than they would outside.

Allen grabbed his chest and fell against the display case at his side. Tanneman glanced at the window. Nothing.

A third bullet made certain. Tanneman carried the body around to the back of the display so it wouldn't be seen. Brushing his coat for unseen dust, he shoved the wrapped gun into his pocket and walked out. A few steps away, he remembered leaving his watch and returned to get it. Two women passed and he nodded and greeted them in German. In the alley, he removed the beard and old hat, replacing them with his goatee and derby.

After a leisurely supper, Tanneman reentered the hotel and went directly up the stairs. He had seen Judge Cline with three men at a table across the room. The restaurant had been humming with the discovery of the murdered watchmaker. No one could think why he would be killed. The clerk didn't notice Tanneman's arrival, as he was discussing something with two guests.

On the second floor, Tanneman found the shadows at the end of the hallway to his liking and waited for Judge Cline to return from supper. In his hand was a knife.

Just as the magistrate opened the door to his room, the ex-Ranger jumped him from behind and slit his throat. Judge Cline was dead before Tanneman dragged him into the hotel room, all the way to his bed, shutting the door behind them. Without lighting a lamp, he laid the body on a small floor rug and locked the door behind him as he left.

Quietly, he walked down the stairs to the clerk's hideaway room. The bucktoothed man was snoring loudly. Tanneman shoved a mask, the powder-burned towel and bloody knife under the bed. Silently, Tanneman retreated from the room. He couldn't resist a chuckle, then chastised himself for making noise.

Judge Cline's body wasn't found until the next morning when the maid went in to clean. His neck had been cut and the rug was crimson. San Antonio was panicked. Four murders in two days! Participants on both sides of the land fraud case were suspected and questioned.

After washing, shaving and dressing, Tanneman slipped out of his room and down the lobby stairs. The lobby was filled with worried guests. A weary-eyed Marshal Timble was talking to his three deputies. He was unshaven, his shirt was badly wrinkled and his vest was closed on the wrong buttons. The only thing that looked clean was the gun at his hip.

Tanneman was totally stimulated by the drama of this; the lawman had jailed him only a handful of days earlier. Could he pull this off? In his heart, he knew people saw what they expected to see. As far as Marshal Timble was concerned, Tanneman Rose was dead.

"I saw something . . . something bad at the Gleason," Tanneman said, almost whispering, to the closest hotel customer. "I'm staying here. Couldn't sleep last night, you know. Too much food. Too much whiskey."

Nodding, the fat customer chuckled and pointed at himself.

Tanneman explained he saw the clerk take off a wooden mask just before he went into a room on the first floor.

"Looked like he had a knife in his hand. Not sure," Tanneman continued. "Light wasn't good. The mask was a weird-looking thing, but I didn't think anything of it at the time. Not until I heard about Judge Cline's death this morning—and the district attorney last night. Some man in a wooden mask, I was told. Awful. Just awful."

"Oh my God! We should tell the peace officers. Oh my!" The fat man held both hands to his chubby face.

Tanneman frowned. "Good idea, but you'll have to do it. I'm late for a meeting."

"Certainly. Certainly. It's my duty."

After eating a fine breakfast of a medium-rare steak and two over-easy eggs at the Colonial restaurant, Tanneman rode quietly out of town. For a moment, he considered finding a way to ambush the marshal, but decided it was a foolish risk. Things had gone well. The town was mesmerized by the sudden arrest of the Hotel Gleason clerk. Gossip running through the town said he had been found with a mask, bloody knife and a towel with powder burns—and he would have had a key for the judge's room.

Tanneman would stop and pick up all the hidden bank money from a cave not far from Portland's place before heading to Mirabile's ranch. Revenge. It was truly sweet, he told the spider jar sitting on the chair beside him in the restaurant. Carefully, he withdrew the folded list and crossed off four names.

Moving west, Tanneman Rose stayed on the main roads. However, he did stop at a farm to refill his supplies and, in the process, killed the farmer and his wife. Fresh buttermilk was a special treat afterward. He took it as a sign of providence. Buttermilk had been his favorite drink when he was a Persian shaman. He was certain of it.

Chapter Twelve

Time Carlow cleared a low rise and saw the town of Bennett in the distance. He knew his real home was wherever his uncle was. Not here. This town had never wanted him. Or his mother. Or his friend. Looking back on it, he guessed his uncle had pressed to make Rangers out of Dornan and himself to place the two young fighters where he could keep an eye on them. He grinned at the thought. The town of Bennett must have been stunned to hear two of their Irish riffraff had become lawmen.

He passed the schoolhouse and noted it had recently been repainted. The clear voice of the teacher carried to his ears as he rode by. Carlow smiled. He and Shannon had definitely not been the teacher's pets when they were in school. Entering town, every building called out with a story from yesterday. He passed a long street of false-fronted buildings with framed awnings and eight-foot-wide wooden sidewalks.

Little had changed, Carlow thought, since his last visit. He rode past the livery stable and waved at the operator, an old friend. He passed the dance hall. Two churches. Saw the hotel sported a new name, The Peabody. Then he nodded approvingly that the general merchandise store no longer declared it was Pickenson's; the name over the storefront was Longworth's.

J. B. Pickenson was the crooked mayor Carlow had confronted during the Silver Mallow Gang war.

A freight wagon squeaked and groaned past him; the driver looked over twice at Chance, not believing his eyes the first time. A string of saloons blurred as Carlow continued to ride through. Only one caught his attention—the Corao. It looked even grayer than the last time he had seen it. He and his mother had lived upstairs for a few years; Kileen had gone to the war and then with the state police. Carlow never knew what his mother did to keep them from starving . . . until much later. It wasn't something he wanted to remember.

He noted the Alamo Saloon was no longer the last building before open land resumed. Three more buildings had joined the parade. Carlow welcomed the return from yesterday. He passed a building with the sign over it that read: Wittlock & Carlson Land Attorneys and Real Estate Agents. That reminded him to tell them of the status of the Portland Rose ranch. He dared not look down the street to where he really wanted to be—Jacobs's Millinery. That was where Ellie worked. Duty must come first, he reminded himself. He could barely contain himself, though. How great it would be to see her!

Many townsmen looked up; several recognized the young Ranger and smiled; several recognized him and didn't. Irishmen were barely tolerated in this town— or any other. The gentry preferred blacks to Irish for domestic help. A stagecoach grumbled past and slammed to a stop at the telegraph and stage office.

The abrupt halt made Carlow notice the telegraph office. He eased his horse in that direction, pinning his badge in place on his coat lapel. Going into the small office, his Mexican spurs rippled on the floor as he entered. A grim telegraph operator looked up and held up his hand to indicate he was busy. Seeing the badge, he gave a tired smile and motioned that he was taking a message. In the corner, an acne-spotted teenager sat quietly; Carlow guessed he was working as the operator's runner.

Carlow folded his arms. His message to Captain McNelly would be one of failure. They hadn't found any stolen money. He winced. Sending that kind of message was not something he liked doing.

"May I help you, Ranger?" the operator said cheerily, after finishing with his just-received telegram.

"Need to send a wire."

"Sure. Say, you're not Carlow or Kileen, are you?"

Carlow nodded. "I'm the first one."

"Thought so. There's a message for you here somewhere. Came a few days ago." The operator flipped through a stack of paper. "Oh yeah, here it is. It's to both of you. From a Captain McNelly."

Carlow accepted the paper and read:

TANNEMAN ROSE KILLED IN JAIL
ESCAPE . . . STOP . . . DEPUTY KILLED IN
ATTEMPT . . . STOP . . . ANOTHER DEPUTY
FIRED FOR BEING DRUNK ON DUTY . . .
STOP . . . ADVISE ABOUT STOLEN MONEY . . .
STOP . . . MCNELLY

Tanneman Rose dead? That was hard to accept. The ex-Ranger was shrewd and tough. Had a local deputy killed him? Which one? Peter Gaggratte or Henry Stevenson? Which one had been fired for drinking? Carlow wanted to ask McNelly if the death had been thoroughly checked, but assumed it had or the captain wouldn't have reported it that way. Kileen would be bothered by the news, he decided.

After sending a wire to McNelly about not finding the money, Carlow hurried to Jacobs's Millinery. He reined up at the hitching rack and told Chance to remain with Shadow. At the last minute, he decided to leave his guns and unbuckled his heavy gunbelt, leaving the rig resting around his saddle horn. He grabbed the folded locket and his last letter and shoved them into his long coat pocket.

After checking his breath with a cupped hand, Carlow walked across the planked sidewalk, removed his hat and stepped inside. It took his eyes a second to adjust to the gray of the small store. It looked like it always had. Walls were decorated with drawings done by the late Mr. Jacobs.

Mrs. Jacobs saw him before he saw her. "Time Carlow! God Almighty, it is you. How are you, son?"

Smiling widely, the older woman jumped up from the chair where she was sewing and rushed over to greet him.

He was fond of the older Jewish woman; she had actually helped fight off the Silver Mallow Gang with a shotgun. Kileen had told him of her courage after the young Ranger had regained consciousness.

"Are you passing through, Ranger Carlow? Or on the trail of some more bad men?" she asked, stepping back from their short embrace.

Carlow smiled and told her what he and Kileen had been doing.

The older woman smiled widely and shook her head. "Time, I'm so proud of you. Mr. Jacobs, bless his soul, always said you would turn out good."

"Thank you, Mrs. Jacobs. He was a special man, always nice to us, even when we were pretty wild." He swallowed. "I was hoping to see Miss Beckham. Does she still work here?"

Blinking her eyes rapidly, the older woman glanced away for a moment, then returned her attention to Carlow's smiling face. "Why, yes, she is. She's in the back. Only Miss Beckham is now Mrs. Thomas Wittlock. Married, oh, about six months ago. A very nice wedding it was." She started to touch Carlow's arm, but her hand stopped halfway.

Married? Ellie was married? The news hit him like a bullet and he thought he was going to retch. He swallowed to hold back the bile. He wanted to run. Anywhere. How could he have been so stupid to think she was waiting for him? How could he think she wanted to marry *him*?

Ellie came into the room, her attention on the blue dress in her hands. She lifted her gaze to inform Mrs. Jacobs that the dress was ready, but she saw Carlow and dropped the garment. Her gasp popped into the air; her hands went to her opened mouth.

Carlow bit his lower lip. "Good . . . afternoon . . . Ellie. It's . . . good . . . to see you."

The older woman rushed over, picked up the dress and said she needed to get something from the back. Both Carlow and Ellie watched her leave, delaying their next encounter as long as possible.

"Mrs. Jacobs told me. You're married now," Carlow said, fighting to control the emotional fireworks within him.

A tear escaped from her right eye.

"I sent you a letter. Over six months ago," she mumbled. "I wanted you to know . . . why." She licked her lips. "Thomas is a good man. Thomas Wittlock. He has an office here in town. Real estate and land. He's good to me—and to Jeremiah."

His face said he hadn't gotten the letter.

Her gaze locked into his for a moment before dashing

away. "Jeremiah needs a father, you know." Her eyelids fluttered to hold back more tears. "And I was . . . lonely. So lonely."

Carlow nodded, finding no words. His throat was jammed with angst.

"I wasn't even sure you cared anymore—or were alive." Her voice trembled, then found some strength. "You didn't write me . . . for a long time."

"It isn't easy. To write," Carlow managed to say, motioning with his hands. "When you're on the trail of outlaws." He held up his last letter and returned it to his pocket. "I brought my . . . last letter. Doesn't matter much now, though." He slammed on his hat.

Her fingers drew circles on the edge of Mrs. Jacobs's table. Finally, Ellie explained that worrying about him, wondering where he was, what he was doing, if he was all right—all that had made her realize she wouldn't be comfortable married to a lawman. The strain of anxiety would just be too much.

"I would've quit the Rangers."

Ellie shook her head. "No. No. You couldn't. You shouldn't. Texas needs men like you—and your uncle." She tried to smile and change the subject. "How is Old Thunder?"

"He's fine." Carlow shoved his hands into his coat pockets and his right touched the wrapped locket.

Withdrawing the small gift, he held it out to her. "Here . . . for you. A wedding present."

Tentatively, she accepted it, slowly unfolded the cloth and studied the locket within. "It's beautiful, Time," she said softly, continuing to look at the jewelry. "But I can't accept it."

Carlow's face was gray and the corner of his mouth trembled. "W-Why n-not?"

She refolded the material over the necklace and held

it out for him. "You know why. It is a gift you should give to the woman you love."

"I just did."

The words jolted her fragile presence. She shivered, as if trying to shake them away. She started to hold the small presentation to her bosom, stopped and extended her hands again.

Carlow tried to regain his poise, but everything in him was shouting. He took back the package.

"I-I h-have . . . a gift for Jeremiah. In my gear," Carlow said, not daring to look at her. "M-may I bring it in—so you can give it to him. Sometime. It's a small knife in a beaded sheath. Comanche beadwork."

Ellie's shoulders shivered. "No, I don't think so, Time." She looked at him, trying to smile, but not achieving it. "He would love it. Especially from you. But it's important right now that he not receive gifts from any man except his new . . . father."

"Any man—or just me?"

"Please, Time. Please understand."

Carlow folded his arms. "I do understand, Mrs. Wittlock. I really do." Unfolding them, he touched the side brim of his hat with his right hand. "Good-bye. I truly hope you have . . . a wonderful life."

Without waiting for her to respond, Carlow spun and headed for the door. He grabbed the handle, paused and spoke into the door. "Please tell Mrs. Jacobs, for me, that it was good to see her." He pulled on the door and stepped outside.

After jamming the gift into his saddlebags, he yanked free the reins and swung into the saddle, without moving his guns. He directed his horse out the way they had come. Chance trotted beside horse and rider.

His mind was black. Black. Completely emptied of thought, memory or concern. His body was slowed with anguish and gradually his mind filled with thoughts driven by Ellie's rejection. Dark thoughts. How could he have ever thought she was in love with him? Why had he been such a fool to think she would wait? He hated this town and it hated him. Bennett had taken his mother and his best friend. He would never come back.

As he rode past the Corao, something in him snapped. He swung the horse back toward the saloon, dismounted and flipped the reins around the hitching rack.

"I'm going to have a good-bye drink, boys. Last time I'll see this town. Stay, Chance. With Shadow." He took the gunbelt from his saddle horn and slung it over his shoulder as he headed for the saloon door.

Chapter Thirteen

Every man in the smoke-stale saloon turned to look as the young Ranger stepped inside. Bad memories of growing up here lurked in every corner of the large room, ready to rush at him. The place had changed since he had been in it as a kid. Certainly it looked a lot smaller.

He knew most of the men—and yet knew none of them. Not really. He reminded himself that few would consider him a friend. Most would be happier if he weren't there—the saloon or in the town. For an instant, he wanted to run. For another, he wanted to shoot at the large mirror behind the long bar. But he did neither, forcing himself to keep walking.

A new Corao owner had placed the emphasis on gambling. Two faro tables, a large roulette wheel and a cluster of card tables controlled the main area. All were filled with customers. Card games occupied three other tables. A pool table was also busy, as was the bar itself. Painted women served drinks and offered other services upstairs.

A loud victory cheer roared from a square-faced businessman playing cards at the closest table. The bearded man in a flat-brimmed hat next to him said to shut up and deal.

"Hey, Mick, who yah after this time? Got us a new mayor. You can have him, though. He's no good," the businessman yelled and looked at his table companions for approval.

Chuckles supported his claim.

Next to him, the bearded man added his own salutation. "Yeah, get rid of Longworth for me, will ya? I'd like to own that general store." He slapped the back of the man to his left.

Nervous snickers mixed with an occasional guffaw, but Carlow paid no attention as he walked to the bar. Two men saw him coming and left, leaving a wide space. He eased next to the bar and laid his heavy gunbelt on it. The blond-haired bartender pushed his spectacles into place and moved toward him.

Pushing his tongue against the side of his mouth, the bartender asked, "Should I put your guns . . . with the others, sir?"

"That's the law, isn't it?" Carlow growled. But the last time he had given up his guns in a saloon, it had proven a dangerous step. State lawmen were exempt from any local ordinance concerning weapons anyway. Giving up his guns was an idea he had gotten from Kileen, simply to show a town courtesy. He still liked it in spite of the risk.

"Whiskey. Irish, if you've got it." Carlow motioned toward the underside of the bar and laid down a coin.

"Yes, sir. Yes, sir." The bartender carried away the gunbelt as if the guns might jump at him at any moment.

Swallowing his nervousness, the bartender returned with the requested whiskey and a glass. He popped the cork from the bottle and poured. "It's our best, sir. Finest Irish."

Carlow laid down a second coin and asked the bartender for another glass. "Join me, will you, in a toast to Bennett—and yesterday."

"Gladly, sir."

The bartender poured himself a drink. Carlow mumbled something in Irish and held out his glass to clink with the bartender's.

"To Bennett, Texas. May she always shine," Carlow said.

"To Bennett, Texas."

Smiling, the bartender downed his glass and said, "How about another, Ranger? This one's on the house."

"Thanks. Then I'd better be going. Got a long ride ahead of me."

At the far end of the bar, a well-dressed man in a tweed suit and narrow-brimmed hat asked his friend, "Who is that? Don't remember seeing him around."

The thick-mustached friend pulled on his ear and explained the situation, adding, "You weren't here then."

"Guess not."

Next to them, a cowboy yanked his hat harder onto his head, gulped the rest of his beer and said quietly, "I'd walk real careful 'round that fella. He's the one got Silver Mallow. By himself. Over in Presidio, it was." He examined the empty mug, as if expecting it to somehow be refilled. "His uncle is a Ranger, too. Big fella. Nobody messes with him neither." He wiped his hand across his mustache. "Pretty sure he killed eight Mallow Gang owlhoots while they were in the jail. Our jail. Yeah, eight. That was after the gang shot up the three other Rangers guarding them. He was one of 'em. A night from Hell it was, yes sir. Proud to say I helped the big Ranger drive those bastards out of town."

He ran his forefinger around the rim of his empty mug, hoping his tale would bring the offer of a refill from the listeners. "Didn't have anything to do with the killing of those in jail, though."

From the northern corner of the saloon, a big cattleman named Connor Atkins stood and walked toward Carlow. His hard face was twisted by hate and reinforced by whiskey. A full beard hid most of his pockmarked face and a wide-brimmed hat shadowed his face. His wide shoulders and heavy arms spoke of a man used to having his own way. Atkins's eyebrows argued with each other. Both fists were clenched and held at his sides.

Unaware of the advancing man, the young Ranger sipped his whiskey, letting its heat drive away some of the agony of Ellie's rejection. It hurt as badly as anything he could ever remember. But the hard-nosed discipline built into him would not let the false sense of the liquor lull him into more of it. He would check with the telegraph operator to see if new orders had arrived, then ride out and make camp somewhere. He would head for Angel's in the morning. If Kileen and Angel wanted to spend more time together, he would ride on. Somewhere.

A heavy hand gripped Carlow's right shoulder.

"What'd you come back for, Carlow?" Atkins demanded, his dark eyes reddened by the smoke of the saloon and hours of drinking.

Without turning, Carlow replied, "Heard the Corao had good Irish whiskey. Who wants to know?"

The grip tightened.

"I want to know. The Roses are my cousins. Heard tell you boys shot 'em all down in San Antone," Atkins snarled; his thick eyebrows collided in the middle of his forehead.

"News about outlaws travels fast," Carlow said without turning around.

"An' Thomas Wittlock is my friend."

"I'm sure he appreciates that. Whoever he is," Carlow said, taking another sip of his drink.

"Turn around an' look at me, dammit," Atkins said, pulling on Carlow's shoulder. "You can't come waltzing into this town and try to steal his wife."

Carlow finished his drink and set it down on the bar. "Go back with your friends, mister. It's been a long day and I don't have any interest talking about things I don't know anything about."

"You calling me a liar?"

"Didn't call you anything," Carlow said.

Atkins yanked Carlow backward, spilling him onto the floor. Carlow's head hit the floor and stunned him. The big man swung a heavy boot at Carlow's unmoving head. Blinking away the daze, the young Ranger grabbed the man's lunging boot with both hands and shoved it upward.

Jolted off balance, Atkins thudded to the floor, his hat flying toward Carlow.

The young Ranger gathered himself and knelt, trying to shake off the rest of the dizziness seeking control of his head. There wasn't much time, as the bigger man was surprisingly agile and already rising to his feet. Carlow lurched forward and upward from his kneeling position, unleashing a ramrod blow into Atkins's face with the top of his head. The big man's nose crunched and blood splattered on both of them.

Someone grabbed Carlow from behind as he stood. Instinctively, Carlow slipped out from under the grasp, spun and slammed his left fist deep into the stomach of the surprised, bald-headed cowboy in a floppy hat. A right jab to the same area was a blur. The second adversary staggered, grabbing his midsection for breath that wouldn't come. Carlow followed with a left uppercut to the man's jaw that snapped his head backward.

Flailing his arms, the cowboy reeled. Carlow drove his right fist into the cowboy's stomach. The cowboy's legs wobbled and he toppled over, face-first.

A savage blow to the side of Carlow's head staggered him. A third man, a stocky, thick-chested cowboy, followed his sneak attack with another blow that pounded the left side of the Ranger's face. Carlow swung wildly, not striking anything, but it bought him a few seconds to clear his head. The stocky man came at him again, fully cocking his arm and intending to knock the Ranger out.

Sudden fear rattled through Carlow. This wasn't some attempt to run him out of town; these men intended to maim or kill him. Recovered, Carlow pushed the blow away with his right arm and delivered a powerful left cross to the cowboy's unprotected chin, followed by a devastating right hook to the same area. A tooth flew from the man's mouth, followed by spurts of blood. The stocky cowboy went down like he had been dropped by a buffalo gun.

Atkins was back on his feet, pushing away the baldheaded cowboy still holding his stomach with both hands. The saloon was tensely quiet, except for a drunken businessman who kept yelling, "Kill the Mick bastard!"

Carlow's left eye was already swollen and nearly shut. His eyebrow was split and bleeding. He turned to face Atkins and knew he could not go down, no matter how many came at him. To do so meant permanent damage. A kick could blind him. Or break his back.

Confident, Atkins strutted toward Carlow. "Gonna

make you sorry you ever came back to Bennett, you Mick sonovabitch," the big man roared. "You're gonna find out what happens to men who come to town and try to steal our women."

"Well, partner, you obviously have me confused with somebody else," Carlow snapped, "but go ahead. I'm looking at you this time. Your two friends have already tried."

As Atkins began a roundhouse swing, Carlow drove his boot into the big man's groin. The pain exploded through him like a lightning bolt. Atkins leaned over to try to ease it and Carlow clubbed him in the back of the neck with his fists doubled together.

Atkins grunted and collapsed, slamming against the floor of the saloon. His head bobbed and was still.

Carlow spun toward the bald-headed cowboy, who shivered and raised his hands in front of himself. His mouth was red and full.

"P-please . . . no more. No more," he muttered, waving away his intention to continue the fight, then moving his hands back to the ache in his stomach.

Carlow turned toward the second cowboy, being helped to his feet by two customers. The cowboy was too groggy to stand; his legs wobbled and he sat back down, his head bouncing against his chest.

"Get up, you bastard. What's the matter? Don't you like to fight a man who's facing you?" Carlow snarled and looked up at the two would-be helpful customers. "Maybe one of you would like to step in? Or both. Come on, all of you. Come on." He wiped away the blood from the cut over his eye, trying to manage its flow away from his eyesight. His uncle had long ago taught him the art of boxing and it had kept him safe more than once. But Ellie's rejection reentered his thoughts and made him even angrier.

Bursting through the saloon doors came Mrs. Jacobs, holding her shotgun. Her flinty gaze took in the scene and a small smile followed.

"What are you doing in here, ol' lady?" a voice challenged.

"Yeah. You shouldn't be in here."

The rest of the saloon was silent. Her reputation with a shotgun was well known.

Mrs. Jacobs straightened. "Ranger Carlow, are you all right? I see three men can't take a Ranger." Her smile became a grin.

"I'm fine," Carlow said, glancing at his raw and bleeding knuckles, then touching the side of his face.

"Figured you were. I appreciate you comin' by to see me earlier," Mrs. Jacobs continued. "A friend came and said you were being attacked by this fool Atkins and two of his thugs. That's all Bennett needs. More foolishness." She looked around the room. "On behalf of the town, please let me apologize for their behavior." Her eyes stopped on a councilman.

"Yes, dear Mrs. Jacobs, you are right," the councilman said, standing slowly. "Ranger, we respect what you Rangers do for Texas—for us. Thank you. Thank you very much." He motioned toward the awakening Atkins. "I believe Marshal Ballis should handle this from here."

Carlow looked over at the bartender and motioned for his gunbelt. "That's not necessary. I won't be pressing charges." He accepted his weapons from the white-faced bartender. "It's clear Bennett doesn't like Irish Rangers—and I will oblige the town by leaving." He turned to Mrs. Jacobs and thanked her for caring.

She smiled and whispered, "I'm so sorry, Time. Ellie should have waited." She patted him on the arm and added, "Bennett is proud of you."

As he belted on his gunbelt, an acne-spotted young man came into the saloon and stopped. He was surprised at the scene. Finding his voice, he declared, "Ah, Ranger Time Carlow, sir."

"Yes?"

"I have a telegram for you. Just came in. From Captain McNelly."

Carlow wasn't surprised. McNelly tried to keep his men informed. The operator assistant worked his way through the tables and handed the folded wire to the Ranger. Carlow thanked him and tipped him a coin. The saloon was gradually returning to its normal state. Atkins was helped to a chair; his two henchmen were largely ignored.

Staring at the young Ranger, the telegraph runner hesitated, then said, "Y-you're bleeding, sir. Around your eye. It's . . . swollen . . . sir." He glanced around. "Are you all right, s-sir?"

"I'll be better when I leave this town," Carlow snapped, looked at the assistant, and said, "That's not correct. Bennett is a fine town. I grew up here."

"I-I know that. Y-you're a l-legend around here."

Carlow smiled and the assistant hurried out.

Opening the paper, Carlow read:

RANGERS KILEEN AND CARLOW . . .
STOP . . . PROCEED AT ONCE TO MIRABILE
RANCH . . . STOP . . . MAKE HIM A RANGER
AND RIDE FOR SAN ANTONIO . . . STOP . . .
JUST GOT HERE WITH FORCE . . . STOP . . .
RANGER DECONER JUDGE CLINE
PROSECUTOR JOHNSON KILLED HERE . . .
STOP . . . ROSE JURYMAN KILLED . . . ONE
KILLER IN WOOD MASK ARRESTED SO
FAR . . . STOP . . . LIKELY ROSE GANG GOING

AFTER MEN CONNECTED TO HIS
ARREST . . . STOP . . . FARMER AND WIFE
KILLED OUTSIDE OF TOWN . . . STOP . . . DO
NOT KNOW IF RELATED . . . STOP . . .
EXPECT MORE GANG TROUBLE . . . STOP . . .
WATCH YOURSELVES . . . STOP . . . MCNELLY.

After staring at the paper, Carlow returned it to his coat pocket and stepped outside. Behind him, the chatter was reinvigorated as customers gathered around the three striken men, each with a version of what had just happened. Mrs. Jacobs was a step behind.

He couldn't believe what he had just read. Pig Deconer had been a friend, a good friend. He hadn't even been on active duty. Judge Cline and Johnson were dead, too. And another man he didn't know, but a man who done his duty.

What was going on? The main connection between four of those murders was obvious, as McNelly had observed: all were tied to the arrest and conviction of Tanneman and Hillis Rose. Maybe it was just a coincidence. Both were dead. So why now? Besides that, Carlow had seen no signs of a gang riding with Tanneman and Hillis, other than the two brothers—and they were dead, too. Was there really a gang? Kileen thought so; evidently McNelly did, too. Enough that he would stop in San Antonio instead of heading on to the border.

"Time, I'm so sorry. That must have been bad news," Mrs. Jacobs said, studying his raw, taut face.

He explained what the wire had said; his shoulders rose and fell in an unspoken sorrow.

She was silent as well, leaving him to his grief, then decided she must speak. "I can't give you any help with that awfulness, Time. But I do know that problem in the saloon wasn't Ellie's husband's doing. He's a very nice man. A good man."

"I'm sure he is, Mrs. Jacobs." His mind barely returned to the fight.

He walked to his horse and yanked free the reins.

"Your hands and face need tending. They're bleeding!" she said without moving toward him. "Your eyebrow, it's cut."

"I'll be fine. Isn't the first time."

She shook her head. "Lordy, how well I know that. You and your friend Shannon used to get into scrapes about every day, it seems to me." Her smile was forced. "I remember you two running around, just looking for trouble. And usually finding it."

He bit his lower lip, but didn't speak, then decided to retrieve the locket and knife from his saddlebags.

"Mrs. Jacobs, I would like you to take these back with you. To Ellie, ah, Mrs. Wittlock," Carlow said, extending the wrapped brooch and the sheathed knife. "That makes the gifts from you, not me. Tell her to sell them if she wants to and buy something else. That's fine. I don't want them." He paused. "Tell her to let her husband give the knife to Jeremiah. That all right with you?"

Looking down at the offered presents in her hands, Mrs. Jacobs said softly, "She talked about you. Every day. She cares for you. Even now. It's just . . ."

"I'm sure it's for the best." He swung into the saddle.

A broad-chested man burst through the saloon doors. His pipe looked like it was part of his face. His round face was beet red and framed by long muttonchop sideburns. He saw Carlow and pulled the pipe from his mouth.

"Ranger Carlow! Please, a moment." He hurried to the mounted Ranger. "I'm Topper Gustavson, editor of the *Bennett Gazette*. A moment, please."

"How are you, Topper?" Carlow responded, crossing his arms on his saddle horn.

"I'm doing well," Gustavson said, then saw Chance beside Carlow's horse and pointed with his pipe. "My God! Is that . . . a wolf?"

"Part. He and I fit together real well."

"I should say." Shaking his head, Gustavson held out his hand. "I just wanted to thank you for ridding our territory of that awful Silver Mallow. Did a big story on it. Got the information from the *Presidio News*. You know, hometown boy makes good."

Carlow shook his hand. "Thanks, Topper. But I doubt Bennett would want to claim me. Besides, I had a lot of help."

"Inside there," Gustavson motioned toward the saloon. "That's not the way Bennett feels about you—or your uncle. Not at all." He waved both arms vigorously. "I've heard all kinds of stories about what you did for Bennett and the cattlemen around here. I know there are some who don't like the Irish, but those . . . don't count." He returned the pipe to his mouth and puffed on it vigorously.

Carlow nodded, his face unreadable.

Mrs. Jacobs licked her lips. "Ranger Time Carlow is a very special young man, Topper. Texas is very lucky."

"If you want to press charges against those three, I'll stand as a witness." Gustavson frowned, reinforcing his intent.

"Appreciate that, Topper," Carlow said, "but no. Got more important things to do."

Carlow told him about the telegram and Gustavson gulped his dismay and asked if he could report the news. The young Ranger shrugged his shoulders and said that was Gustavson's business, not his.

"Got to be riding. Good to see you again, Mrs. Jacobs," Carlow said. "Nice to meet you, Topper."

"You, too, Ranger," Gustavson said. "I'm going to do a story on that fight. It was really something to see."

Shifting his weight in the saddle, Carlow glanced at Mrs. Jacobs. "I wish you wouldn't, Topper. Some innocent people might get dragged into it."

"I don't understand."

"I know you don't. Trust me. Bennett doesn't need a story like that."

"Aren't you going to stay in town? At least for supper?" A small tear gathered at the corner of Mrs. Jacobs's eye.

"No. Need to get going." He gave a weak wave and nudged his horse into an easy lope. Chance yipped and followed.

Holding the gifts to her bosom, the old woman watched him leave and murmured, "You're a good man, Time Carlow. Bennett doesn't know how good. Neither did Ellie."

Gustavson looked at the older woman. "You like that young Ranger, don't you?"

"Yes, I do."

"Man, he sure handled himself inside. Don't think I've ever seen anything quite like it. Why do you think he didn't want me to write about it?"

Mrs. Jacobs turned toward him and smiled. "Someday I'll tell you."

Chapter Fourteen

Time Carlow let Shadow have his head as he rode without thinking. Occasionally, Ellie's face would break through and he would hear again: "I wasn't even sure you cared any more—or were alive. You didn't write me . . . for a long time."

His face was sore, his left eye nearly swollen shut, his eyebrow throbbing, and his knuckles cut and puffy. He wasn't aware of how long they had ridden, or even the direction. But when Shadow stopped, he nodded.

They were beside the creek where his mother and best friend were buried, only fifty yards downstream. Carlow's initial focus was a timbered creekline off to the left. Twisted underbrush and saplings butted up against the greasewood, cottonwood and willow trees. An occasional pecan tree stood proudly. As far as he could see was grassland, dotted with cattle. Open range.

He dismounted and began unsaddling the fine animal. He led the horse to the creek and let him drink his fill. Chance joined him as he soaked his sore hands, then his battered face in the water. The cut in his eyelid had closed and was now only sore. Afterward, he used his saddle rope to tie Shadow to a small cottonwood with enough room to graze. He wiped down the horse with his saddle blanket, stopped and looked around. Dusk was closing in. Sounds of nightfall were beginning to come alive. He didn't mind. There was nothing about this day he wanted to remember.

For an instant, he wanted to ride back to Bennett and tell Ellie that he loved her and that she should go with him. That thought was followed by an emptiness he had known before. When his mother died. When Shannon Dornan had been killed.

He stared up into the graying sky and screamed, a sound like a wounded wolf.

Shadow's ears straightened and he tensed. Chance turned to look at him, as if seeking a brother. His body shook and his arms fell to his sides. Even his soul ached. For the first time, he realized he hadn't slept under a roof since being in Angel's house when he had been wounded. All he owned were some guns, bullets, a knife, travel gear and a good horse. What he made as a Ranger went into a bank account, except for living expenses. Kileen had almost forced him to do that. Long range, a horse ranch of his own. Like Mirabile. That would be years coming, he decided. More likely, a bullet would find him first—and no one would care. Except for his uncle.

Enough, he finally told himself. Enough of feeling sorry for himself. He wasn't the first man to be rejected by the woman he loved.

He forced himself to gather firewood and soon had a small fire going. The fire was cradled within a narrow but shallow ravine, to hide its light. He had lived too long in the wilds of Texas not to be careful. His fire soon took Ellie's letters and the one he had carried to give her. A small cast-iron skillet warmed some salt pork and cut-up wild onions he had secured days earlier. He gave most of the meat to Chance and threw the onions in the fire. He wasn't hungry. Coffee didn't taste good either. He started to pour the rest of the pot to douse the remaining coals, but decided against it. He might want coffee in the morning.

Gathering his blanket from the saddle, he grabbed his Winchester from its sheath and carried them away from the dying fire and his munching horse. Kileen had taught him the wisdom of that. After laying out the blanket, he returned for his saddle to use as a pillow, just as he had done countless times before.

He unbuckled his gunbelt and removed his hat, boots and leggings, but left on his long coat and pants. He should clean his guns, but didn't want to. He didn't want to do anything and lay down with his hand carbine next to him. Crickets had begun their night serenade. He loved the sound, but tonight it just made him feel lonelier than ever. Chance wandered close and finally lay down next to his master. A pale moon was working its way into control of the sky. He closed his eyes, but the day's awfulness rushed into his mind.

His face was sore and his hands swollen from the fight, but that wasn't bothering him. What was chewing on his mind was the fact that the men in town would brag they had run him off. It shouldn't matter, he kept telling himself. But it did. The town may not have liked him—or his uncle—because they were Irish, but nobody sent him away.

Nobody.

He knew his uncle wouldn't agree, although Kileen had a long history of dealing with this kind of problem directly. Kileen might say Carlow should ride on, but the big Irishman wouldn't have done it himself. Not like this.

Sleep wouldn't come.

He sat up. The crickets were silent.

Chance was immediately alert.

"It's all right, boy. Just me. You settle down," he whispered and patted the wolf-dog on the head. He crouched and slipped toward a gathering of rocks, taking his hand carbine with him. His bare feet didn't like the uneven ground, but he barely noticed. Chance trotted at his side, then stopped, growling in his throat.

Someone was there! Off to the left was a tree's shadow with lumps where they shouldn't be.

Hushing Chance again, Carlow was certain more were out there. Wandering thieves? Or more trouble from town? He was betting on the latter as he eased behind the cluster of rocks to determine his next move. To his left, the trail wound like a broken finger, pointing northward through a wall of proud trees. He studied the shadows extending confidently, stroked by moonlight.

A man was standing beside a large oak. Looking closely, Carlow could see the thin line of black that was the man's rifle at his side. Two more men were a few steps away, also with rifles. He guessed it was the bunch from the saloon. Their intent was obvious. Right now, they were trying to see where he might be. His fire offered little help, its brightness extending only three or four feet. They hadn't seen him, didn't know where he was.

Studying the terrain for the best route, he decided to loop them and come up from behind. It would take longer, but he was more likely to get close before being noticed. Yet every noise seemed loud as he crept closer. Every rustle of his coat seemed like a roar to him. Every touch of his bare feet on the hard ground seemed like thunder. Every escaping breath was a recital. Even Chance's crouching advance sounded like a galloping horse.

Still, the men didn't notice. They whispered to each other, trying to decide how best to proceed. The big man in the middle had to be Connor Atkins.

Another voice answered, but Carlow didn't recognize it.

He knelt beside a fallen log and watched a ground squirrel scurry away, squeaking obscenities at being disturbed. Carlow lifted his head around the end of the log and considered the next phase of his advance. Ahead of him was a maze of trees, rocks, dead branches and hardy weeds.

No sign of the waiting men was evident from this angle. Carlow knew it was unlikely there would be, until he had completed at least a half circle. He told Chance to remain where he was. Minutes later, he had worked his way around to a cluster of undergrowth and small boulders gathered for a meeting only they understood.

Belly down, he sorted through the gray shapes ahead. There were four, not three. One was definitely Atkins. The bald-headed cowboy and the stocky man were also there. A fourth he didn't recall seeing before. The man was his height, wearing a business suit. A hawk nose was the only feature Carlow could distinguish from the night's shadows. A favorable sliver of moonlight indicated his pants were tucked into long boots. In the man's hands was a Springfield rifle. Carlow had a funny feeling this was Thomas Wittlock, Ellie's new husband.

The men were facing the other direction, toward his camp. Waiting longer would only increase the likelihood of his being discovered. He raised the hand carbine. It was moderately comfortable in his stiffened fingers, but he couldn't grip the handle as tightly as he wished. He would wait to cock the weapon until the last second. The noise would definitely give away his position.

He slowly released a deep breath through his closed mouth. As he stood, the gun barrel clanked off of a triangular-shaped outcropping of a boulder and the resulting noise clamored for attention in the night. Carlow froze in place. A glance at the boulder made him realize a shard of moonlight nestled where he had hit it. He shook his head at the coincidence.

If the noise had any effect on the four men, it didn't show. Satisfied that his mistake hadn't changed anything, Carlow resumed his stalking, being more careful this time not to hit the rocks. In a dozen catlike steps he was ten feet from them.

"Evening, gentlemen," Carlow growled and cocked his hand carbine, holding the butt against his right thigh, and added, "Don't turn around. Drop your guns. Do it now."

All four froze.

The stocky cowboy muttered, "It's four ag'in one."

Carlow fired and relevered. The bullet spat up dirt inches from the man.

"You're right. I'll get lead into three of you before anyone turns around. Who thinks he'll be the lucky one?"

Three rifles bounced on the ground. Connor Atkins gripped his weapon, his fingers tightening and loosening.

"Well, Atkins, you're not as smart as I thought you were," Carlow said. "You just made yourself my first target."

The big man rolled his shoulders and let his rifle slide to the ground.

"Now your gunbelt, Atkins. You, too, Baldy."

The loosened gunbelts thudded on the ground.

"Think you're pretty slick, don't ya, Irishman?" Atkins snorted.

Carlow didn't like their calmness. The man he thought was Thomas Wittlock kept glancing over at Atkins.

A hidden gun.

"Slicker than you might think," Carlow said. "For an Irishman." He quietly moved three steps to his left. "Take out that hideaway pistol, Atkins. With your fingers. Move real slow. I'm getting tired of all this."

Glancing at Wittlock, Atkins's shoulders rose and fell. His right hand moved slowly toward his waistband. Just where Carlow had guessed it would be.

Carlow moved again. Three more steps to the left.

Atkins raised his left hand slowly into the air; his right was unseen. The big man spun toward where he thought Carlow was standing. The Ranger's movement was enough to give him an edge.

Atkins's derringer roared orange flame into the darkness.

Carlow said, "You don't deserve it, but I'm giving you another chance, Atkins. Your cousins would be alive today if they hadn't tried shooting it out with us." He motioned with his gun. "You've got another bullet in that thing. You can try to cock it and be dead—or drop it and live."

"Shoot 'im. Shoot 'im," the stocky cowboy muttered.

Atkins shivered and tossed the gun toward Carlow.

Carlow walked over and picked it up. He glared at the stocky man. "You, the one with all the advice. Here."

He threw the derringer at him. The man's hands moved toward the flying weapon, but not fast enough. It bounced off his stomach and fell away.

"Pick it up. I'll give you a chance," Carlow snarled.

His face was dark with fury; the soreness around his left eye was throbbing worse than before. "More than you bastards were going to give me."

The stocky man shook his head.

"What about you, Baldy? Wanna give it a try?" Carlow pointed his hand carbine at the man's midsection.

"N-no sir, not me. No sir."

Licking his dry lips, Carlow said, "You know, I could shoot all of you. Right now. Most would, I reckon. Nothing worse than dry-gulchers."

"W-who are you?" Thomas Wittlock quivered.

"You already know who I am. Who are you?"

"Ah . . . Thomas Wittlock. From Bennett. I'm a respected businessman there."

"And why are you—and your friends—sneaking up on me?"

Wittlock hesitated and looked away. Right now he would rather have been almost anywhere else. Anywhere.

"I asked you a question."

"Ah, we . . . ah, we came out here to see you. To talk with you."

The laugh that came from Carlow was more of a panther snarl than a jovial response. "Come on now, Wittlock. You can do better than that."

"It's . . . about my wife. Ellie." His words trailed off.

Carlow shook his head. "You left your bride's bed to come out here just to talk with me? Come on, Wittlock. I'm not one of your idiot friends here."

Atkins's face tightened.

"Yeah, Atkins. I said you were an idiot."

Finally, the bald-headed man blurted, "It wasn't my idea. Honest. Atkins paid me an' Shorty. We were supposed to rough you up. Get you away from Bennett."

"I'm not in Bennett."

"I know. I know." The bald-headed cowboy was waving his arms now. "Mr. Wittlock was behind it all. Paid us. Thought you was gonna take his wife 'way." He folded his arms and looked at Atkins, then at Wittlock, and jerked his chin down to reinforce his statements.

"Well, I'll take it back, boys. It's Wittlock who's the biggest fool." Carlow waved his gun in the businessman's direction. "Anyone who knows Ellie . . . Mrs. Wittlock . . . knows she wouldn't make a commitment like marriage—and break it. Not for anyone."

The bald-headed man looked at Atkins and frowned.

The stocky cowboy, Shorty, snorted. "I told you so."

"Well, gentlemen, here's what we're going to do," Carlow said. "We're walking back to your horses. They must be just over that ridge."

Minutes later, the fivesome were approaching the four tied-up horses. Carlow ordered each man to free his horse and give it a hard slap on the rump. The animals whinnied, snorted and bolted for town.

"Now, you boys will have a nice long time to talk this over," Carlow said. "I'm letting you off real easy. Think about that, too. I could arrest all of you for attempted murder of a state lawman. But I won't. Just think of it as my gift to Ellie on her marriage."

His eyes narrowed. "But if I see any of you again, I'm going to kill you." He paused. "All except you, Wittlock. Ellie's too special a gal to be a widow. Again. And Jeremiah's too good a kid. You take care of them, Wittlock. They deserve better than you. But that's what they signed on for."

With a glance in his direction, the four men began walking toward town, grumbling and cursing at each other.

"Let them go, Time," Carlow said to himself. "It

doesn't matter what they say about you in Bennett. It doesn't matter that they'll claim to have run you out of town. It doesn't matter what Ellie thinks. Not anymore."

Carlow watched until they became blurs, then turned and decided to move his camp. He didn't think the men would return, but there was no reason to be careless.

Chapter Fifteen

Leading Shadow, Carlow moved his camp south several hundred yards, even wading across the creek to make it more difficult to ride up on him. He dumped the gathered guns in the water.

He stretched out and tried to sleep. The side of his face and eye were pounding. Finally he gave up on the idea and got dressed. He needed to return to Bennett and wire McNelly so the captain would know his message had been received and the two Rangers would head to Mirabile's ranch. Their leader deserved that, Carlow told himself. The fact that he would be seen returning to Bennett would just be a coincidence, he added.

Dawn was stretching itself over the land as Carlow rode into Bennett. He rode down the main street with his wolf-dog trotting proudly, as if he understood the reason for the return. As the young Ranger passed the string of saloons, he heard voices declaring his presence. Surprised voices. He tried to force his tired mind to think about the murders in San Antonio. Why did he resist the idea of a Rose gang? Just because he hadn't seen them? It sounded like a gang at work. How many?

He pulled up at the hitching rack in front of the busiest restaurant in town and went inside, reminding Chance to stay with his horse.

Ellie sat at a back table with her husband, Thomas Wittlock. With them was a gray-haired man with a thick mustache. He eyed Carlow as he entered and said something to the couple, who had their backs to the door. Both turned to see. Ellie smiled and an uneasy Wittlock nodded. Gaslight from the wall slashed their faces and flirted with her light brown hair, rolled into a tight bun. Her blue eyes glistened with interest in him.

Ignoring their attention, Carlow forced himself to look for an open table. The back of his neck was hot. He reminded himself this was exactly what he wanted. He sat down at one of three open tables; this one was to the right of the door. A shaggy-haired waiter brought coffee and asked for his order. Eggs over easy, bacon and toast. He was surprised at how good it sounded and took a sip of the hot liquid.

"You're one of the Rangers who grew up here, aren't ya?" the waiter asked, pushing a free hand through his unruly hair.

Carlow took another sip. "Yes, I am. Time Carlow's my name. What's yours?"

"I'm Russell Erickson. We went to school together for a year. A long time ago," the waiter said quietly. "Don't suppose you remember?"

Setting down the cup, Carlow rose from his chair and held out his hand. "Of course I do. Where are my manners? Too early, I guess. How are you, Russell?"

"How are you? Looks like they roughed you up."

"Did you get a good look at them?"

The waiter chuckled and said he had, then explained he was working two jobs and hoped to get married after he was able to handle it financially. He clerked at the general store in addition to waiting tables at the restaurant. His goal was his own ranch.

Glancing at Wittlock, he said, "I'm glad you came to

town. Atkins and his two thugs have been going around town, saying they sent you packing."

"Did you see how they came into town this morning?"

"No. Why?"

Carlow explained; his eyes darted toward the Wittlock table, then back to Erickson. The waiter slapped his thigh and laughed loudly enough that two tables of men stopped eating and looked over.

"Oops. I'm supposed to be seen, not heard," Erickson said. "I'll get your order going. Wait 'til I tell the boys in the back." He laughed and hurried away.

At a middle table in the back corner, four members of the town council finished their breakfasts and strolled through the restaurant, acknowledging diners and stopping to greet them. Carlow guessed their importance from the way they were handling themselves. When they came to Carlow's table, the four hesitated and three of them went on.

The fourth, the town's banker, cleared his throat awkwardly. "Mornin', Ranger. I'm Simon Seikerman. I'm on the town council."

"Mornin' to you, sir." Carlow made no attempt to hold out his hand.

"Heard there was some trouble in the Corao yesterday," Seikerman said, and paused.

Carlow deliberately took a sip of coffee and said nothing.

The tight-faced banker pulled on his coat lapels, brushed off an imaginary piece of dust and said, "Bennett is a peaceful town. We don't take much to bar fights and ruffians."

Carlow looked up at the man; the Ranger's eyes sought the banker's face and the townsman was immediately uncomfortable.

Speaking loudly, so everyone in the restaurant could hear, Carlow said, "Seikerman, you're talking to the wrong man. I didn't start the fight. Atkins and his two men did. But you already know that. Atkins said he was a friend of Thomas Wittlock. He's right over there. Go ask him why they came at me."

He cocked his head. "While you're at it, ask Wittlock why the four of them tried to sneak up on me last night. On the trail. To kill me." His fingers touched the coffee cup and his fingers encircled its rim. "Ask Wittlock what happened. Why he and his friends had to walk back to town without their horses. Or their guns."

He sat back in the chair. "As a matter of fact, you and your fellow councilmen might want to say thanks— for me not pressing charges and bringing more shame on Bennett. How about attempted murder of a state lawman, for starters?"

Chuckles rippled through the restaurant, followed by low murmuring.

Seikerman started to say something, but Carlow stopped him. "Go away, Seikerman. I'm leaving town right after I wire Ranger headquarters to find out where I'm needed next. But I'll be back." He paused. "Atkins and his two clowns had best be gone when I do. I've been as understanding as I care to be. I don't like men who sneak up and try to maim me."

Completely flustered, the banker pulled again on his coat lapels, straightened his back and left the restaurant.

Shortly after that, Erickson brought Carlow his breakfast.

"Man, that was wonderful! Absolutely wonderful," Erickson said as he refilled Carlow's coffee cup. "Stuffed-up toads. All of them."

Carlow grinned. "Thanks, Russell. I'm sure you're the only one who thought so."

Leaning over again as if to pour more, Erickson said, "Don't be so sure of that, Time. A lot of people think you're the best Ranger in Texas. Hey, I don't think many had seen Atkins get whipped before, much less the three of them. Not everybody has a problem with the Irish, you know."

Someone came walking up behind them and Erickson excused himself and went to another table to see what they needed. Throughout the restaurant, most had returned to their meals; a few, though, continued to watch.

"Good morning to you, Ranger. Didn't know you were in town," said the gray-haired man from Ellie's table, holding out his hand. A star was evident on his lapel.

"Name's Carlow. Time Carlow, Marshal." The young Ranger accepted the greeting and noticed the shoulder holster under the lawman's coat.

"Heard plenty about you, Time. I'm Penniston Ballis," the lawman said, adjusting his glasses. "Came from Uvalde. Might have heard of me. I broke up the cattle war over there. About ten years ago." His shoulders jumped slightly, as if a current had run through them.

"Heard about that. You did well, Marshal Ballis."

"Thanks. A lot more quiet here since you boys got rid of Silver Mallow and his bunch." The lawman's shoulders jumped again. "What brings you to Bennett?"

Everything in Carlow wanted to say that he didn't care what Bennett did, but he knew better than that. A Ranger represented Texas; his personal problems were just that, personal. Kileen had told him so. Often.

"Just riding through, Marshal," Carlow said. "Rode into Bennett because I grew up here. That's all." Carlow answered the unspoken question. "You can tell Wittlock not to worry. I don't blame him for his friend's stupidity."

"How long are you staying?" Ballis folded his arms.

Carlow smiled. "I could take offense at that, Ballis. I'll be riding on as soon as I finish my breakfast and wire my captain. Well, I might go to the general store for some supplies."

"Do you need some tending for that eye? Looks pretty mean."

"It'll be fine. Been hurt worse."

Ballis wasn't sure how to respond, then surprised Carlow when he asked the Ranger if he wanted to press charges against Atkins and his men. He looked relieved when Carlow said he didn't. Then Ballis turned pale, when the young Ranger repeated his threat from last night about seeing them again.

"B-but that would be m-murder, Ranger."

"No. That would be justice," Carlow said, sipping his coffee. "If you want to help, tell them now would be a good time to leave town. I'll be back. They better not be here when I come."

Without another word, Ballis returned to Wittlock's table and shared his conversation. Ellie glanced back at Carlow and he was glad he wasn't looking.

The meal tasted good. Very good. Trail food wasn't nearly as tasty. Neither he nor Kileen were particulary good cooks, although the big Irishman thought he was. Carlow was nearly finished when both Ellie and Wittlock got up from their table and headed out. Ballis remained at the table, drinking coffee. They stopped at his table and Carlow put down the last remnant of toast and looked up.

"Mornin', folks," Carlow said, and avoided looking at Ellie. "Enjoy your walk, Wittlock?"

"Time, please, Thomas has something he wants to say." Ellie's face was a plea. From her expression, he thought it was the first time she had been told of yesterday's fight in the bar and last night's attempted ambush. Her face was a mixture of fear, anger, disbelief and embarrassment. Dimples dominated her cheeks, now flushed with the range of emotions going through her. Her eyes went to Carlow's bruised face and darted away.

"Of course."

Looking around, then at Ellie, Wittlock said, "I came over to apologize. I had no intention of seeing you hurt. I . . . just wanted you . . . to leave." He licked his lower lip; his shoulders rose and fell. "It was my fault. I should've guessed Atkins wouldn't do things . . . well, politely."

Staring at the tall man with long sideburns, curly hair and a prominent hawk nose, Carlow responded, "Wittlock, the only reason you're sorry is because it didn't work. Your friends got whipped instead of me. Athough they tried real hard." He held a hand to his bruised face. "And your attempt to ambush me last night failed. Ellie might believe that crap—or think she has to, but nobody else would. Move on, you're . . ."

"That's not true, Time," Ellie interrupted.

"Look, Ellie, what you do with your life—and Jeremiah's—is none of my concern. You've made that quite clear," Carlow said. "But don't try to make me believe your husband is sorry."

She stood, red-faced, for a moment, then trounced out.

Fuming, Wittlock started to leave, but Carlow's

command to stay stopped him. The young gunfighter unnerved him greatly.

"Wittlock, there's a ranch not far from here. Owned by Portland Rose. Atkins told you he's dead, I'm sure," Carlow said, sipping the rest of his coffee.

"No, he hadn't shared such with me or my associates." Wittlock folded his arms, wishing he could be almost anywhere but here right now. "We don't talk much."

"Interesting friendship."

"However, I believe I know of the place. Kinda run-down, as I recall. Why? You looking to buy it?"

"No. As I said, Portland is dead. So are his three brothers. They were caught robbing banks." Carlow looked at his cup and decided he wanted more. "Don't know who owns it after that. Maybe Atkins. Said he was a cousin. Just thought you ought to know."

Wittlock thanked him, said he would look into the matter, excused himself and hurried away.

Carlow waved Erickson over for some more coffee.

A few minutes later, Carlow walked out of the restaurant and headed for the telegraph office. The young assistant, sitting on a chair against the wall, greeted him warmly. Carlow returned the greeting.

"How may I help you, sir?" the thick-mustached operator asked, tugging on his white shirt to pull back the cuffs.

Carlow sent a wire to McNelly telling him his order had been received and would be followed, paid for it and left. As he cleared the small office, a boy came running toward him.

"Ranger Carlow! Ranger Carlow!"

It was Jeremiah. The boy dashed up to him, almost out of breath. In his hand was the beaded sheath knife.

Carlow watched the boy approach, partly glad to see him and partly wishing he hadn't. It would only make leaving harder.

"Ma gave this to me. Just this morning! It's beautiful," Jeremiah said. "She said you gave it to her to give to me."

Carlow wasn't sure how to respond. "Well, I'm glad you like it, Jeremiah. Remember you have to take care of it. That's a man's knife. It's no good if it's dull."

"Yes, sir! I will. I promise."

Jeremiah studied the young Ranger, bit his lower lip and said, "I thought . . . maybe . . . you were . . . going to be . . . my new pa." He squinted back emotion and the freckles guarding his face ran toward his wrinkled nose. "But . . . I already . . . have a new pa."

"Yes, you do," Carlow patted the boy's head. "You'll be able to do all kinds of things together."

Jeremiah looked at his scuffed boots. "Yes . . . sir."

"Well, you greet your mother for me," Carlow said. "And your new father."

"Are you going . . . away?"

Carlow felt emotion jump to his throat. For an instant, he couldn't speak. "Ah, yes, Jeremiah. My uncle— Thunder Kileen—is waiting for me. We've got our orders."

Jeremiah twisted his shoulders. "Will you . . . come back?"

Carlow knelt beside him. "Of course I will, Jeremiah. But you have lots of good things waiting for you—and your mother. You won't remember me in six months." Jeremiah shook his head, unable to speak.

Carlow pulled the boy to him and hugged him. "I'll miss you, too."

The boy wiped his eyes with his sleeve and stepped back. "I almost forgot. Ma wanted to see you. If you had a minute, she said. She's over at Mrs. Jacobs's store, you know."

"Sure, Jeremiah." Carlow stood. "Do me a favor, will you?"

"You bet."

"I'll walk over to the store—and you ride Shadow over there for me. Tell Chance to come with you. All right?"

The boy almost jumped out of his patched overalls. "Oh, wow! That'd be great."

Inside the millinery store, Carlow looked around but didn't see either Mrs. Jacobs or Ellie. He turned to leave; it was probably something Jeremiah wanted to have happen, not something requested. Carlow had been foolish to think so.

"Time? Oh, I didn't hear you come in." Ellie stepped around from the back room. Her eyes sought his. "Thank you for coming. I didn't think you'd want to . . . after all that awfulness." She shook her head. "I don't know what got into Thomas. He's a good man, Time. Really, he is."

Carlow was irritated. Had she asked him to come over to tell him this? His voice carried the feeling. "Mrs. Wittlock, I've got to be riding. Did you need something?"

Her face pale and closing in on tears, she revealed what she held in her right fist. Carlow's locket. Slowly she put it around her neck and looked at him.

"Time, I decided I want to wear this, if it's all right with you. I wanted to tell you. I want to remember our moments together," she murmured. "That's why I gave Jeremiah the gift and told him it was from you." Her bosom swelled with feelings she knew could not be released. "I wish it had . . . worked out. I guess I resent . . . the Rangers taking you from . . . me."

"Well, ah, that's nice," Carlow said, and stepped backward toward the door. "I hope you have a good life, Ellie. You and Jeremiah. I really do."

It wasn't what he had expected and he knew staying there would only be a mistake. He loved her. He wanted to hold her and tell her that. But it was too late for that. Too late.

"I . . . ah . . . better leave, Ellie. Else I'm liable to grab you and kiss you and tell you that I love you."

She half turned, her eyes closed. "Please . . . go."

He spun and left without hearing her choked affirmation: "I . . . love you, Time."

As he strode onto the sidewalk, an anxious Jeremiah came forward with Chance at his side.

The boy started to say something, but Carlow saw a reflection from a dark figure across the street beside the general store. A gun! Atkins!

"Jeremiah, get inside. Now!" Carlow drew his hand carbine. "Down, Chance. Down, boy!"

The boy hesitated and Carlow shoved him down and stepped in front of him. Chance dove on top of the boy.

Orange flame spat from the figure—and from a second-story window to his left.

Both shots missed. One splintered the sidewalk; the other slammed into Mrs. Jacobs's storefront. Carlow leaped off the sidewalk and to his left, to direct the gunfire away from the boy. He held his gun butt against his thigh with both hands and fired, levered and fired again, then again and again.

The silhouette fired at the middle of the street, tumbled off the sidewalk and was still.

Carlow ran across the street, toward the downed figure. Atkins was dying. The young Ranger kicked the Winchester at the man's side into the street. Orange flame spat again from the upper window, cutting Carlow's coat sleeve. Another cut the bottom of his long coat floating out behind him. Carlow threw himself next to the general store and fired into the window, emptying his hand carbine.

As suddenly as it had started, the gunfire ended.

Ellie opened the door slightly and screamed for Jeremiah to join her. The boy responded, bringing the wolf-dog with him. Blood was leaking from a splintered piece of wood that had struck the animal in his lower back.

"Come on, Chance," Jeremiah said, and looked up at Ellie as he entered the shop. "Ma, Chance is hurt. You gotta help him. He covered me. So I wouldn't get shot. He's a wonderful dog. He's my friend."

Carlow jammed new loads into his gun. Where was the other Atkins thug? Had the man lost his nerve? Or was he just waiting for the right opportunity?

From the sheriff's office came Marshal Ballis with a shotgun. Two strides behind him was a skinny deputy with another shotgun.

"Ranger, what's going on?" Ballis yelled when he saw Carlow standing against the building. "Are you hit?"

"Don't think so. Atkins and his friends tried one more time," Carlow yelled. "That's Atkins." He pointed his gun toward the still figure below him. "There's another in the hotel. Been quiet for a while. Don't know if I hit him or not."

"You raise quite a ruckus when you come to town, Ranger."

"Stay there. I'm going into the hotel," Carlow shouted. "Watch the back door."

The terrified hotel clerk told him what room the shooter was in and handed him a key, and Carlow bounded up the stairs. The clerk managed to say only one man had taken the room and paid in advance. At the door of 215, Carlow paused and shoved the key into the lock. He waited, stepping to the side of the door, then pushed it open. And waited.

Nothing.

On the floor beside the window sat the stocky cowboy who had been with Atkins the previous night. His right arm and shoulder were soaked in blood. A Winchester lay a few feet away.

"D-don't shoot, R-Ranger . . . please."

"I won't—unless you make a move for that gun."

"I-I w-won't. H-had enough. T-told 'em you would be tough to k-kill."

"Good for you."

Carlow kicked the rifle away and demanded to know if the man had a pistol. He said he didn't. Carlow examined him and decided he was telling the truth. The young Ranger leaned out the window and yelled to Marshal Ballis, "Going to need a doctor up here."

Carlow sought a lamp from the bedside table. Its trembling light did little to drive away the grayness of the room.

"How bad is it, Ranger?" the man asked, patting his shoulder with his left arm and staring at the blood on his hand.

"Don't know. Where's your friend? The bald-headed one?"

"Jake didn't want any part of this. He went back to Atkins's ranch this morning. I think he's gonna keep ridin'. Didn't like any of this."

Carlow opened the lone closet. "Tell me why I should believe you."

"Guess you shouldn't." The cowboy's face was white. "Oh my God, it hurts somethin' awful."

"Tell me one more thing. If you're lying, I will find you," Carlow said. "Is this more of Wittlock's doing?"

The man groaned and pleaded for something to stop the pain.

"I asked you a question."

"I h-hurt s-so bad. Oh, Lord."

"Answer me or I've leave and you'll bleed to death," Carlow spat.

"Y-yes, T-Thomas w-was afraid his n-new wife would run off with you," the man whimpered. "Paid us two hundred each to kill you. On top of the fifty to . . . ah, beat you up. Don't know how much he p-paid Atkins. They're friends, ya know."

"Yeah, I know."

Heavy footsteps made Carlow turn toward the open door, and Marshal Ballis and a man Carlow assumed was a doctor entered. Grimly, the sheriff told him there would be no hearing; it had definitely been self-defense.

Minutes later, the young Ranger walked out of the hotel. Atkins's body lay where he had fallen. Carlow's mind was whirling with conflict. Wittlock had paid to have him killed. What should he do? Jeremiah deserved a father; Ellie deserved a good life.

Halfway across the street, he saw Jeremiah open the store door and run toward him. Chance was at his heels. A white bandage signaled the wolf-dog had been hurt, but not badly, it appeared.

"Are you all right?" Jeremiah asked breathlessly. "I was worried."

"So was I, Jeremiah."

The boy explained what had happened to Chance and that his mother had removed the splinter, treated the wound and bandaged it. Carlow knelt to examine his wolf-dog and patted him gratefully.

"Tell her I appreciate that, Jeremiah," Carlow said, and headed for his horse.

Jeremiah's face turned from worry to sadness. "Chance saved my life. He jumped on me. He was going to take a bullet. For me."

"Reckon he thinks a lot of you, Jeremiah." Carlow bit his lower lip and looked away.

"Got to go, Jeremiah," Carlow said, trying not to let the boy's eyes change his mind. "There's a gang killing good people. I've got to find them."

"I know Ma would like you to stay. So would Mrs. Jacobs. I heard them."

"That's real nice. You take good care of your mother, all right?" Carlow pulled the reins from the hitching rack and swung into the saddle.

He couldn't remember feeling so weary. It wasn't just from the lack of sleep. Ellie's marriage lay on his mind like a boulder. So did the realization that her husband had tried to have him murdered. He tried to focus on what was ahead and couldn't. If it were any other situation, any other man, he would have him arrested for murder. He couldn't. He wouldn't. Ellie had made her choice. Arresting Wittlock would only make things worse for her. That would be his real gift to her—and to her new husband.

"Good-bye, Jeremiah," Carlow said, and kicked his horse into a lope.

Chance barked at the boy and ran after them.

The boy stood and watched him go, twin tears racing down his cheeks.

Carlow stopped his horse and reined him toward the Wittlock & Carlson Land Attorneys and Real Estate Agents law office. He jumped down and stomped inside.

Thomas Wittlock looked up from his desk, trying to

appear busy. He had watched the gunfight from the street. Under several sheets of paper was a Smith & Wesson revolver. He had taken it from his desk drawer this morning. At one moment, he had thought he might be able to join in the shooting without anyone realizing it. He had quickly discarded the idea when he saw Carlow in action.

Carlow folded his arms. "Wittlock, I should have you arrested for conspiracy to murder. Don't say anything." He pointed with his left hand. "And, for God's sake, don't try to go for that gun. Ellie doesn't need to be a widow. Again."

The businessman stared down at the papers, then lifted them, acting surprised at what he saw. He shivered and dropped the papers, holding his hands away.

"Do you realize your new son could have been shot out there?" Carlow's voice was barely controlled. Rage coated each word. "You stupid fool."

"I-I d-don't . . ."

"I said, don't talk. I know you paid them to kill me. I know it," Carlow snarled. "Jeremiah needs a father—and Ellie deserves a good husband—or you wouldn't walk away from this." He cocked his head to the side. "If you knew anything about Ellie, you'd know she'd never leave you. For me, or anyone. No way." He rubbed his chin. "If I ever hear about you mistreating either of them, I'll come back—and finish this." He took a deep breath to release the venom within. "Now, get up off your butt and go down to Mrs. Jacobs's to make sure they're all right." He spun to leave, then wheeled and turned back. "Almost forgot. Portland's ranch. If there's no legitimate heir—and there isn't—I want that ranch to go to Russell Erickson. He's a good man—and he needs a break." Carlow glared at Wittlock, who couldn't bring himself to look at him. "Whatever he's got saved should be enough to buy the place. Right?" Carlow took a step forward. "I asked you a question."

"Ah, yes . . . right."

"Good. An' if there are any back taxes, you'll take care of them. Right?"

"Right."

"Good. I'll be checking." Carlow spun again and left.

Wittlock leaned down and vomited into the open drawer.

Chapter Sixteen

A late afternoon sun was stretching itself over the land as Carlow rode up to Angel's adobe house. His face and hands were sore from the fighting, but the swelling around his eye had retreated. Worse, his soul was aching. He wouldn't have come to Angel's place so soon, but the telegram had indicated they needed to ride.

He had kept Shadow at a steady pace, but the big horse loved to travel fast and long. Chance was barely in sight. Twice Carlow had stopped to give his horse a breather and to let the wolf-dog catch up, once near the grave sites. The small wound on Chance's back didn't seem to be bothering him, but Carlow had checked it anyway.

Stepping from the doorway, the big Irishman waved and hailed him warmly. "*Dia duit!*" Kileen's gunbelt was thrown over his shoulder.

Carlow tried to smile at the old Irish greeting of "God to you," and replied, "God and Mary to you," in Irish, as was the custom.

"*Dia is Muire duit.*"

The big Irishman was more than a little surprised to see his nephew so soon, but it didn't take long for Carlow to share the news about Ellie and the orders from McNelly's telegrams. Kileen was more interested in what had happened to his nephew. By the time Angel came outside, Kileen knew the whole story and was saddened for his beloved nephew and disturbed by the news about the killings in San Antonio, especially the death of their fellow Ranger.

"What ees thees?" Angel declared, waving her arms. "Why ees my two *hombres* lookin' so . . . how you say it, long in the faces?"

Carlow licked his lower lip and told her the same story. Immediately, she rushed to him, hugged him and said, "She ees not *bueno* for *mi hijo*. No." She held his bruised face with both hands and stared into it. "Eet does nothing to be sad. You must ride away from eet. There is *mucho* to love about life. Angel knows."

Patting her hands with his own, Carlow said, "It's good to see you."

"Come in!" Angel exclaimed. "You an' Beeg Thunder come in while Angel cooks ze fine supper. Then maybe we should ride to Bennett—and straighten some people out," Angel said, her dark eyes dancing. "There ees some who need thees straightenin'." She cocked her head. "I weel straighten thees *Señorita* Ellie. You straighten *Señor* Wittlock."

Carlow looked at Kileen and shook his head.

"No, we cannot be doin' such."

She grinned widely—and wickedly—and kissed Kileen, then hurried inside.

"Maybe you should settle down. Here. With Angel," Carlow said. "She is a good woman. You are good for each other."

Gazing down at the just-arriving Chance, Kileen said, "We be talking about it. Angel an' me. But not yet, me son. Not yet." He slapped Carlow on the shoulder. "We be Rangers, ye know."

"I don't understand what's going on," Carlow said.

"Aye, women can be difficult to know, me son."

Carlow chuckled. "No, I mean these murders. They have to be connected to Tanneman in some way. It's too much of a coincidence."

Silence indicated Kileen either wasn't ready to talk about it or had no idea of what was happening either.

"What be happenin' to the spirit wolf?" Kileen asked, kneeling to pet Chance and changing the subject.

"Oh, he got hit with a sliver of wood. From the sidewalk. He was lying on top of Jeremiah to protect him when the gunfight was going on. Ellie fixed him up good."

"Ellie did, did she?"

Kileen stood and made a two-inch gap with his thumb and forefinger. "A wee bit o' hot coffee would be good, me lad. Aye, 'tis a bad thing when a fine Ranger be killed. An' a judge and district attorney. An' the good lad who stood for juryin'. Especially in a town like San Antonio."

Carlow slapped the reins against his own leg. "Captain must think ol' Julian is their next target. His telegram almost says that." He motioned toward the corral. "Better get saddled. It's a long ride to his place."

"Easy, me lad. Easy," Kileen said. " 'Tis nowhere ye be goin' with that fine hoss o' yours. Hot and sweaty he be. Too good a hoss to be run into the ground, lad. Ye know it's the truth me be speakin'." He laid a big paw on Carlow's shoulder. "Tomorrow. First light. That be soon enough."

Carlow shook his head. "You're right. I wasn't thinking." He turned to his horse and rubbed his nose. "You think Julian will ride with us again? He just gave all that up."

Kileen's face was a full frown. " 'Tis unlikely he be turnin' down the captain hisself, me lad."

"Yeah, he warned us to be on the lookout. While we ride."

"Sure 'n we will be," Kileen said and motioned toward the corral. "Ye be puttin' up your fine steed there. After a good rubdown. No water 'til he's cool."

Carlow smiled. He knew better than his uncle how to care for a horse.

"Did you ever hear any mention of a Rose gang? From the banks they robbed?" Carlow folded his arms, holding the reins with his hand.

Kileen glanced at the house. "Aye, don't ye remember? There was talk about a gang hidin'. Outside, they were. Waitin' to be shootin' any o' the lovelies who came out of the bank too soon." He crossed himself and added, " 'Tis the workin' of the Rose gang all right. The bloody blaggards." He stared at his nephew's face again. "Angel be havin' some salve that'll do yourself good."

The two Rangers entered the eastern gate of Mirabile's small ranch and knew immediately something was wrong. Morning sun was on their backs. They were weary, but alert. The ride had been hard, having left as soon as Kileen could pull himself away from Angel. Their overnight camp had been a good one.

"Hold it right there, strangers." The command was harsh and supported by a levered Henry in the hands of a young man. Beside him was an older Mexican with a similar weapon.

Both Kileen and Carlow held their hands away from their bodies.

"We be comin' to see Julian. An old friend he be. Of the Rangers, we are," Kileen stated.

"Rangers? Where are your badges?" the young man demanded, waving his gun.

"They be in our pockets," Kileen answered. "Not a good idea to be wearin' the fine things while ridin'."

The young man looked like he didn't understand. "That a wolf with you boys?"

"No. He's not," Carlow said.

"I was thinking about shooting it."

"Good thing for you that you didn't try." Carlow's voice was thick with threat.

The young man frowned. "Looks like you've already been in a fight."

Carlow smiled. "Yeah, I have."

"Aye. He be whipping three thugs who attacked him," Kileen said proudly. "Aye, three."

The conversation was interrupted by a graying woman bursting from the ranch house.

"It's all right, Nelson. Those are friends of Julian's. When he was a Ranger."

She walked past the two armed men and directly to Kileen, who swung down and gave her a hug.

"Julian's been murdered, Thunder," she said. Her eyes were too dry to cry more. "We buried him yesterday."

"By all that's holy, when did this awful thing happen?" Kileen's eyes glared at the two waiting men.

Mirabile's widow was the only witness. Three days ago, he had been shot to death outside of his corral, just after breakfast. From long range, a hillside a hundred yards away. She said the killer had been wearing a long black coat and had a rifle with a scope and a sling. She had seen the weapon clearly when he stood up and tipped his hat at her and yelled out the German greeting, "*Guten Tag!*" His hair had been long, stringy and gray under his hat. He had ridden away on a gray horse, in the direction of the town of Strickland.

"Had a full mask over his face. Made of wood, I think," she continued.

Carlow stared at her, not believing what he was hearing. This couldn't be. Was there really a gang taking revenge on the men who had stopped the Rose brothers? He swung down from his horse, introduced himself and said he had always admired Julian Mirabile's approach to duty. He told her why they had come, of the other recent murders by masked men and the possible gang connection to Tanneman and Hillis Rose. He didn't mention the captain's orders; asking Mirabile to become a Ranger didn't matter now.

Her face was a mixture of shock and sadness. "Y-you should have been here . . . three days ago. I-I thought h-he was through with all t-this . . . violence." She turned away and held her hands to her face.

Carlow suggested Kileen walk her to the house while he talked with the two men. The big Irishman put an arm around the weeping woman and led her away, talking more softly than Carlow had ever witnessed.

Quick introductions determined the younger man was Julian's son, Nelson; Carlos Mide, the Mexican, was the only permanent hand. Neither had seen the murder; they had been working cattle. Carlow guessed the killer had planned it that way. He tied up the two horses at one of the corral posts and told Chance to stay with them.

As they walked, Mide asked about Chance and Carlow told him—in a handful of sentences—how the two of them had met up. He left out the part about Kileen thinking the wolf-dog was actually his friend's spirit. Nelson was interested in knowing if Kileen's statement about Carlow beating three men was true; Carlow explained what had happened, but left out why, as well as the subsequent attempt to kill him.

Nelson and Mide took the young Ranger to the killer's place of concealment, an elevated rock shelf that gave a perfect view of Mirabile's ranch house and surrounding buildings and corrals.

The killer had been there most of a day, judging from the empty cans. Carlow saw that the man had smoked a pipe; there were three places where he had emptied the burned tobacco.

Tracks from the man's getaway horse had no particular distinction, only that they headed toward the closest town, but there couldn't be many gray horses there. The most puzzling part of this crime was why the killer had ridden an easily identifiable horse, especially when he was clearly headed for a town.

After examining the surrounding brush, Carlow walked back to the two grieving men and asked, "Any strangers around recently? Anybody who'd profit if your dad were out of the way?"

"No to both, I reck . . ." Nelson said, then stopped as Mide touched his shoulder and reminded him of the peddler who had come by a week ago.

"Oh yeah, Carlos just reminded me," Nelson continued. "There was an old peddler with a wagon full of things to sell. Came by the ranch about a week ago. It couldn't be him, though. He was one-armed, sounded kinda slow. In the head, you know. Might've been from Missouri. Had one of those funny drawls."

"Ever see him before?"

"No, can't say that I have. Of course, peddlers come and go, you know." Nelson scratched his boot toe along the rock. "Should've stayed home. Should've stayed home."

"Hey, you've got nothing to apologize for." Carlow reached out and held Nelson's arm for an instant. "You were doing what your father wanted you to do."

"Doesn't help much."

"I know. I'm sorry."

"What are you Rangers going to do now?" Nelson Mirabile asked.

"Ride for Strickland and talk with the marshal there, first. Ranger Kileen knows him," Carlow said. "Learn what we can. Then we'll wire the captain with the news."

"Oh, he knows Lark, huh?" Nelson said. "Strange one, he is. One of them Brit soldiers come over here."

"That's what I hear."

"We'd like to ride with you," Nelson said, patting his rifle.

"*Si*, we ride, *Señor* Ranger," Carlos Mide affirmed.

Carlow studied the two men. "Thanks, Nelson, Carlos, but you need to stay here. With your mother, Nelson. She needs you more than we do right now." He paused and his tired shoulders rose and fell. "Besides, we don't know if he might circle back."

"*Si*."

"All right, I guess."

"I know it's hard, Nelson," Carlow said. "Your father was a great Ranger. Taught me a lot. We won't stop until we find the bastard who killed him."

Nelson's face was pinched to hold back emotion. "So you think this is a gang that was led by those Ranger brothers."

"Looks that way."

Nelson frowned. "You don't sound convinced."

After looking away for a moment, Carlow returned his gaze to the young Mirabile's. "I don't think the

Roses had a gang. Others do. But I can't give you a better answer than that."

"Wish you'd been here earlier."

"So do I."

Chapter Seventeen

The two Rangers left the Mirabile ranch hurriedly. Kileen couldn't resist pointing out that a gray horse was bad luck for everyone who saw it—and the killer would be no exception. Both Rangers were impressed with the widow's attention to detail under such duress. Kileen decided her keen eye was a fitting reaction from the wife of a former Ranger. He also managed to indicate that she was a fine-looking woman.

Carlow ignored the remark; something more important was chewing on him mind.

"Thunder, I don't think Tanneman and Hillis had a gang, other than Portland and Barnabas," Carlow blurted. "I think Tanneman somehow faked his death and escaped. I think it's him we're chasing."

Kileen looked like he had been hit in the face. "Meanin' ye be that Tanneman hisself has come back? He lived once before, ye know. A shaman he were. In Persia. Long ago. Aye."

Biting his lower lip, Carlow said, "No, he hasn't come back from the dead. I don't think he ever died. I think he escaped. We need to have that whole 'death while escaping' thing checked out better. Tell Captain about it when we wire him."

Kileen rubbed his unshaven chin. "Ye want me to be

tellin' the fine captain that Tanneman Rose be not dead?"

"Yes. Let's hear the details of that escape. The whole thing." Carlow motioned with his left hand. "Tanneman's shrewd enough to set it up, Thunder. He loved the theater. That's about wearing costumes and changing the way you look. Think about it. It's the only thing that makes real sense."

Kileen's face indicated that he didn't believe his nephew was right. Silence was his only recourse. The idea was far-fetched. How could he tell McNelly what his nephew thought? Kileen worried the captain would away take Carlow's badge. They rode on without speaking.

Finally, the older Irishman looked away and said, "Time, me son, let's not be tellin' the fine captain of your . . . idea. Not yet. Let's find where this killer has gone, then we'll know better. Aye?"

Carlow brushed the neck of his black horse and glanced at his uncle. "Sure."

An hour past noon, Strickland was an angry town. Texas Rangers Time Carlow and Aaron Kileen eased their tired horses into a walk as they entered the agitated settlement, too drained themselves to be surprised by the gathering crowd around the bank a block away.

"Looks like some folks are riled up at the bank. They're either giving away money or there's been a robbery. Want to bet which?" Carlow's light blue eyes studied the crowd ahead with only passing interest. His gaze could be gentle or intense, friendly or cold, could search a man's soul for truth or track an outlaw through Hell.

"Aye. Be a holdup. No bettin' from your handsome uncle o' this fine day. Just happened it be, I be judgin'.'"

"Wonder why they aren't going after the robbers?" Carlow frowned, trying to make sense of the angry gathering. "You think this Marshal Bridgeport's already on their trail?"

"Well, knowin' Lark Bridgeport, he probably be not yet awake." Kileen rolled his shoulders to ease the fatigue. His sweaty shirt and long coat strained to stay with his heavily muscled frame.

"Doesn't sound like much of a lawman, Thunder."

"Don't ye be judgin' Lark so quickly, me son." Kileen studied the crowd, spotted a wagon team of dirty white horses at the far end of the yelling men, and pointed. "Ah, but look there. 'Tis more bad luck it be. Ye must spit three times an' be lookin' for a dog."

Carlow frowned. "There's a dog right behind us, Thunder. More or less."

He loved his uncle. Sometimes though, Kileen's superstitious ways were a bit much to handle. Half the time he thought his uncle just made them up to fit what he wanted to have happen.

"Aye, so it be. Chancey, we're glad you're here, boy. Ye be savin' us from a bad spell," Kileen declared and stared back at Chance following a few strides behind. With great ceremony, Kileen spat three separate times toward the ground.

The great beast's tail hung down from weariness, his tongue slung low between white teeth. A few people on the planked sidewalk, heading for the bank, stopped to stare, wondering if a large prairie wolf were stalking the two men. One young woman gasped and asked her male companion what they should do. The nattily dressed man told her it was none of their business and urged their brisk continuance.

In the distance, a train headed Strickland's way. The town itself was booming with flour mills, a planning mill, three newspapers, a carriage factory, an ice plant, two foundries, doctors, lawyers and even a fire department and a flourishing theater. It was truly a focal point of commerce that had been gaining steam since the war.

The two Rangers really didn't want to get involved in any Strickland matters, regardless of how important the town was becoming. In fact, they preferred to avoid the matters of any town. Anywhere.

"Can't be more than two or three grays around here," Carlow said. "No matter how big Strickland's gotten. 'Course he's probably already left town. Or, more than likely, never stopped. But somebody might have seen him."

"A back-shooter on a gray hoss be a dark trail, I fear, laddie." Kileen slapped trail dust from his long coat, more amazed than annoyed at the puffs that came from it. "Maybe the wee people will scare him into letting see his blackguard face."

Carlow glanced at his uncle and resisted asking if a gray horse was unluckier than a white one. "Looks easy enough, Uncle. We find a gray carrying a slinged rifle—and we have him."

"Beware o' the gray, laddie. Beware o' the gray."

Not interested in pursuing this discussion further, Carlow shifted his weight and nudged his black horse toward the group near the bank. He really wanted a few minutes of relief from the saddle while he sought information from the Strickland marshal. They didn't expect any help from Marshal Lark Bridgeport, but they had to start somewhere. A gray horse shouldn't be too hard to track down. Surely somebody had seen a stranger come and go on a gray horse. Nor did they expect to find the man in town. Not after three days.

"Well, guess we'd better ride over and see what's happening. Maybe we'll get real lucky—and it'll be the same man," Carlow said, not believing his own observation.

A hot meal and a little rest before continuing their search for the murderer would have been welcome, yet the young Ranger knew they wouldn't leave the town without helping to find the bank robbers. Long black hair cascaded over his shoulders. His mustache was surrounded by an unshaven chin that only made him look more aggressive than he did naturally.

"Lucky, is it now? Never thought meself be hearin' such from his sweet nephew." Streaks of trail dust had settled on Kileen's puffy face hours ago. Fresh dust from slapping his pants had recently joined the collection.

A man driving a loaded farm wagon came toward them, slowed and shouted the news that the bank had just been robbed and no one had seen the crime except those in the bank. The robber had escaped undetected. Marshal Bridgeport was on his way to form a posse.

"What did he look like? Did anyone get a look at his horse?" Carlow asked.

Pursing his lips and reining in his wagon horse, the farmer shook his head. "No, suh. Don't think I heard. Sorry."

Both Rangers touched their hat brims in response as the farmer went on.

Coming close behind was a creaking freight wagon. Chance growled at the passing rumble and Carlow told the wolf-dog to be quiet. The younger Ranger wondered why the town's lawman was so slow. Kileen was again philosophical, pointing out that the robber might have been smart enough to wait until the marshal had been occupied elsewhere.

"We shan't be leavin' the fine folks of Strickland in need."

"So these folks just want to gripe, but nobody's trying to find out which way the robber went." Carlow shook his head. "That's really going to help."

"Aye, 'tis a worthy observation, laddie. Why don't ye be sharin' that wee bit of wisdom with them?"

"I intend to," Carlow said. "Maybe, at least, somebody from inside the bank knows something."

"Aye."

Two miles back, the killer's tracks had blended with others headed for Strickland. He was definitely in town or had been. Of that, the Rangers were certain. First, they planned on checking the rifles carried on any gray horses hitched to the racks and at the livery. There wouldn't be many grays and even fewer would be carrying a rifle with a sling. If such a combination was found, it was a cinch they had their man. A black coat would be gravy. Same with the man's gray hair.

Carlow couldn't imagine why the killer would remain in Strickland, but Kileen advised him that he might not think anyone was tracking him. Carlow kept the thought that the killer was Tanneman Rose to himself. It had to be, although the description certainly didn't sound like him. Maybe he had gray hair now. Did Tanneman know any German? Why had the killer yelled out something in German?

This masked killer on a gray horse was the best—and warmest—lead they had, regardless of who it turned out to be.

Outside the Strickland Hotel, a small, wiry man watched them from the porch with unusual interest. He glanced down at a pad of paper in his hand, scribbled furiously, then looked again at the two well-armed men, this time concentrating on the bigger Ranger. A strange smile entered the writer's face.

Neither Ranger noticed the reporter as they concentrated on a sign in the general-store window. A familiar, hateful sign: No Irish. No Coloreds. No Mex. No matter how often he saw that message, it always brought a hiss from Carlow's clenched teeth. That was followed by a knowing chuckle from his uncle, as usual.

"I don't get it, Thunder. Guess I never will," Carlow snarled. "How can you hate all people like that—when you don't even know them?"

"Aye, 'tis a puzzle of life, me lad," Kileen said. "Folks be likin' to hate, I guess. Easier for some. If they be any Injuns about, ye can figure the sign would be includin' them, too."

A squatty businessman at the outer edge of the crowd glanced back at the two advancing Rangers, then whispered something to the taller man beside him. In a hot minute, the crowd swarmed toward the two riders. Some brandished guns, while others yelled threats and encouragement to their comrades.

"Should we put on our badges?" Carlow asked, shoving his hand into his vest pocket.

"Aye. 'Tis bank robbers they think we be. Strangers, 'tis enough we be."

The men never wore badges on the trail; badges only served as giveaway reflections there.

"Hold it right there. You two are under arrest," announced the squatty, pumpkin-faced businessman, trying to make his voice more forceful than normal. The result was a raspy honk.

He looked around for support and got it from some of his fellow townsmen. The closest waved a Civil War Navy Colt.

"You think you can rob our bank and just ride through with nobody noticing?" he continued, "Uh-uh, boys, this is Strickland. We know how to handle crooks. Won't the marshal be surprised when he sees what we've done!"

"Leave your gun be," Kileen whispered to his nephew.

"What is this?" Carlow snapped back, his hand still in his vest pocket.

"Just a wee bit o' nonsense."

Everything in Carlow's tanned face wanted to attack. Chance growled his support from near the back legs of the young Ranger's horse.

Carlow's earliest memories included Kileen teaching him the value of patience, particularly in a fight. It always seemed to work best when Kileen told him that Carlow's late father, a man the young Ranger had never known, had had such qualities.

"Easy, me son, easy," Kileen muttered, without taking his eyes off of the accusatory businessman. "Tell Chancey to stand easy hisself."

Chapter Eighteen

"That's enough, Chance," Carlow commanded the growling wolf-dog behind him. He eased his right hand away from his vest and laid it on the saddle horn; his left, holding his reins, followed.

Kileen straightened his wide back, making his six-foot-two, 220-pound frame look even bigger, and cocked his head to the side. Nothing in his manner was threatening; both hands rested on his saddle horn. "Me lads, 'twould appear ye be having' a wee bit o' trouble."

"Wouldn't you know it, a Mick. A goddamn Mick." The crowd buzzed with supportive remarks as it drew closer to the two Rangers. "Watch out. That young one looks like a Comanche."

Carlow couldn't hold back a laugh. It hurt the bruised side of his face. The swelling had gone down, however, leaving only streaks of purple and yellow around his left eye and on his cheek. He'd heard that observation about his heritage before, but he was all Irish. Black Irish. The only things that weren't Irish about him were his lack of superstition and the absence of a brogue, which had been his late mother's doing.

Stepping alongside Kileen's horse, the businessman grabbed the reins with his free hand; his eyebrows saluted the bold move. For the first time, he noticed the wolf-dog trailing Carlow. Chance's snarling white teeth made the man look away and whisper a silent prayer.

"Sorry to disappoint you, mister, but I'm Irish, too," Carlow said. "And we're Rangers."

"Rangers? That'll be the day," the squatty business-man said to the man next to him. "Border ruffians is more like . . ."

Thud!

Kileen's boot exploded into the posturing man's chin and drove him back into the stunned mass. The businessman's thick fingers released the reins with a jerk. No one thought to catch his limp figure and he collapsed in the dirt.

A blur of color, Chance unleashed his own attack on the next-closest man, slamming into the surprised townsman's chest and sending him sprawling. The man's Civil War Navy Colt popped from his hand and stood momentarily at attention in the air, before thumping to the ground a few feet away. The wolf-dog pounced on his chest and stood on him. The dog's dark unblinking eyes searched the terrified man's face for any sign of further aggression.

The man swallowed his own vomit.

In the same instant, Carlow drew his hand carbine and levered it one-handed, with the shortened stock against his thigh. The movement was smooth and quick. Gasps followed. At the back of the group, a farmer in overalls turned and ran.

"The rest of you idiots drop your guns. Do it now," the young Ranger demanded.

Carlow's gun sought the head of the man he judged most likely to shoot. Most didn't wait for the Ranger's heated gaze and immediately released their weapons.

"You with the big hat, either use that pistol or get rid of it. I'm too tired to mess with a bunch of fools." Carlow acknowledged the group with a slow movement of his gun barrel. "Let him go, Chance."

A quick bark preceded the wolf-dog's retreat. He bounced from the downed man's stomach to his previous position beside Carlow's horse. As the beast spun back into place, he snarled his defiance.

Glancing down at the pistol in his hand, the man in the tall-crowned hat dropped the gun as if it were heat coming from the stove.

The bearded storekeeper standing beside him, holding a rifle, hesitated.

"Ye be droppin' the Springfield now." Kileen directed his own just-drawn, long-barreled Colt at the storekeeper. "'Tis too fine a day to be dyin' for nothin'. Ye be uncockin' it first, lad."

Shaking visibly, the bearded man eased down the hammer on the single-shot rifle, bent over and carefully laid the gun on the ground, inches from his feet.

"That be a good lad."

Behind him, a man gagged, turned away and retched on his own boots. The men closest to him stepped away in disgust. With Kileen's approval, both Rangers pinned on their badges.

"What the bloody 'ell is going on here?" A clipped voice with the telltale sound of a British upbringing brought an immediate split in the group to reveal a stumpy man in a rumpled suit, fresh-collared shirt and food-spotted cravat. He was eating gumdrops from a small sack.

Marshal Lark Bridgeport's white and brown hair was mostly covered by a hat that had once been a proud derby, but was now little more than a gathering of black. Strings of hair poked out from under it like straw from a scarecrow's head. The bulge in his patched tweed coat, on the left side of his chest, had to be a shoulder-holstered gun.

"Well, well, 'tis a sight for me ol' eyes. Marshal Bridgeport hisself," Kileen bellowed. "What are ye feedin' the fine folks of Strickland, Lark? They be a bit riled up 'bout strangers."

The British lawman shook his head and motioned toward the bank, smiling without meaning to do so. "Jolly what! I say, if it isn't the great Ranger Kileen 'imself. 'Ow fascinatin' you should show up at this grand moment of our need. Our fine bank 'as been bloody robbed. A sticky wicket, it be."

One tall man found his courage. "Yeah, where were you when all our money was being taken, Marshal?"

Bridgeport ignored the question, walked up to Kileen and held out his hand. In his other fist was the sack of candy. Kileen grabbed his hand enthusiastically and introduced the British leader to Carlow. Bridgeport made a foppish bow and Carlow nodded.

"Would appear you have had a run-in with something, son," Bridgeport said, his eyes sparkling.

"Aye, Lark. Ranger Carlow, he be attacked by three thugs. He whipped them all." Kileen liked making the statement.

"Blimey! That is exceptional."

The young Ranger remembered his uncle saying Bridgeport had fought with the British Royal Marine Light Infantry in India. It was difficult to match this graying, out-of-shape figure with the image of that fierce fighting unit.

As if reciting what he had had for breakfast, the Strickland lawman explained what he knew about the bank robbery. A lone gunman had accosted the bank president, Gerald Douglas, at his home, and had come with the president into the bank through the back door. Patting his cheek with his fingers, Bridgeport noted that the bank president was not an early riser and the bank itself had been open for several hours. The gunman took the money from the opened vault; stuffed certificates, coins and some small sacks of gold dust into his saddlebags; and made his getaway. Again, he had gone out the back, taking the president with him, and then leaving President Douglas at the rear.

The shaken bank executive hadn't recognized the bank robber, who had covered his face with a full mask made of wood. However, he had long, gray hair, wore a wide-brimmed black hat and rode a gray horse.

Kileen mumbled that a gray horse was, indeed, bad luck.

Bridgeport pondered the idea for moment before continuing. According to the bank president, the robber had carried a rifle with a scope and sling. Bridgeport said it sounded like a Pedersoli rifle to him. He knew the gun, owning one himself.

"Your fine bank president, did he be sayin' this blackguard be wearin' a black coat?" Kileen asked, leaning over to make his point. "Or be smokin' a pipe?"

" 'Is clobber included a black coat. A long one, at 'is knees. No pipe. At least, no one mentioned it, by golly. 'Course 'e had a mask on. That would make it difficult to smoke such," Bridgeport chirped. "Said the fellow was a little taller than he was, Mr. Douglas did, yes he said that. Mr. Douglas, our bank's head executive, is only a bit taller than me." He indicated the relative height difference with his hand.

"Oh yeah, almost forgot, 'e had a German manner of speaking." The marshal waved his arms vigorously and the movement caused him to remember the sack in his left hand.

"Blimey, I forgot my manners an' all. Would you be carin' for a gumdrop? Fresh they be." He took one from the sack, popped it into his mouth and held out the sack.

"No thanks," Carlow said, shaking his head.

"Thank ye, Lark, but I be fine," Kileen responded and asked, "Aye, be there not a wee hole in the mask for his mouth?"

"Hmmm. Didn't ask. Probably. I don't know," Bridgeport responded. "We can ask Mr. Douglas." He took another gumdrop from his sack.

Carlow watched the crowd fade away except for the bearded man, who leaned over twice, trying to regain the nerve to retrieve his rifle. "Just leave it there, mister. You can come back for it later. After we're gone."

"Y-yessir. Sure . . . I will." The man backed away from his gun, his arm still extended toward it, then spun around and half ran down the street.

"What's a clobber?" Carlow eased down the hammer on his gun and holstered it. He was satisfied the crowd had thoroughly dispersed, except for three men standing outside the bank. Carlow guessed one of them must be Gerald Douglas, the bank president. They might learn more from him than from continuing discussions with the marshal.

Bridgeport glanced in the direction of the retreating man as he continued, "Clobber. Ah, uniform. Clothing, if you please, Ranger Carlow." He smiled at his own use of British military slang. "'Aving spent my life with the RMLI, mostly in India, I 'ave a tendency to talk like a swaddy."

Cocking his head, Carlow waited.

"Ah, yes, the Royal Marine Light Infantry . . . and a swaddy is a soldier."

The marshal continued, "Mr. Douglas even asked if

I still 'ad my fine gun, thinking it looked just like the robber's. Assured 'im I did, that my rifle was resting in my closet at 'ome." Bridgeport paused and giggled. "Of course, I made a bloody beeline to the residence shortly thereafter to make certain of the gun's continued presence. And, ta-da—there it be in all its glory." He struggled to keep from smiling. "Oh, and there may have been a second fellow, watching from outside the bank. The witnesses aren't clear on the matter."

"Your bank robber be soundin' like the man who murdered a fine rancher a few days ago. A former Ranger," Kileen responded. "The killer be usin' such a gun—and riding a gray horse, he be. We be trackin' the blaggard."

"Blimey, a busy boy, it would seem." Bridgeport giggled and felt sorry for it. "Would that be the rancher Mirabile?"

"Aye. What do you be knowin' o' the sad thing?"

Frowning, Bridgeport explained that a cowhand from a neighboring ranch had brought the news yesterday.

"Are you going to gather a posse? I don't suppose you know which direction he went?" Carlow was annoyed by Bridgeport's self-amusement. The marshal pointed toward the other end of town, watching a young man in his late teens walk toward them, trying to build his confidence as he advanced.

Kileen frowned, but said nothing.

Bridgeport smiled again. "Yes, a group of armed citizenry rode out immediately, led by one of my fine deputies. Before I arrived. Gallantly all, bellowing their vindictiveness. You colonials are a bit impetuous, you know. Actually, that may be the most cruel of bloody jokes played upon our avenging angels." He reached into his sack and gathered a handful of candy and slipped the pieces one at a time into his mouth as he talked.

"What do you mean?" Carlow's eyes flashed annoyance.

"Shortly after they left, all claiming loudly of immediate success and bloody retribution . . ." Bridgeport stopped, pushed another gumdrop into his mouth and chuckled, before going on. "A young lad came to me and told of a lone rider in a black coat—on a gray horse—clearing the hills to the east, where the boy 'ad been watching some sheep." He giggled loudly. "Isn't that a bit much?"

"Could've been just another gray horse," Carlow observed.

"Ah yes, it could 'ave been. But the boy said the fellow was 'olding a rifle with a sling. Long hair under his hat. Gray. 'E couldn't see his face. The bloody mask again."

"How come this blackguard let the lad go?" Kileen asked.

"Blimey lucky 'e was. Said the rider didn't see 'im. The boy was kneeling down, checking one of 'is lambs."

Carlow looked in that direction. "That would mean he's headed for the hill country. Good places to hide up there."

"Before there, as well," Bridgeport corrected. "There's a 'eavy stand of fine trees a few 'ours ride from 'ere. I've enjoyed the scenery more than once." He giggled and selected another piece of candy from his sack. "A small cabin can be found there, as well, if one knows where to look. A worthy place to doggo for the night." His stare sought Kileen's for approval.

"So what about your posse?" Carlow frowned. He didn't ask what "doggo" meant, assuming it was English military slang for "hide" or "sleep."

"Oh, I sent an enthusiastic galloper out after them. As soon as I knew." Bridgeport raised his chin to support his claim of action. "It was the least I could do."

"Close to it, anyway," Carlow growled.

Bridgeport folded his arms in front of his chest. "Ranger Carlow, I think I did well under the circumstances. Warned the bank's owners of the laxity of their chief executive several times, I 'ave. It should not 'ave been a surprise that the bank was violated in this way." He cocked his head to the side. "Myself, I keep no money there." He turned toward Kileen. "Come to my favorite establishment for some good food and drink before you 'ead on—you and your angry associate. Steer's 'Ead rivals the finest English taverns—and the wenches are much nicer." He giggled again. "An' the Gem Theater, ah, a Shakespearean troupe is in town. *Othello*, they're doing. 'Ear it's really good."

"Be thankin' ye for the kind offer, Lark, but we best be gettin' after him," Kileen answered. "Dark be his friend, not ours. A three-day lead he once be havin'. 'Tis shorter now, 'twould seem."

The British lawman asked why the Rangers had gone to Mirabile's ranch and Kileen explained the situation, leaving out Carlow's suspicion that the man behind the killings was Tanneman Rose. Carlow listened, but made no attempt to add to the description.

"Bloody tough business, yours." Bridgeport shook his head. "Will you be minding if I bring along some support to 'elp in this endeavor?"

"You mean a posse?" Carlow was still watching the young man coming toward them, now more purposefully. As far as Carlow could tell, he wasn't armed.

"Blimey, what else?"

"They'll get in the way."

Kileen glanced at his nephew and frowned. "Easy, me lad. Mind your manners. The good constable can be comin' with us if he's a mind to. 'Twould be much to our likin'."

The young man from town stepped up to them and announced with as much bravado as he could muster that he wanted to go with the posse. His voice gave away his age by cracking in midsentence.

Bridgeport put his arm around the man and cocked his head upward toward the Rangers. "Ah, the Imperial Yeomanry is gathering already." He turned back to Kileen. "By the way, there's a man—and 'is lady—who live in that cabin I mentioned. They're real loners. Never come to town. Farmers, sort of. Got some 'ogs. Milk cows, too. 'E's been suspected of bringing someone else's cow home for eating from time to time. Not proven, mind you. From Germany. Long gray hair. Thick glasses. Speaks with a German accent. Waulken is the name. Alben Waulken."

He looked like a man sharing a private joke, smiling slightly.

"Does he own a rifle with a scope? A gray horse?" Kileen asked intently, ignoring the obvious reaction.

"That I not be knowing." Bridgeport shrugged and examined his sack to see if any candy remained. "Never seen 'im with either. Never seen either 'e or 'is lady in town, for that matter." He cocked his head. "But I haven't exactly been spending afternoon tea there. It's out of my jurisdiction."

"Not ours," Carlow snapped, annoyed at Bridgeport's manner.

Bridgeport nodded agreement and pointed at Carlow's wolf-dog. "Be this scary fellow with you?"

The young Ranger cocked his head to the side. "Yes. You have a problem with that?"

Shaking his head, Bridgeport chuckled. "Naw, I do not. 'E bloody well fits you, it seems to this bloke."

Chapter Nineteen

Letting the gray thoroughbred have its head, Tanneman Rose passed four quiet farms and mostly open plains. He knew this country well, having spent most of a week combing the area, disguised as usual as a traveling peddler with a thick Missouri twang. Selling goods from his rickety wagon was an ideal way to move about a region without raising suspicion. No one cared where this odd man came from or where he was going. It had also produced the perfect foil—Alben Waulken.

With his field glasses, Tanneman had observed Mirabile for two days. This yielded a pattern of behavior Tanneman had used to catch the rancher alone. Disguised as the reclusive farmer, he had executed his plan and then headed for Strickland. The bank robbery had gone well; the bank president was a predictable buffoon.

Tanneman had planned the crime as a reinforcement of his disguise as the long-haired German in a black coat, riding a gray horse, carrying a Pedersoli rifle. He had expected a posse to follow his easy-to-read trail, which would lead directly to Alben Waulken's isolated cabin. The news of Julian Mirabile's death would catch up with the local law soon enough. Maybe it already had. However, it was necessary to pin both crimes on the unwitting man living at the edge of the timberline.

Tanneman would leave the rifle on the man's property, along with the black coat and the wooden mask. The long gray wig and pipe he would keep for another time. Actually, the only thing he didn't like about his current strategy was leaving the gray horse behind. He had actually purchased it from a rancher outside of San Antonio in need of immediate cash.

Laughing as he rode, Tanneman Rose revisited his discovery of Alben Waulken. It had happened almost by accident. Except he didn't believe in accidents, only fate. He had been looking for the right person to set up and, behold, there he was. Alben Waulken lived alone with his wife at the edge of a wooded area, scratching out a few crops, raising hogs and milking a couple of cows. Through careful questioning as he peddled his wares, Tanneman learned Waulken was suspected of stealing an occasional steer for eating. Better yet, the couple never went to Strickland, so nobody there knew them well. Long gray hair and a pipe were simple props he already had that would be hidden along with many others inside his peddler wagon.

Waulken's thick German accent was memorable and easy to imitate. Tanneman liked having someone blamed for his assassinations when possible; it gave the law a sense of accomplishment—and kept them from probing further.

"Perfect, *Herr* Waulken, *du* vill never know vhat *ist* happening to *du*," Tanneman muttered and chuckled at his imitation. He touched the jaguar necklace beneath his shirt. A suitable replacement for the original was secured in a small town he passed through. A Mexican trader had three, just like his first necklace; he had bought all three.

Tanneman's peddler's wagon was well hidden in the forest not far from Waulken's small cabin. Once there, he would reapply his well-developed disguise as a downtrodden peddler and head back to San Antonio. Planning for the execution of the next man on his list would begin. Probably Marshal Timble—or the jury foreman. Unless Carlow and Kileen showed up unexpectedly. He smiled. Just like in his dreams.

"Mirabile, you bastard, I waited a long damn time to put a bullet in your head," Tanneman muttered. "Sitting there in the courtroom. Smiling at me. You bastard."

Town was well behind him and forgotten. He had ridden in sight until he saw the young shepherd. That sighting would bring the posse in the right direction—and his trail could be followed by anyone. Anyone.

"Good. Good," he said, passing a fifth farm, where a man was still working in his field.

Tanneman rode slowly past the south edge of the man's pasture. The farmer's description would aid the posse. Of course, he wouldn't identify the rider as Waulken. He would only state that a black-coated rider—in a full mask—had ridden by on a gray horse. Tanneman grinned and kicked the animal into a smooth lope to move out of range of any further identification.

At the last instant, he avoided the temptation to holler out *Guten Tag!* The farmer might know Waulken well enough to recognize it wasn't his voice.

Suddenly his anger at his former comrades for trying to send him to prison burst through. "Rotten hog meat. Filthy mattresses. Working every stinking day. Being whipped. You bastards wanted me to live like that. Now you'll pay." The tirade slipped into a chant only he knew.

Lately, his dreams had been filled with images of Pakistan and a dark hut that had often appeared in his reveries. He assumed the hut had been his home in his previous life. In the dreams, he often changed from a spider to an owl and back again.

An hour of riding took him across the darkening land. He eased past a string of trees lining a fat creek, through a spongy swale of slick wet grass and slipped over a broken hill. A man-high rock passage was the prelude to an open spoon of level earth with a small cabin settled within it. Shadows were twisted and angry around him as he reined up beside a scraggly oak tree thirty yards from the house.

Tanneman dismounted, removed the mask and studied the cabin. He had to be careful not to scratch his nose as he removed the mask. He had already done that with one of them.

A feeble light at the only front window was enough to assure him that the couple were inside. Snickering, he muttered that their lives were about to change. Forever.

With a deep breath for reassurance, he removed a canvas sack filled with oats from his saddle horn. Quietly, he led the gray horse toward what passed for a barn, slipping past a pen of comfortable hogs and a buckboard wagon. The door was ajar and he pushed it open slowly to avoid any squeak. The mount went easily into an empty stall next to two worn cubicles, each containing a disinterested milk cow. Next to them was an old brown horse. It was used to pull the wagon, he guessed.

Looking around, he found a bucket and emptied the sack into it, to assure the horse's silence. He had carried the sack just for this purpose. He wouldn't take the time to unsaddle the animal, only removing the saddlebags carrying the bank money and laying them outside the stall. He laid the black coat over the stall door, propped the Pedersoli rifle against the post and flipped the hat, then the mask, on top.

He decided it might fall off and bring the Waulkens, so he laid the wooden disguise on the ground. It had felt good to take the mask off; the closeness to his face always brought unwanted sweat. Besides, his vision was limited through the eyeholes. Actually, he preferred disguising himself and not using the mask, but when he wanted to lay blame on some poor fool, like now, it was important to use the mask and leave it.

He lifted the heavy saddlebags over his shoulder. Why give away such treasure? He would add it to the pile of bank money hidden in the wagon. A cave near the ranch had been a perfect place to keep it. Not even Barnabas, with his childlike mind, had guessed where it was.

There was plenty of evidence already. Satisfied with the picture he had created, he cleared the barn. With gleeful eyes, he glanced down at the pistol rig strapped to his waist. The stiff holster was handsomely accented with woven layers of tan cowhide and soft doeskin throughout the base of dark-brown hard leather. He had bought it from a penniless Mexican and had never seen another like it.

He drew the Colt with the cutaway trigger guard for swifter firing, and checked the loads. He had modified the gun since taking it from the luckless traveler the night he escaped. His fingers caressed the barrel with its filed-off sight and reholstered the weapon. The presence of the gun, any gun, was always comforting.

Even in the dark, the forest was an old friend as he entered. An owl saluted as he entered and he smiled at the welcome. He raised his hand in tribute and whispered, "Good to see you again, Hillis. We missed you. Portland is here with me. Haven't seen Barnabas. He may not return so fast, you know. It doesn't always happen that way."

Had he been an owl once?

To his right were the remains of an old campfire. Lighting the pipe resting in his pocket would taste good, but he decided against it. Even a tiny spark could be seen by a knowing man from a long way off. Something rustled to his left, then disappeared. Presumably a squirrel. He worked his way along a path most men would not have seen in the daylight, but the opening had been wide enough to drive his wagon to the hiding place. Most men riding by the forest would not believe a wagon could ever move through the trees.

Minutes later, Tanneman rose out of a dry creek bed inside the stretch of clustered trees. Smothered within this fortress of trees and overgrown brush was a shallow arroyo connected to the creek bed. He was no more than a half mile from the Waulken cabin, although it could just as easily have been ten miles, as well concealed as it was.

Within this land crease were his wagon and its two unharnessed horses. The two animals—an older bay and a chestnut with two stockings—raised their heads at his advance, then resumed their grazing. Both were hobbled and tied to the wagon on long lead ropes. After laying the saddlebags on the wagon seat, Tanneman buckled the harness into place, keeping the hobbles on for the moment.

Working from the back of the wagon, he sought a small mirror and a bottle of glue to help hold his fake beard he used to disguise himself as the peddler. Deftly, he began to apply the lotion onto his flat cheeks and down onto his thick chin.

" 'When devils will the blackest sins put on, They do suggest at first with heavenly shows.' " He muttered the Shakespeare passage again. His shrill laugh turned the bay's head toward him, its ears cocked for understanding.

The only thing bad about this glue was that it was difficult to scrub off, but that was better than having his beard sag or fall off. Finally satisfied with the transformation, he applied fake eyebrows over his own. The arching brows were full and thick, giving an instant scowl to his gray-blue eyes and long eyelashes. Then he inserted tiny rolls of cloth between his lower jaw and cheeks on the inside of his mouth. The cloth was definitely better than the paper he had originally used. The effect made his face more full, but wasn't uncomfortable.

From a trunk came stomach padding with long strings he used to attach it around his waist and over the back of his neck. Then he added the worn suitcoat of gray woolen heritage, stringed tie and the battered derby, completing his peddler's appearance.

He decided it was prudent to hide his supposedly removed arm, even though no one was around. It was good discipline. He moved the Colt to his waistband where it could be easily reached. His normally light brown hair was already dyed black to match the beard. There no need to change his pants or boots; both were his regular attire.

"Y'all need some pots today? Got some fine pots an' pans." He practiced his affected delivery and felt the jaguar teeth neckace under his clothes for reassurance.

The Missouri drawl, delivered in a high-pitched voice, was effective, as was the slump-shouldered manner in which he carried his body. So was the limp he had perfected using an old cane. Most people with whom he came into contact when disguised as the peddler referred to him simply as "the peddler." In this disguise, he had no name and never offered one. He chuckled. No one had ever asked.

When this revenge was all over, he would retire to New Orleans, perhaps, and underwrite, direct and play the lead in a production of *The Merchant of Venice*, his father's favorite play. It would be a grand tribute to the man. Tanneman decided he would attribute the performance to his father's memory, citing him as a visionary in theater, in the printed program.

Satisfied with the day's actions, Tanneman removed the hobbles from his wagon horses and returned to the wagon seat. He checked the jar with the spider and was pleased to see it was moving around. Two dead flies he had placed in the jar before leaving were gone.

"You won't believe who I just saw, Portland. Yeah, it's Hillis. He's an owl, you know. Came to watch."

Making certain the jar was secured among the wagon's possessions, Tanneman repeated his ritual chant and jigged the horses into a trot. He rode for an hour through the forest. His horses needed no encouragement. They were well rested. The load of man, wagon and goods seemed to disappear into the pounding hooves.

Several loose books continued to slide around. The hidden sack of money bounced and moved sideways. It angered Tanneman that he had not been able to secure either the books or the money sack. The creaky buckboard bounced and leaned as they traveled into the night. Folded clothes, linens, coils of rope, bridles and a saddle, pots and pans, boxes of tobacco, the trunk holding all of the stolen bank money, horseshoes and bullets, and a few guns slid around and behind him as he reined the wagon to a stop.

"Why not?" he said aloud, grabbing the spider jar so it wouldn't be turned over.

Both horses sought the location of the words, then stood quietly, waiting for more instructions.

Most times he hadn't been in a position to watch the payoff of his meticulous efforts, to see the set-up man arrested and taken away while protesting his innocence. This time he could. Easily. He could easily watch, unnoticed, from the edge of the woods and see what happened at the cabin when the posse arrived. Even if he was seen—and he wouldn't be—he would simply pretend he was still working his trade.

It was too joyful to pass up. He would leave for San Antonio after that. Reining the horses, he turned back toward the cabin.

Chapter Twenty

After an hour of hard running, Carlow and Kileen eased their horses into a land-eating lope that led them past sunset and into the night. To save the weary wolf-dog's legs, Carlow had carried him across the saddle. Chance seemed to enjoy the transportation and licked Carlow's hand.

The trail of the man who had robbed the Strickland Bank was too warm to stop. Even in the growing darkness, hoofprints told a story fairly easy to follow. They were headed directly for the forest Bridgeport had mentioned. The British lawman and his posse were coming behind them, or so he had promised. Neither Ranger was interested in waiting. Carlow figured a bunch of trigger-happy volunteers behind them could be more trouble than the outlaw or outlaws ahead of them. Bridgeport had assured the Rangers that he would only bring men who had fighting experience, except for the teenager who had volunteered. The British lawman didn't have the heart to turn him down.

In an unnecessary statement, Bridgeport had said the Rangers didn't need to wait for them to catch up; the posse was more for the town to feel good about itself. He had full confidence in the Rangers apprehending the robbers and returning the bank's money.

Carlow realized he was trying to set them up to take the blame if the money wasn't recovered.

Curling in and out of a mile-long string of cotton-woods lining a struggling creek, the two Rangers passed a spongy swale of slick wet grass and slipped over three broken hills. The bank robber's trail was clear, even in the pale moonlight. Rather than a hurried escape, it appeared to be a planned one.

"Aye, 'tis an old man's thinkin' that our lad'll be stopping at that cabin Lark be tellin' about," Kileen volunteered, motioning toward the north.

"Looks like it," Carlow said. "Looks like he's the man who lives there, doesn't it?" He rubbed his hand along the tired wolf-dog's back. "What would a man like Bridgeport be doing out here—to discover such a man and such a place?"

"Doin' his job, me thinks."

"Do you think he really sent a messenger after the posse?" Carlow peered into the hillside ahead, trying to determine if any of the shadows belonged to a man.

"I'd be sayin' so. Ol' Lark, a strange one he may be, but I've never known hisself to lie." Kileen took a flask from his coat pocket and downed a long swallow. "Leastwise, not when it be counted." He made no attempt to offer the small container to Carlow and slipped it back into his pocket.

"So when do you think we can expect the posse to catch up with us?" Carlow asked sarcastically, removing his boots from their stirrups, allowing them to hang free for a few minutes to let his legs relax.

"Me not be knowin'." Kileen wiped his mouth with the back of his huge hand. "Many o' them lads be re-discoverin' the wonders of home an' hearth, I reckon." He motioned toward the dark shapes that were the forest ahead of them. "Hmmm, on me sweet mither's grave, this be a place where the wee people be livin'."

"Do they ride gray horses?"

"Don't ye be foolin' with your sweet ol' uncle, laddie."

Looking around, Carlow said, "Thunder, do you think the Captain was certain about Tanneman's death? I still think he's alive—and behind all this madness. Nothing else makes sense." He rolled his tired shoulders and glanced at Kileen. "I don't know who we're following, but Tanneman's got to be involved. I'm sure of it."

Kileen's drained face twitched. "The captain hisself wouldn't be sayin' so, if it weren't." He looked around. "Of course, Tanneman Rose be a dreamer. Return in another form, he might be." He bit his lower lip. "Ye know, the Navajo, they talk of the skinwalker. A witch who can change into a crow. Or a wolf. Or a man." He shook off the idea as a shiver rattled through his shoulders.

"If he's dead, Thunder, he's dead. I think he's alive—and setting up innocent men to throw everyone off track. There's no Rose gang and you know it."

They rode through the man-high rock passage and saw the small cabin resting on the flattened open land.

"Rein up," Carlow said in a hushed voice.

"What?" Kileen reached for his holstered gun.

"I'm thinking we'd better expect a guard along here somewhere." Carlow stopped his black horse. "Easy, Shadow. Whoa."

Kileen frowned but did the same, watching the younger Ranger slip from the saddle and lift Chance down. Immediately, he began removing his spurs. Dismounting himself, Kileen secured his reins to a branch, keeping the horse's head tight enough that it wouldn't attempt to graze. He did the same with Carlow's black. After a swig from their canteens, they poured water into the crowns of their doffed hats and offered the refreshing liquid to their mounts.

Chance rubbed his nose against Carlow's leg. The young Ranger poured more water into his hat and gave it to the tired wolf-dog. He patted the fierce animal on the head, ordering him to wait with Kileen and told his uncle to stay where he was until he gave the all-clear. Carlow would go on ahead and see if a sentry had been posted. Or maybe he would see the man they sought. For the first time, both men noticed the new full moon in the darkening sky was heading toward its full circle.

"Much to be wary about with the moon, me lad, ye be knowin' that." Kileen motioned with his head. "Don't be pointin' at it. The man there gets angry—at bein' pointed at."

"I can understand that. Don't like being pointed at either," Carlow said with a grin.

" 'Tis a good time to be killin' the pig." Kileen rubbed his unshaven chin. "When the moon is becomin' her full se'f, makes the fryin' bigger." He took a long breath as if preparing himself for a most serious statement. " 'Course, the moon in her full can make a man crazy, ye know. Best not to tempt her."

Facing the yellow orb, Kileen tipped his hat and uttered, "Lady Moon, I hail thee." He repeated the phrase two more times and added, "Me father—and your mother's—would go outside the house and bow nine times to the new moon. Aye, he did so every time."

Carlow looked up, half a grin on his tanned face. Many Irish he knew had tendencies to believe in, or at least talk about, things beyond their control, but Kileen was certain of every one of them. Sometimes, Carlow wondered how his uncle made it through the day with all the interlocking and contradictory superstitions he followed. Silently, he thanked his mother again for making certain such tendencies hadn't made their way into his thoughts.

"Touch your money. In your pocket, son," Kileen continued, still looking into the dark sky. "Turn your smallest coin upside down. 'Twill make sure ye do not run out."

"Stay here until I give a holler." Carlow laid the second spur over his saddle horn. He hesitated, then thrust his hand into his pocket. There would be no rest until he followed his uncle's superstitious counsel.

"That's a good lad. Make a wish now. Keep it a secret and it will be given ye." He added, "A blade, not a bullet." Kileen wanted to caution him about being careful, but knew it would sound like he didn't have confidence in his beloved nephew.

"I want him alive," Carlow announced. "We need to find out if he's Mirabile's shooter. Who knows? We might even find Tanneman here. Wouldn't that be something?"

"Aye. May be more than one, laddie. 'Member Lark speakin' of a possible second robber."

"I remember."

In seconds, Carlow had disappeared into the darkness surrounding them. Even the bright moonlight couldn't find him. Kileen shook his head at the swiftness of his young protégé. "Aye, the strike of the Celtic warrior, he be gifted with," Kileen muttered. He thought about taking another swig of whiskey, then decided not to.

Drinking on duty was not allowed, but Captain McNelly had never paid any attention to Kileen's indiscretions. Probably because Old Thunder could outfight any three or four Rangers put together. Except for Carlow. Ranger Time Carlow might be young, but his reputation for battle savvy had already outstripped all but Kileen and one or two other veteran state lawmen.

An owl saluted the big Irishman as it glided through the night. Kileen watched the wide wings and tried not to think that the Comanche thought the bird was a ghost. Could it be somehow related to Tanneman? He shook his head to drive away the thought.

"Ye be lookin' out for me nephew now." Kileen looked at the moon and growled, then pulled his pistol and tapped the barrel three times against the trunk of a nearby oak.

Both horses' ears twitched toward the sound to assure it was not harm coming. He tried to think about Angel Balta and her warm body, so he wouldn't worry about his nephew. Patience was a trait hard earned by the big man. Hard earned. One he had diligently taught his nephew, or so he told himself.

He looked down at Chance sitting quietly. "Shannon, me be countin' on ye to watch over me nephew."

Chance cocked his head to the side and stretched his head out on his legs.

Nearly soundlessly, Carlow worked his way through the trees, alternating his attention on shadows ahead and on the ground for anything that would make noise if stepped on. His tracking skills were more the result of the guidance given by a Mescalaro Apache years before, than that of Kileen's teaching. Carlow and Kayitah had become friends after the young Ranger whipped three white men who were beating on the Apache in a nameless town along the western edge of Texas.

Later Kayitah had been shot down by the U.S. Cavalry in an attack on a small village, and Carlow had sought his body for proper burial. With Kileen's support—and McNelly's—the army unofficially allowed him onto the site of the pitiful massacre. Carlow's best friend, Shannon Dornan, had joined him. Less than a year later, Dornan had died and Carlow had been badly wounded in the Silver Mallow Gang's ambush.

Breathing through his teeth to avoid the sound giving away his advance, Carlow patiently studied the forest as he darted from tree to tree. He could see well, even though the forest cloak lay heavily on the land. Moonlight knifed its way through most of the branches, providing shards of yellow seeking gray rocks and downed branches. Night sounds filled the dark, a good sign that no one waited. And so far, he couldn't see anyone on guard.

Strings of smoke from the cabin's chimney were caught in the cloudless sky as if weaving the handful of aggressive stars together. The yellow light gracing the inside of the cabin yielded two shadows. Carlow stopped behind a fat tree to determine his next move. To his left were a weathered barn and a hog pen. It would make sense to determine whether or not the gray horse they followed was in the barn.

He crouched beside a fallen log and watched a jackrabbit scurry away. Ahead of him was a thick maze of trees, rocks, dead branches and hardy weeds surrounding the barn. No sign of any outlaw sentry was evident from this angle. Carlow knew it was unlikely there would be, until he had completed at least a half circle. He hoped Kileen would remain where he was and not get anxious, for this would take longer than he had expected. But to do it any other way would be to invite a bullet. Slowly, he worked his way to the barn's doors, past a buckboard and a pen of softly grunting pigs. A favorable embrace of moonlight indicated the doors weren't locked, only shut.

Waiting longer would only increase the likelihood of the shadows in the cabin being suspicious, so Carlow drew the Colt from his sidewinder holster and shifted it to his left hand. He leaned over and, with his right, pulled the war knife from its sheath in his Kiowa legging. If necessary, the silence of the blade would be preferable to a gunshot.

He darted forward, but didn't see a rusty hoe left from tending the field and he kicked it into the barn. Carlow froze in place. Would it arouse whoever was in the cabin?

If the noise had any effect on the cabin's inhabitants, it didn't show. Finally satisfied his mistake hadn't changed anything, Carlow slid inside the barn and let his eyes become accustomed to the even darker situation. His gaze took in a gray horse, then the wooden mask, black coat and Pedersoli rifle. He walked over to the horse, which was still saddled and sweaty. The two cows and a brown horse in the adjoining stables looked like they could use some grazing time, but that wasn't his concern.

Heavy footsteps interrupted his examination. Carlow thought it must be Kileen, but a smart man was always careful. He stepped back into the shadows with his Colt ready in his hands. If this wasn't his uncle, he would first try for a quiet surrender. He fingered the sharp blade in his right fist. Firing would be a last resort.

Chapter Twenty-one

The advancing shape was as huge as the bootsteps indicated and it soon became Thunder Kileen. Moonlight painted his craggy face into an Irish savage. Kileen stepped into the barn, not yet seeing Carlow. The long-barreled Colt looked like a toy in his big fist. His blustery challenge was a general threat to whoever might be in the barn. Chance was at his side.

"Be prayin' on the soul of your sainted mither that ye be knowin' where Ranger Time Carlow be," he snorted, "and that ye have not been so foolish as to attack hisself from the back."

"I'm right here, Uncle. There's no one else here."

Kileen jerked his head toward the gray figure he loved. "Aye, be knowin' ye be there. All along."

"Of course." Carlow surpressed a smile, then showed Kileen what he had found. "The gray horse has just been ridden. Still saddled. A Pedersoli rifle. A long black coat. And a wooden mask. Looks like we've got our man."

Kileen stomped over to the post and grabbed the rifle. "So this be the gun that shot me friend Mirabile." He spat at the gun and dropped it.

"Looks that way," Carlow said and motioned toward the cabin. "There are two inside. I couldn't tell if one of them was Tanneman."

Rubbing his chin, Kileen took a half step back. "Ye be forgettin' Tanneman, me lad. So there be two in the wee cabin? A second robber at the bank be right, then. Are ye sure there are not more? We don't be knowin' how many are in the ol' Rose gang." Kileen turned, walked away and stopped at the barn's entrance. "Would ye be willin' to listen to an idea your uncle be having?"

"I always listen to you, Thunder."

"Aye, an' then be runnin' off to take on the Devil hisse'f."

With that, Kileen suggested that he go ahead alone, acting like he was a drunk who was lost. To reinforce his idea, he took another long pull on his flask. He thought it would be unlikely they would be able to sneak up on the cabin without being seen. After he was inside, Carlow could close in as well.

"What if they don't wait to find out you're drunk an' lost?" Carlow asked, rubbing his hand across the folded black coat. "At least one of those boys knows how to shoot, Thunder."

"Is it me actin' skill ye be questionin' now?"

Carlow shook his head. There was no reason to argue. Kileen's way was the approach they were going to use. It usually was—and it was usually right.

"Just wobble a lot. You know, weave back an' forth." Carlow imitated his suggestion.

"Be lookin' like ye know what it is to be full of the spirits, laddie." Kileen smiled and patted his nephew on the shoulder.

Carlow resisted the idea of saying he had learned by watching his uncle. His head nodded toward their back trail. "What about Marshal Bridgeport and his posse?"

Kileen had obviously forgotten about them. He

dragged his boot in a line between himself and the younger Ranger. "If ye be hearin' them, have 'em wait by our hosses." He pursed his lips and shook his head. "Nay, bring Lark with ye. He be good in such as this."

"Are you sure?"

"Aye, the lark be a bird of good luck."

"Think you just made that up," Carlow said.

Kileen smiled a full jack-o'-lantern grin and walked away.

"Get it done, Thunder. I'll be watching."

The evening's growing coolness felt good as Kileen walked slowly toward the hideout cabin, already weaving from one side to the other. It took longer than it would have otherwise, and almost made him dizzy. He rolled his tongue across his lips. Whoever was inside would likely have seen him by now, so he stood still and weaved back and forth before continuing.

What would he find waiting? He wondered why men wishing to hide would build a fire, but only someone close would catch it. He tried to remember if Tanneman liked fires or if a blaze was somehow connected to the man's reported past life. He didn't think his nephew was right about this one, but it paid to be cautious.

Now he was being too cautious, he told himself. For luck, he touched the closest tree three times and wobbled forward. Methodically, the habit of being prepared for any situation took over his mind. The trials of many battles—both with guns and his fists—had left him with a set of practiced instincts. There was nothing casual about battle—or his readiness. It only looked that way. He rehearsed the actions he would take if a shot was fired, or, preferably, if he spotted someone about to shoot. He imagined the Colt in his hand as he dove to the ground.

Carlow would be covering his advance, but he might

not be able to see clearly. Kileen dismissed that thought. Of course he would. Carlow could see a crow in the middle of the night.

Yellow light seeped through the edges of the closed window shutters and out of the small watch holes in the center of each shutter. Slowly, he pulled a black cigar from his coat pocket. Both hands were deliberately kept in sight. After pretending to drop it, he leaned over, letting his eyes search the cabin for movement or the glimmer of gunmetal.

Seeing none, he searched for a match, lit it and dropped the flame, found another match, and finally drew deeply from the cigar, finding calmness as he let the smoke curl in front of his hard face. A trickle of sweat skidded down his dried cheek but left no mark.

"H-hey-ish, the c-cabin!" he yelled from fifty yards out, his hands still held away from his sides to further indicate his nonaggressive intentions.

His voice took on the sounds of someone filled with whiskey. No one answered. From under his hat, another sweat trickle followed the first. He blotted it carefully with his shirtsleeve.

"H-hey-ish, inside! I be alone an' hungry. D-don't know—" *Hiccup.* "—where I be this night. C-can I come in?" *Hiccup.* "A gentle Irishman I be," he yelled, pleased at his fake hiccups. He stood, weaving, fifteen yards from the planked door with the leather strap hinges. "Got me own whiskey. Irish it be."

"*Vilkommen*, Mick—but *du* keep your hands var I see dem."

Kileen didn't recognize the voice, but it was definitely German in accent. "T-that be a most gentlemanly—" *Hiccup.* "—offer. Best invitation I be havin' in a long spell." He took the cigar from his mouth and waved it gloriously.

"Var *ist* your hoss?"

The door opened and the silhouette of a gray-haired man with glasses filled the space.

"Uh . . . left her, I did. Tied to a tree. Back there. Yeah, me think so."

An uncomfortable laugh followed.

"Kileen's me name," the big Ranger growled, holding out his hand as he approached.

Alben Waulken received Kileen's hand with a strong grip, smiled thinly and said, "*Du kommen* from town? Var are *du* headed?"

"Aye, came from Strickland. Hopin' one o' the ranches be hirin' 'round here. That be where I was headed."

Waulken laughed again. The German had a thick head of hair that touched his heavy shoulders. Mostly gray. Water hadn't touched his hair or face recently. He looked like a man who had spent his life struggling with the land—and the land had won. An old pipe grew from the corner of his mouth, its smoke curling about his rugged face. Kileen guessed the man was in his late forties.

"Aye, S-Strickland. Been a-drinkin' there since the wee morn," Kileen said casually. There was no reason to lie about it. "Ye hear 'bout the bank bein' robbed there?" It was an impulse; he wanted to see how the man would react.

Waulken straightened himself in what Kileen judged was genuine surprise. "*Das ist* vhy I do not put *der* gold in there."

"On me mither's grave, I didn't do it." Kileen wiped his mouth. "Leastwise, I donna remember nothin' like that. Nossir, I didn't."

Waulken removed his pipe and chuckled again, more comfortably this time.

From an adjoining room came a tired-looking woman. Her hair was as gray as Waulken's, but had been tied in a bun at some point during the day. Her shape was thick with age, yet there was a strength about her that was appealing. Her smile was hesitant. Shy.

"*Das ist mein frau*, Margareitte," Waulken said. "Mama, this is Kileen. He comes from Strickland. Looking for cow work he be."

"*Guten Abend*," Mrs. Waulken said with a slight curtsy.

"Aye, 'tis a fine evening, ma'am." Kileen's eyes brightened.

Inside the log-lined cabin, a blackened stone fireplace held a fat, crackling fire. The room reeked of fried food and sweat. Sitting on the fire's edge was a coffeepot, its tantalizing aroma mixing with the other smells. A single oil lamp was doing its best to push the shadows into the corners.

Kileen was surprised at the condition of the cabin's interior. The main room was sparsely decorated, but lovingly clean. Every corner of the hard-earth main room had been freshly swept. A rag rug, obviously handmade, attempted to cover what it could of the floor. Even the hard-working fireplace had been recently scrubbed to remove soot from its stone foundation. Two chairs and a threadbare settee completed the room.

The northern split-log wall featured an oil painting of hill country in the spring. It looked like West Texas. Kileen wondered if it could be Germany, instead. An adjoining room held a bed and a chest of drawers. No rug.

It was definitely a home, although a poor one. A home, not a hideout.

As far as Kileen could see, there was no gun in the house, just the rifle left in the barn. The big Irishman looked around the small house. Could anyone be hiding? Where? There were no closets. No large food bins. Certainly no curtains to stand behind. From where he stood, he could see the lone bed—and underneath it.

"Are *du* hungry, Kileen?" Waulken asked politely. "We haff eaten our evening meal, but I am certain *Frau* Waulken could find something for *du*."

Margareitte Waulken nodded agreement. "*Ja. Du* be needin' something in *der* belly, besides *der* whiskey." She smiled.

Kileen's eyes blinked twice before he responded. He hadn't expected any of this. Had Waulken gotten revenge by shooting Mirabile? For what? Being accused of stealing one of his cows? Why did he think he would get away with robbing the bank? Certainly, the big Irishman could see why the man would want the money. Maybe it was time to lay it on the line.

Kileen cocked his head. Had that been Carlow's face briefly at the window? Where was he, anyway? Kileen glanced again but the window was black, and he realized he should concentrate on the task at hand. His fat fingers touched the acorn in his pocket. Good luck to carry such, he told himself. Reassured the little people were with him, he took a deep breath and announced his real intention.

"Waulken, I am Texas Ranger Aaron Kileen. I've come to arrest ye for the murder of Julian Mirabile— and the robbin' o' the Strickland bank," Kileen's face was hard; his eyes shoved their way into the German's face. He reached into his coat pocket with his left hand, withdrew his dull Ranger badge and showed it.

Kileen's heavyweight prizefighter frame was coiled, as he expect the German to explode into violence.

Smoothly, his big right hand drew the revolver and cocked it, as his left fist, holding the badge, dropped to his side.

Waulken looked like a man who was going to vomit. His wife was white, frozen in place.

As the big Ranger's Colt took a visible position in his fist, the door slammed open and Ranger Time Carlow and Marshal Bridgeport entered. Carlow held his sawed-off carbine in his right hand and the mask from the barn in his left. Both men wore their badges on their coat lapels.

Bridgeport was a few steps behind Carlow, holding a double-barreled shotgun. Behind him charged Chance, as refreshed as if he had been resting all day.

"Well, did ye enjoy your fine Sunday afternoon buggy ride? It be takin' ye so long to come to me aid?" Kileen growled and slipped his badge into place on his coat lapel.

"Watching from the window." Carlow motioned with his gun. "You didn't seem to be in any trouble." He glanced down at Chance and told him to stand at his side.

"Blimey, I should say not. The old sweat would seem to 'ave it all tied up in a bow," Bridgeport chimed in. "Captured the bloody bloke. On the peg, he be. Now all we need is to recover the queen's gold." He looked at the stunned Waulken. "It will go easier on you, mate, if you turn the money over to us."

Carlow guessed "on the peg" meant "under arrest."

"I-I don't know vat *du*—or *der* big Kileen *hier* be talkin' about." Waulken shrugged his shoulders and glanced at his terrified wife. "P-please . . . I do *nicht* know. W-we are quiet people. W-we . . . I haff hurt no one. I haff *nicht* robbed any bank. I haff *nicht* taken any cow. P-please."

The younger Ranger challenged the German's response by reciting what they had found in the barn.

Waulken was incredulous and said he didn't own a gray horse, or a black coat, or fancy rifle—or any kind of mask. He turned to his wife and pleaded for her to say something.

She found her voice, swallowing hard. "*Meine Herren*, I believe *du* haff made *der* great mistake. *Mein* husband has *nicht bien* gone from our house for *der* week. He has *bien* planting . . . *der* crops. Do you *nicht* see *der* fine furrows?"

"Ma'am, I'm sorry to have to contradict you. Ranger Kileen and I, we're trying to find a man who killed a rancher not far from here. Three days ago. A friend of ours." Carlow studied the couple for any reaction. "The rancher's wife described him as wearing a black coat, riding a gray horse—and carrying a rifle, just like the ones we found in your barn. She said he sounded German."

Margareitte Waulken's eyes widened into huge circles. She tried to speak, but could not find words. Only the shape of her mouth gave any indication she was attempting to respond.

"That's the same description the bank president gave us—of the man who robbed the bank," the young Ranger continued, motioning in the direction of town. "Oh yes, both said the guilty man wore a wooden mask. Like this." He held up the mask with his left hand.

"Blimey. Coincidence, she makes such a lovely mistress." Bridgeport grinned.

"Oh yeah, the man we're after . . . he smoked a pipe," Carlow continued. "Like you do."

Waulken's face ballooned into a red ball and he began to wave his arms in frustration. "*Nein*! *Nein*! *Nein*!

I did *nicht* to do these awful things. *Warum*? *Wer kann . . . nein.*"

Studying the farmer, Kileen asked, "How long have ye been part of the Rose gang?"

Waulken stared at him. "I know *nicht* vat *du* are saying to me. I know *nicht.*"

"Holy mither of Mary, the Rose gang, ye know," Kileen growled. "Men who be following Tanneman—and Hillis Rose. Before they died. Bless their black souls. Men who be seeking blood for their dying."

Scratching his head, Waulken turned toward his wife again and asked her if she had ever heard of this Rose gang. Her response was fiercely negative.

Carlow tried a different approach, following what he was beginning to believe. "What direction did Tanneman ride from here? How long has he been gone? An hour? A day?"

Kileen's expression was clear; his nephew wasn't right—and shouldn't be asking such questions.

Behind them, the sounds of stirring brought a reaction from the three lawmen: Kileen swung his pistol in the direction of the noise; Carlow turned toward the sound with his hand carbine; and Bridgeport lifted his shotgun to his shoulder.

A furry yellow and gray cat ambled into the room, meowed its introduction and continued on as the lawmen stared, then looked at each other, then back at Waulken.

"You didn't answer my question. How long ago did Tanneman ride out of here?" Carlow said. "Do you know where he was headed?"

Waulken looked like he was going to cry and muttered a long German statement that the three lawmen assumed was a negative response.

"Alben, you can go with us peacefully—or 'andcuffed,"

Bridgeport said, lowering his gun. "It is your choice, mate."

Margareitte finally found her voice. "I would go with *mein* husband." Folding her arms, she declared, "Ve *nein* to let *der* volf into our *haus*."

"Sorry, ma'am. He isn't a wolf. Not all, anyway," Carlow said, and motioned for the wolf-dog to go outside.

Reluctantly, Chance turned around and left the cabin.

"Waulken, how do you want to ride to town? You and your wife?" Kileen asked, his voice trapped in a strange sense of gentleness.

"Your gray's still saddled—and doesn't look too tired," Carlow said, cocking his head to the side.

"*Das ist nicht mein* horse." Waulken's face reddened again. "I haff a *braun* vagon hoss and *der* vagon. Ve go in *dat*."

Chapter Twenty-two

From behind the dark treeline, Tanneman Rose watched the two Rangers, Marshal Bridgeport and the Waulkens exit the small cabin. He grinned in satisfaction at the sight.

"Perfect. Perfect," he muttered, then squinted to get a better look at the hulk of a Ranger leading the group and the younger gunfighter with him. It had to be! Ranger Kileen and Ranger Carlow! Ah, his trip to Strickland had truly been a rich one.

His next kill would be those two, the Rangers who had first confronted him, arrested him and then killed his brothers, supported by the others. Tanneman had assumed he would have to return to San Antonio and draw them to him by killing more on his revenge list. And now, here they were. Providence was, indeed, blessing his way.

After they had been killed, only one more Ranger would remain on his revenge list: Captain McNelly himself.

Tanneman glanced back at the wagon. The gun wasn't in sight, but he knew it was there, ready for Kileen and Carlow. A new model Sharps rifle with .50-70 centerfire cartridges.

He needed to get a closer look to make certain. The two Irish Rangers would likely be in town for a few days to help oversee Waulken's trial. Maybe they would provide some predictable pattern of behavior that would leave each Ranger vulnerable and alone. Did he dare get that close? What if they recognized him? His ego told him that they wouldn't. People saw what they expected to see. In this case, they saw an eccentric peddler.

Now at Carlow's side, the wolf-dog growled at something unseen in the forest as they headed for the barn.

"What is it, boy?" Carlow said, peering in the direction of the dark woods. "I don't see anything."

Clicking to his horses, Tanneman headed out of the forest. "Aho, the cabin," he yelled in his best Missouri-laden voice. "Kin I be a'sleepin' in yo-al's barn tonight? Nothin' will I be a'usin'. Bin a long day, sure nuff. Got no place to stay."

He grinned, then forced himself to remove the smirk. He was well enough known in the region now; it wouldn't seem strange that he was riding at night. Or seeking lodging. The hidden fingers of his right hand assured him that his gun was close, if needed.

Carlow took two quick steps to his right and peered into the night, holding his hand carbine with both hands.

Chance continued his deep growl, his back hunched and ready.

"Steady, Chance. Steady."

The fierce animal continued to growl.

A few seconds behind, Kileen drew his pistol and aimed it at the advancing clatter of hooves, wagon and harness. Bridgeport pointed his shotgun at Waulken.

"Jolly what, that's just the bloody peddler," Bridgeport responded. "Been around for a week or so. Selling stuff to farmers and ranchers," Bridgeport informed the Rangers. "A little goofy in the 'ead, I suppose, but 'armless. 'Eard he was from somewhere in Missouri. Sounds like one of them. Looks like the war took a good piece o' 'im."

"What's he doing out here at night?" Carlow asked, lowering his gun to his side.

Still growling, Chance moved next to Carlow and rubbed against his right leg.

Carlow leaned down to scratch Chance's ears, without taking his eyes off the advancing wagon. "It's all right, boy. It's all right."

"Blimey! Who knows where 'e bloody stays when 'e's around?" Bridgeport responded. "Looking for a place to doggo this night, it sounds like."

Confident of his abilities, yet on edge with the importance of the performance, Tanneman pulled up a few feet from the group, keeping his face in the shadows as best he could, and avoided looking directly at either Ranger. The eyes could reveal what was hidden elsewhere, he thought.

"Would yah mind if'n I be a'sleepin' in yur barn tonight, suh? There's a bit o' a chill in the air. I won't be usin' nuthin', I promise. Got my own oats fer me hosses. Be gone afore daybreak, I will."

Waulken stared at the lawmen, then shrugged his shoulders. "*Ja. Du* may to sleep there." He started to add more, then decided against it.

"I sure does thank yah. Yes, suh, I does,"

He was certain now it was the two Rangers. He would kill them in the next day or so, then leave for San Antonio. If he could do it without arousing suspicion, it would be a most rewarding trip. Inside he was tense, yet totally energized. This was the ultimate performance! A reckless move, of course. Unnecessary. But that was what made it so exciting. He wanted to tell Portland what was happening, but knew he must wait until these people were gone.

"Waulken, since you won't tell us where the bank money is," Bridgeport announced, refocusing his attention on the German farmer, "I'm going to 'ave my posse search your place from top to bottom." He grimaced. "Might mess things up a bit. Like I said, it would be easier on you if you told us where you 'ave it 'idden."

"I haff *nein geld*. I haff told *du* that before." Waulken frowned and jerked on the handcuffs in frustration. "Does our *haus* look like a place wit *geld*?"

Kileen turned toward Margareitte and spoke softly. "Ma'am, we be sorry to have to be doing this. It be our duty, ma'am."

Both Carlow and Bridgeport were surprised at the caring statement.

She nodded and wiped away the trace of a tear from her cheek. A stoic firmness came to her face and she continued to walk.

Shifting his weight on the wagon seat, Tanneman touched the spider jar and asked, "Have I a'come at a bad time, suhs? I see yah be lawmen. Rangers two o' you be. I kin be movin' on."

Bridgeport was the first to respond. "No, peddler. That's fine. Mr. Waulken has given permission to sleep in the barn. A kip. Ah, a bed in the barn. No food. No going into the Waulken home. We'll be 'ere for a few minutes and then be leaving."

He turned toward Carlow. "Would you be a fine lad and go tell the posse we're coming? They're waiting out by the big rocks."

Trying hard not to show his displeasure at the condescending request, Carlow glanced at Kileen, then headed into the darkness. Chance followed, eager to keep up. The young Ranger stopped and turned back. The wolf-dog bounded on for a few steps, then halted.

"Thunder, do you want me to bring your horse?" Carlow thought for an instant and added, "How about you, Marshal?"

"A nice lad, it would be."

"Thank you, son. One of the possemen is 'olding mine. A gentle brown walking 'orse, he is," Bridgeport said. "Better it is to be calling out to the vedettes when you get closer." He rubbed his chin. "Ah, riders on sentry duty. Some of those mates might be bloody jumpy." He waved his hand. "Welcome you are to get into the candy in my saddlebags. Some fine caramels."

As Carlow resumed his walk, his gaze sought the peddler again. Did he know this man? From where? Probably he and Kileen had passed such a peddler along the way. He resumed talking to Chance as he walked.

False dawn was touching the wood-framed buildings as the two Rangers rode toward the main intersection of Strickland and to the city jail. Alongside, in the buckboard, rode a silent Waulken and his wife, with Marshal Bridgeport driving and munching on caramels. Behind the wagon was tied the gray. Inside the wagon bed was the black coat, Pedersoli rifle and a wooden mask. And Chance. It had been Carlow's idea to let his wolf-dog ride there. He hadn't asked for permission.

Strung out behind them was the posse, who had decided searching in the dark was a waste of time. A return to the Waulken cabin in the daylight would yield better results.

Sleep was flirting with Carlow and he had caught himself dozing in the saddle several times. A few minutes ago, the Celtic cross on the silver chain had slipped out from under his shirt, clinked against the saddle horn and jerked him awake.

He was always amazed at the stamina of his uncle, who never seemed to tire. At least not when he was on duty. The big Ranger had taken at least three swigs from his flask during the ride. That, too, had not seemed to bother his endurance. Carlow had seen Bridgeport nod off once and Waulken had nudged him with his elbow to awaken him.

"Do ye recall if we first be seein' the new moon lookin' to our right—or to our left?" Kileen broke into Carlow's sleepy mind. '"Tis a bad thing to be seein' from our left. Or through a branch. Did we see it through a branch?"

"Thunder, I really don't remember. Honest, Uncle, I don't."

"Aye, well, take out one o' your coins an' spit on it. Both sides. Do it now, laddie. Just in case."

Carlow's shoulders jerked slightly, but he knew better than to delay. It would only mean the next problem they had would be attributed to his lack of compliance with whatever his uncle felt was necessary to change the forces of nature.

Kileen was already spitting on his coin in an exaggerated ceremony as they rode. The young Ranger reached around his gun belt and secured a coin from his pants pocket. Feeling quite silly and hoping no one in the wagon turned around, or any of the possemen behind them noticed, he quickly spit on the money and pushed it back into his pocket.

"Aye, that be a close one," Kileen muttered. "Be glad we did not see it through a window."

Carlow shook his head and decided not to ask what such an action might bring.

Music from a tiny saloon piano accompanied them

for a block, then stayed behind. A shout of gambling achievement burst from another saloon and both Rangers swung guns in the direction of the noise. A woman's forced laugh from inside released them from the distraction. A drunken cowboy stopped to watch the silent riders pass, then slipped back inside.

A similarly inebriated townsman, dressed in a suit of blue velveteen and now crusted with dirt and dried vomit, watched them. As they rode by, he raised his half-filled glass of beer in tribute, burped, then stumbled and sat down hard on the planked sidewalk. He looked around to see who had yanked him. Seeing no one, he drank the rest of his beer from his new sitting position.

Carlow glanced at the hotel and wondered if he and Kileen would get a nice sleepover before heading to San Antonio. They needed to wire McNelly to update him on Mirabile's death, the bank robbery and the subsequent arrest. Carlow planned on asking him to check into Tanneman's supposed death. He looked over at Kileen and saw that he, too, was gazing at the hotel. Whatever was going through the big Ranger's mind caused his broad shoulders to rise and fall with its passing.

Both Rangers' moods were dark. Part of it was the lateness of the hour; part was the absence of any sense of victory. Neither expressed his thoughts as they rode into the mostly quiet town.

A part of Carlow half hoped to see Ellie Beckham and her young son, Jeremiah, standing on one of the wood-planked sidewalks to welcome him. But the rational side of his mind knew that didn't make any sense. She was married and lived in Bennett. Still, he watched the mostly empty streets as they rode. His face wasn't readable to anyone except Kileen.

He glanced again at his uncle. The big man's twisted face was a telltale sign he was bothered by something and not just tired. Impulsively, Carlow reached into his vest pocket to touch the acorn where it was jammed alongside extra cartridges, two pieces of hard candy and an old silver watch. Kileen had given the acorn to him with the observation that carrying it would give him good luck and a long life. It hadn't helped Shannon Dornan, Carlow had told himself.

In his other pocket were two tiny, flat stones, darkly stained with long-ago blood. A large chip was gone from one of them, where it had deflected a bullet. His Ranger badge was in that pocket now, too.

Carlow loved the hulk of a man riding beside him; he was the father he had never known. To receive praise from Kileen was his greatest reward and letting him down was his worst concern. Right now, he couldn't read what was on Kileen's mind, but it was definitely worry, not lack of sleep.

Just as soon as the thought passed, Kileen gave an indication of his concern. "Mrs. Waulken, with your husband's permission, we will be seeing you to the hotel. Late it be, but they will be giving you a room."

She turned her shoulders toward him slowly. "I have no money for such. I vill be sleeping here." She pointed toward the wagon bed. "If *der* volf vill let me do so."

Kileen swallowed and looked like he had been slapped in the face.

A freight wagon rumbled past on its way north. The driver spat and nodded his head as a greeting. The driver's eyes slid toward Chance, and he shook his head as if disbelieving what he saw. Carlow returned the greeting with his own nod and rode on. They stopped at the hitching rack in front of the small city marshal's office. The weary possemen continued, headed for their respective homes. None paid any attention to the wolf-dog watching them from the wagon bed.

Swinging down, the young Ranger told Chance to remain and waited for Bridgeport to climb down. Carlow patted the long-barreled .56 Sharps rifle in its saddle sheath and drew his hand carbine instead.

Bridgeport and Carlow helped the manacled Waulken from the wagon. Dismounting quickly, Kileen attempted to assist Margareitte, but she ignored the courtesy and climbed down without help, saying something in German to her husband, which no one else understood.

"Mrs. Waulken, you will 'ave to wait outside until we put your 'usband behind bars," Bridgeport announced. "Because of the lateness of the 'our, you may stay in one of the other cells if you wish, for this night only. I will not be able to allow you to remain there after that." He touched the brim of his hat, then offered her a caramel from the nearly depleted sack.

Straightening her shoulders, she nodded politely and waited.

"Ranger, perhaps you can wait with Mrs. Waulken?" Bridgeport asked, looking at Carlow.

The young Ranger bit his lower lip and saw that Kileen was nodding. "Sure, that'll be fine."

"Thank you, son."

Bridgeport and Kileen disappeared inside the office with Waulken a few steps in front of them.

Standing near his black horse, Carlow stroked its head and tried to think of something to say. His mind was dark. Tired. Too tired.

It was Margareitte Waulken who spoke first. "I vant *du* to know I understand vhy *du* must do this. But I vant *du* to know—on *mein* vord of honor—these things

are *nicht mein* husband's." She motioned toward the
wagon bed and the gray horse standing behind. "We
knew *nicht* how they got into our barn. I swear it,
Ranger."

Carlow was uncertain how to respond. Of course,
most criminals claimed their innocence. There was
nothing new in that. But there was something in her
voice, in the way she talked, that made him wonder.

"Well, Mrs. Waulken, how do you think they got
there?"

She stared into his face with a quiet resolution about
her. "*Der* man who did those awful things put them in
our barn—to make *mein* husband *der* one *du* arrest."

"I see." Carlow wasn't sure how else to respond. He
was too tired to work at it. He didn't even want to ask
her about Tanneman Rose. Not now. Maybe in the
morning. When he could reason clearly. It was probably just a dumb idea anyway, like his uncle thought.

"*Du* think about this," Margareitte continued. "*Mein*
husband *ist* afraid of horses. He does not ride *der* horse.
Ever. He had *der* bad . . . ah, accident, as a boy. In *der*
old country. Ah, Germany. He *nicht* ride since then.
Only use *der* wagon. Like tonight."

Before Carlow could respond, a weary Kileen came
through the door.

"Ma'am, there be a place for ye to sleep now," he said
in his gentlest voice. "Blankets be there. No pillow, I be
sorry to report, but I rolled up one o' the blankets. Real
tight an' nice."

Margareitte studied his craggy face, smiled thinly
and accepted his held-out arm.

"*Danke*," she murmured and looked back at Carlow.
"Please to be remembering vhat I haff told *du*. *Ja*?"

Nodding politely, Carlow said, "I will, ma'am. I
promise."

"*Guten*. That vill bring *der* freedom to my Alben. I am certain." Her smile was gentle, like that of a mother addressing her son.

With that, she disappeared inside the jail, holding on to Kileen's arm.

Walking over to his horse, Carlow stroked the mount's neck. His mind didn't want to work, only to sleep. Was Waulken's wife just making up an alibi? Who wouldn't try to save a loved one? Or was someone behind this? Was that possible? Was it Tanneman Rose?

Chance jumped down from the wagon, bounded over and rubbed Carlow's leg. The tired lawman leaned over and scratched the wolf-dog's ears. "Yeah, it's been a long day, my friend. A long day." His hanging cross fell out of his shirt again and he pushed it back.

Kileen came out of the door. "Me lad, Marshal Bridgeport suggests we be sleeping here for what's left of the morn. In another of the empty cells it be." He motioned with his huge right hand. "Hisself says we can be leaving our hosses here—and the wagon. Take them to the livery we be—after we get up."

"I was wondering if you and the marshal were going to leave the Waulkens alone?" Carlow asked. His shoulders rose and fell. "I'm not going to leave Shadow and Chance here on the street. Shadow deserves to be unsaddled and rubbed down. Some grain. Water, too. I'll take him over the livery. I can sleep there, Thunder."

"Oh. Well, if that be your choice."

"It is." Carlow studied his uncle. "An' you will be sleeping with Margareitte Waulken." A smile slipped onto his weary face.

His neck reddening, Kileen coughed and said angrily, "Ye be careful about your wordin', me lad. Lark an' me be guardin' the prisoner."

Carlow swung easily into the saddle. "Don't let any birds inside."

It was a tease about the superstition that a bird coming into a house was a sign of impending death.

"Don't ye be jokin' o' such," Kileen blurted. "Your sainted mither—God bless her sweet soul—herself not be likin' such words from her only son."

Leaning down, Carlow yanked free the reins of Kileen's horse. "I'll take your horse, too." He straightened himself in the saddle. "Just kidding, Thunder. Didn't mean to upset you."

"Me knows ye didn't, me son. A bit edgy I be," Kileen said, almost in a whisper. "Thank ye for takin' me hoss."

Carlow swung his great horse away from the post, with the reins of Kileen's horse in his left fist. His shoulders rose and fell, and then he told Shadow to stop.

"Ya know, Mrs. Waulken told me her husband was afraid of horses," he said, suddenly feeling more tired than ever. "Never rides, except in a wagon. Like tonight."

Kileen licked his lips, felt for the flask in his pocket, then dropped his hand to his side. "How did that bleemin' gray—and the other stuff—be gettin' into his barn?"

"Good question, Thunder. Wish I knew. Maybe Tanneman set this whole thing up. Think about that." He nudged his horse into an easy trot, leading Kileen's tall mount. A whistle to Chance brought the wolf-dog eagerly following.

The older Ranger watched his nephew ride away. He loved the young man as if he were his son, maybe more. Down deep, it pleased him Carlow wasn't superstitious like he was. It reminded him of his sister,

Time Carlow's late mother. In their younger days together, in Ireland, she had always been scolding him about his irrational ways, then giving him a soft kiss on his cheek.

But the younger man's comment about Waulken churned his exhausted mind. Something about this arrest wasn't right. Or maybe it was too right and he was just too tired. He wiped his nose with his coat sleeve and headed toward the jail. The earliest blush of dawn was flirting with the town. Somewhere an owl hooted and Kileen shivered.

Chapter Twenty-three

It was barely past nine when Aaron Kileen came lumbering into the livery, yelling for Time Carlow to wake up.

"Wake up, me lad! Wake up. There be trouble at the jail," he shouted as he hurried toward the bed of hay where the young Ranger lay sleeping. Chance was sprawled out next to him.

"What time is it?" Carlow asked, stretching his arms and yawning. His wolf-dog was immediately on all fours, watching the young Ranger for his next movement.

" 'Tis late enough. A lynch mob be gatherin' outside the jail," Kileen said. His suit and shirt were more wrinkled than usual, from sleeping on the marshal's office floor. "Marshal Bridgeport be alone. Hisself an' his bleemin' shotgun."

"Won't charge yah for the night. Just for the day," the livery man shouted from another part of the stable, as he tossed a pitchfork of hay into an empty stall.

"Thanks. Appreciate that." Carlow stood up, brushed himself off and buckled on his gun belt. He glanced at Shadow quietly eating from a bucket of oats; Kileen's horse was similarly occupied.

"Stay here, Chance," he said, then remembered the

wolf-dog hadn't eaten since gobbling a stick of beef jerky near the Waulken farm.

"Wait a minute, Thunder."

Pushing his hat on his head, Carlow hurried to his saddlebags, still tied to his saddle resting on the stall fence. Retrieving two big pieces of jerky from one bag, he tossed them to the appreciative animal. For the first time, Carlow noticed his uncle was carrying a shotgun, one of Marshal Bridgeport's.

"Should I get my Sharps?" Carlow asked, waving toward his saddle resting over the stall where Shadow stood.

"No. Let's go."

"Give my dog some water, will you?" he yelled as he turned toward the livery door.

"Is he a wolf?" the livery man shouted back.

"Not today."

"Hurry, me lad," Kileen yelled as he exited the livery, waving the shotgun.

Running to catch up, Carlow's concern about the innocence of Alben Waulken pushed its way into his just-awakening mind. Drawing the sawed-off carbine as he hurried, the same questions bounced again into his thoughts.

What if somebody truly had set up the German farmer, leaving all that incriminating evidence? Certainly a recluse like Waulken was an easy target. No one in town would likely speak for him. How could they prove—or disprove—Margareitte's claim that her husband was afraid of horses? What if they tried to force the German immigrant to ride a horse? What if he refused?

Coming alongside his hard-breathing uncle, Carlow said, "Thunder, I think Alben Waulken might be an innocent man. Tanneman's behind all this. He has to be. We've got to check out his attempt to escape from prison. I'm betting he faked his death somehow. I don't believe there is any gang. I know I keep saying it, but it's true. I know it."

"Aye. Be leanin' . . . the same way meself." Kileen tried to smile and talk between gulping for air. "But right now . . . stoppin' these folks . . . we must be doin'."

Down the street they ran, with Carlow easily outdistancing his out-of-breath uncle. He wasn't certain if Kileen's remarks meant he was beginning to think Waulken was innocent or that Tanneman was alive. Right now, neither mattered.

In front of the jail, an angry gathering was taking on a life of its own. Furious men yelled at Marshal Bridgeport to bring out Waulken. Their demand was a fierce litany in the gray morning. A few weapons were raised in the air for emphasis. The town itself was awakening to the uproar. Those watching safely from windows and doorways silently approved of the crowd's desire— or, if not, were afraid to speak out.

Neither Ranger saw a bay horse tied in the alley across the street from the jailhouse. No one noticed a man lying on the flat roof of the two-story J. A. Mosedain Dry Goods and Clothing building next to the alley. In his hands was a Sharps carbine. The barrel moved from Carlow to Kileen and back again. Lying beside him on the roof was a wooden mask.

The younger Ranger was moving too fast to be a good target; Tanneman knew he would have only one chance for now. Kileen would be the better choice. He smiled. How fitting, to kill the one man who believed his stories of reincarnation.

Below the barely visible nose of the gun was a sign proclaiming the name of the establishment, as well as

additional information: Dressmaking a specialty . . .
Hats and Caps and Boots and Shoes.

"Break this up! Go home. Alben Waulken is an innocent man," Carlow yelled as he burst into the crowd
and shoved his way through to the door, swinging his
hand carbine to emphasize the order. He wasn't certain about the latter statement; it just came out.

"*You* go home, Mick. We want our money. If that
German bastard doesn't tell us where it's hidden right
now . . . we're gonna hang his ass." The voice came
from somewhere in the middle of the crowd, emboldened by anonymity.

Others joined the challenge, making certain, however, they weren't close to the advancing Ranger. Carlow joined Bridgeport, standing with a double-barreled
shotgun, in front of the closed jail door. The young
Ranger nodded his support, levered his gun into readiness and pushed two townsmen back with his free
hand.

"Jolly well good to 'ave you with me, son," Bridgeport said.

Carlow ignored the slight. It was different when Kileen called him son. Waving his gun, Carlow yelled a
fierce command that had the men looking at each other
for a decision.

Kileen reached the outer edges of the mob and took
a deep breath to reclaim the wind lost in his hurrying.
He bent over with his hands on his knees to ease the
aching loss. As he bowed, a heavy shot rang out, startling the mob into absolute silence.

Kileen half spun, straightened and fell facedown in
the street.

Hearing the shot, Carlow saw his uncle fall and
yelled, "Oh no!"

Frantically, he pushed and shoved his way back

to the downed big Ranger. "Oh no, Thunder . . . Thunder . . . Uncle . . . Father . . ."

A tall man in overalls stepped into Carlow's furious path and Carlow shoved him away and kept on going. Only the closeness of others kept the man on his feet. His reddened face looked after Carlow for only a moment, and then he joined the reinvigorated throng.

In the doorway of the jail, Bridgeport yelled a command of his own, but the rush of emboldened men took his words away. The British lawman was slammed to the sidewalk and his shotgun kicked aside. The door itself followed, bursting open from the furious charge. Margareitte Waulken screamed, threw open her cell and tried to stop them.

Someone slugged her and she went down.

In moments, the keys were found and Alben Waulken was dragged from his cell, shouting his innocence.

Kneeling beside Kileen, Carlow couldn't remember running back to his uncle. He wasn't aware of the fierce bolt of the mob into the jail. All he cared about was his beloved uncle, lying facedown with a pool of blood growing around him. Crimson fingers reached out to find Kileen's dropped shotgun, Carlow's hand carbine lying beside him and his nephew's Kiowa legging where he knelt.

The young Ranger managed to turn over his wounded uncle, studying the large black hole in his right shoulder. Blood was everywhere. Carlow ripped off his own neckerchief and pressed the wad of cloth against the ugly wound.

"F-forgot . . . t-to tap me sh-shotgun . . . t-three times, me lad," Kileen stammered.

Carlow bit his lower lip and continued to press against the wound. At his side was a worried Chance, nuzzling his leg for reassurance. The wolf-dog had bolted from the barn when he heard the gunfire. Carlow seemed unaware of him. Or of anything.

"A Ranger's dog . . . he be," Kileen muttered. "Came to . . . the sound . . . o' the gun."

Carlow realized the beast was beside him and rubbed Chance's ears. "Good boy, Chance. Good boy." It helped steady his nerves.

Across the street, Tanneman Rose reloaded and aimed, this time at Carlow.

"Damn that wolf! Get out of the way!" he cursed as Chance stood next to the young Ranger, blocking him from Tanneman's view. For an instant, he considered shooting the dog, reloading and trying for Carlow. His heavy slug would likely go through the animal anyway, wounding Carlow, too.

He remembered the young Ranger being quite fond of the beast; shooting him now would bring a wild Carlow into battle, in full rage. Tanneman didn't like that idea. Carlow in a gunfight was not something to bring on oneself. He had seen it.

"He's almost as good as me," Tanneman murmured. "I'll wait."

A minute passed without the wolf-dog moving enough to give him a good shot. Finally he decided it was too risky to wait any longer. Someone would see him if he did, and getting down would be difficult. He could get another shot off; that wasn't the problem. Getting away was. He caressed the jaguar teeth necklace under his clothes and muttered something he considered to be Persian.

He wasn't certain that Kileen was dead, but if he weren't, he wouldn't be alive long. Tanneman crawled back across the flat roof of the building, jumped to the rickety stairway balcony and climbed down the back stairs. He left the mask where it lay. The alley remained as empty as before.

His disguise was one he had used already—a businessman in a three-piece gray suit and a matching bowler. Heavy eyebrows and a thick mustache completed his look.

Waiting for him was the bay horse from his wagon. He shoved the big gun into its saddle scabbard and rode around the backside of the building. He passed two more buildings, then eased into the main street. The mob was in front of him, dragging the struggling German farmer, now with his hands tied behind him.

Tanneman grinned at the effect his Waulken disguise had created, then kicked his horse into a lope. The peddler wagon and the other horse were waiting for him, hidden in a narrow ravine, not far from town.

Kileen placed a wobbly hand on Carlow's arm. "M-me son, the wee things p-pulled me over—or me w-would be gone to the other world." He let go and tried to regain his breath. His eyes fluttered and closed for a moment.

Maybe Kileen was right. Maybe he did have invisible helpers protecting him. Somehow Carlow had never wanted to challenge the idea by thinking about it too much. There were things a person didn't understand in this world, especially those of the spirit. Certainly he had seen happenings that couldn't be explained by anything that made any sense, at least not to him. Maybe it was smart to be a little superstitious. Kileen had said this feeling came from seeing miracles that occurred in everyday life and not recognizing them as miracles. Maybe so.

Trying to calm down, Carlow told himself Kileen's wound was bad, but not fatal. Seeing the first part of neckerchief fill with blood, he took another section and repeated the attempt. He wasn't sure, but thought the bleeding was beginning to slow. Maybe he was seeing something he badly wanted to see.

Kileen's eyes fluttered open again, and the big Ranger said in a halting voice, " 'Twas a . . . b-big gun, me lad. A S-Sharps. Like Rangers b-be carryin'. H-had to come f-from . . . across the street. H-high, it be. A r-roof, me lad. A r-roof."

Carlow shook his head. How like his uncle to ever be the lawman. He glanced at the buildings across the street. He saw nothing, except townspeople gathering to wonder. But he was certain Tanneman Rose had struck again. Why hadn't he seen this coming?

"W-where be M-Marshal B-Bridgeport?" Kileen stuttered.

"Don't know. Don't care," Carlow answered.

Kileen's face became a frown. "No, m-me lad. You be a R-Ranger. First, ye m-must see to our prisoner. We must . . . b-be provin' him innocent. I be thinkin' yourself be right . . . about Tanneman. Comin' after us from the grave he be."

"No, Thunder. He's alive. He's got to be. I think he shot you."

From the doorway came a distraught Margareitte Waulken, waving Bridgeport's shotgun. The side of her pale face was red and swelling; her gray hair had found freedom from her usual tight combing and bounced on her shoulders.

The British lawman was barely conscious, shaking his head and trying to stand.

"Ranger . . . Ranger . . . they haff taken *mein* husband." Margareitte staggered out of the jail. "Please . . . please . . . help us." She ran past them into the main street.

"G-go, me lad. H-help her. I be . . . all right." Kileen held up his hand to Carlow.

As the situation registered for the first time, Carlow looked around, saw no mob and realized what had happened. His mind clearing, he grabbed his hand carbine and stood. Glancing at his uncle, who shooed him away, Carlow began to run. In a few strides he passed the sobbing Margareitte.

Just beyond the last building, an ice cream parlor at the commercial end of town, was a cluster of trees. A black silhouette dangled from a rope tied to the closest cottonwood.

Alben Waulken! The mob had lynched him!

Fear took his legs even faster. He grabbed Waulken's legs and lifted his body with one strong arm, firing his hand carbine twice at the hanging rope near the branch. The second shot clipped the rope and the body fell into his arms. He couldn't hold it and Waulken's body crumpled to the ground.

It was obvious the German was dead. His face was blue, his pants stained with the release of his bowels.

Carlow stood over the body, unable to think or act.

Sobbing, Margareitte caught up, dropped to her knees and cradled Waulken's head against her chest. She rocked and wailed.

Carlow muttered more to himself than to her, "He was innocent. They must pay for this. He was innocent."

Chapter Twenty-four

When a deflated Time Carlow returned to the jail, his wounded uncle had been moved to the hospital. Behind Carlow, a distraught Margareitte Waulken mourned over her dead husband. She would not allow anyone to move the body.

Marshal Bridgeport watched Carlow advance; the only sign of the Englishman having been unconscious earlier was a red mark on the side of his face. He chewed on a piece of toffee from the sack on his desk. One of his deputies stood next to him. The deputy had reported for duty fifteen minutes ago, unaware of the jailbreak until his arrival at the marshal's office. A tall man with long sideburns, he wore a shoulder holster and an oddly shaped, short-brimmed hat.

"Ranger Kileen 'as been taken to our 'ospital, such as it is," Bridgeport announced as the young Ranger walked up. "Dr. Morrison is with 'im."

"How is he?"

"Bloody old bloke should make it," Bridgeport said. "Lost a lot of blood, 'e 'as. Big 'ole in his shoulder. Doc says it went through. Didn't 'it bone. That's a blessing, wot. Won't be going anywhere for awhile." He paused and added, "Bloody well might not have full use of 'is arm, you know. Might." His frown was genuine.

"Thanks for . . . taking him," Carlow said, his shoulders rising and falling. "Alben Waulken was innocent. I'm sure of it." The words tumbled from Carlow's mouth as if they'd been waiting for the opportunity. He glanced in the direction of the sadness at the end of the street.

Benjamin Payne, the tall deputy, responded first, "Y-y-yeah, y-y-you're r-right." He accompanied his stuttering by scratching the back of his right hand.

Without waiting for Payne to explain, Bridgeport told Carlow that a cowboy had come to the jail a few minutes ago. The cowboy had just heard about the arrest of Waulken for robbing the bank. He told the local lawmen that he had ridden past the Waulken farm yesterday morning—about the time the bank was robbed—and had seen the German farmer feeding his pigs. There was no mistaking who it was, the cowboy had said. Or the time. The cowboy had stopped and talked with Waulken for a few minutes before riding on. He had been on his way to another ranch to arrange for round-up cooperation.

"Where is he now? The cowboy," Carlow asked.

"'E's still in town. Bitterman's," Bridgeport answered. "Or that's where 'e was 'eaded anyway. To 'ave a wet." He pursed his lips. "Well, not tea, I suppose."

"Th-th-that m-m-means all of th-th-the m-m-mob have to b-b-be arrested." Payne nodded his head authoritatively and rubbed his hands together.

Bridgeport bit his lower lip. "You 'ave a bloody tough job to do, Ranger Carlow. Find the bloody bastard who shot the good Ranger Kileen." He motioned toward his deputy. "We 'ave a nasty one, too. That mob is guilty of assaulting an officer—and of murder." He lifted his hand to reveal a sheet of paper. "A list of the mob combatants I 'ave 'ere. Just wrote it out a few minutes ago wot. On the peg they will be. My deputies and I will start arresting them. 'Twill not be a good day for Strickland."

"What about Waulken—and Mrs. Waulken?"

Bridgeport shook his head, swallowed the remaining toffee in his mouth and was silent.

Carlow hitched the gun belt at his waist and looked again at the black figures of Mrs. Waulken and her dead husband. A shiver galloped through his body.

"The town must pay for his burial," he muttered. "A nice funeral. Granite headstone."

"Agreed." Bridgeport shook his head.

"Th-th-that's right," Deputy Payne added.

"If Mrs. Waulken wants to stay in town during that time, the town will pay for her room and board," Carlow continued.

Both Strickland lawmen nodded agreement.

"I'd like you to go tell her that. All of it," Carlow said. "I'm going across the street to see if I can learn anything. Then I'm going to see Thunder. And wire our captain."

"Got a strong feeling, son, that the bloody shooter was Mirabile's killer—and our bank robber 'e be, too," Bridgeport said.

Ignoring the marshal's continued use of "son," Carlow agreed and headed toward the J. A. Mosedain Dry Goods and Clothing store across the street. Chance followed closely. Someone watched them from the store window, but made no attempt to come out. Paying no attention to the curious face, the young Ranger walked into the alley.

Horse tracks were easy to read. The shooter had used the back stairway to gain access to the roof. His footprints coming and going were a mute story of the attempted ambush. Then the man had escaped the same way he had come to town, along the back row of buildings. A quick trip to the roof revealed the mask and a large empty cartridge. A Sharps, Carlow thought. He took both items with him and returned to the ground.

Next to the building, he discovered a fake eyebrow. At first he thought it was a caterpillar. He held the fuzzy strip in his fingers, trying to decide what it was. Then it hit him. Of course! It was part of a disguise. Tanneman Rose loved the theater; he talked about it all the time. When they had arrested him, he and his brother had been wearing beards. As far-fetched as it seemed to his uncle, it had to be Tanneman. It just had to be.

Shrugging his shoulders, Carlow placed the eyebrow in his vest pocket, next to the bloodstones, and headed in the direction of the shooter's escape. Every part of him was alert to the possibility that an ambush was waiting. Tanneman would expect Carlow to come. The Ranger looked up at the buildings on both sides of the J. A. Mosedain Dry Goods and Clothing store. They were clear.

Chance gave a yip and hurried after him. Carlow was certain Kileen's shooting had nothing to do with the lynching, other than the fact that it had provided a convenient distraction. He was growing more and more confident the killer was Tanneman Rose. They should have checked into his supposed death. At the time, though, it had seemed right.

As Carlow walked, he saw where the ambusher had returned to the main street. The would-be killer had been in full view for a period of time, probably close to the time of the lynch mob's charge to the trees. Why would someone try to kill Kileen in the middle of town? Even a twisted man like Tanneman? The only answer that made sense was that it was an action of opportunity. The mob. The damn mob! All that confusion had given the shooter the perfect opportunity to shoot Kileen—and escape unseen. The hoofprints indicated the ambusher had left town. South.

But how did Tanneman know Kileen and Carlow were in town? Again, the only answer that made sense was that he was watching them. Had seen them bring Waulken in. Instinctively, the young Ranger looked up.

Tracking him now wouldn't be easy, but it would have to be done. Certainly, Kileen would have enemies; no lawman would be free of them. But the continuing connection to Tanneman's arrest bothered Carlow. Kileen had been a major factor. So had Pig Deconer. So had he. Why hadn't the shooter tried for him? His mind retraced his steps from the barn to the jail. Was it simply that his uncle provided the better target? Or was Carlow trying to tie together something that didn't exist?

Shaking away his concerns, he returned to the J. A. Mosedain Dry Goods and Clothing store and told Chance to wait outside. As he entered, an older woman looked up from an unpainted table where she was working on her new Edward Ward Arm & Platform sewing machine. Her soft smile indicated she was enjoying its speed and convenience as she worked. She was finishing a fancy dress with lace around the collars and cuffs. He smiled and wondered if Mrs. Jacobs in Bennett had a machine that nice. He couldn't recall seeing anything like it.

That made him think of Ellie and he shook his head to lose the painful memory.

The small area was jammed with bolts of cloth. In the back, another woman examined a roll of calico.

The woman was deep in concentration, reviewing how the material would be made into a dress. The north wall behind the table displayed bonnets, ready-to-wears, sewing patterns, boxes of needles, thread and thimbles—even pairs of black silk gloves and green gauze veils. On the adjoining wall were displays of shoes and boots. One pair of Mexican embroidered boots caught Carlow's eye and then he remembered what he had come in for.

Removing his hat, Carlow asked politely, "Is the manager in? I'd like to talk with him. It's about the shooting."

She stood, brushing herself off. "I own this store. How may I help you?"

"Sorry, ma'am. I'm Ranger Carlow. My partner was just shot and the man who did it was on your roof. Wondered if you . . ."

"That can't be. It just can't be," Mrs. Mosedain declared. "Are you saying my establishment had something to do with such an awful act?"

Shaking his head and waving his hat, the young Ranger tried to explain, but the older woman wouldn't listen. The door opened behind him and he turned to meet the incoming person.

"I'm Abigail Mosedain. This is my mother, Mrs. Mosedain," she said, brushing her brown hair back toward the tight bun that held it close. She smiled and sought Carlow's eyes.

"Yes, ma'am. As I was saying, I'm looking for clues. Anything that might help me find the man who shot my un . . . the Ranger," Carlow said, gripping his hat with both hands in front of him.

"I'm very sorry, but we didn't hear anything until that awful gun blast. I knew it was above us." She swallowed, as if recalling the incident was difficult and distasteful. "I heard a slight noise. Across our roof—and down our back stairway." She pointed in the direction of the back of the building. "I ran outside and saw a man was riding away. Behind the building. I went to find Marshal Bridgeport—and he told me you were over here. We must've just missed each other."

"Can you identify him? Was it anyone you know?"

She folded her arms. "No, no one from town. I'm sure of that. He was in a nice three-piece suit. Gray. Broadcloth, I believe. Yes, definitely. His hat matched the shade. A bowler, it was. A red silk cravat. Rather dapper, I would say. Oh, and he had a thick mustache and kinda heavy eyebrows."

"Very good, ma'am. You have an eye for detail. That's most helpful." Carlow smiled and shifted his feet. "Didn't happen to see what kind of horse he was riding, did you?"

She closed her eyes for a moment. "It was a bay. Wasn't young. I have a young bay. It's kept at the livery."

After she asked about the lynching and the status of the bank's money, Carlow explained the situation. Then he thanked her for her help and left. Her eyes followed him, hoping he might turn back to look at her, but he didn't. She began to discuss the encounter with her mother.

Carlow stepped out onto the street and his tired gaze took in the Gem Theater across the street. A traveling troupe was presenting *Othello*, as Bridgeport had told them. His mind skipped along to Tanneman Rose. Then his eyes took in the small symbol adorning the playbill attached to the theater door. A mask! The traditional mask of theater, combining sadness and happiness.

"Of course Tanneman is using a mask. Wooden masks," Carlow muttered to himself. "It's the perfect

way to set up an innocent man. He would be drawn to
the idea. Of course. Why didn't I think of that before?"
He took another step and studied the people walking
along the sidewalks. That meant Tanneman Rose could
be anywhere, disguised to look like someone else.

Carlow saw Marshal Bridgeport walking slowly
down the middle of the street and decided to join him,
pushing his thoughts about Tanneman to the back of
his mind. He was surprised it had taken the British
lawman so long to head for the site of the lynching.

"Find anything useful, son?" Bridgeport looked up
as the young Ranger approached.

"Horse tracks. Headed out of town. The lady in the
dress store said he wore a three-piece suit. Gray broadcloth. Had a mustache. Rode a bay. An older one, it
sounded like." Carlow pointed south, but didn't mention the eyebrow he had found or his growing sense of
who the murderer really was.

The British lawman pursed his lips and stared at the
horizon. "Blimey. Doesn't 'elp much."

"It's a direction."

"Which Mosedain lady did you talk with?"

"Mostly the younger one."

Bridgeport acknowledged that she had come to him
and he had sent her to find Carlow. The British lawman
walked farther, then stopped, his face laden with a
heavy frown. "Why didn't Waulken jolly well tell us 'e
'ad an alibi? That would've stopped this whole thing."

"Don't blame yourself, Marshal. It wouldn't have
made any difference. Not last night anyway," Carlow
answered, staring at Mrs. Waulken ahead. "We would
have still arrested him—'til that cowboy was found."

"Jolly right you be, lad. Never thought about it that
way," Bridgeport said and nodded several times to af-
firm his agreement. "I sent Deputy Payne for the un-

dertaker. Wilson Gibbs makes furniture. Does this . . . coffins and the like . . . on the side."

Finally, Carlow decided to share his growing suspicion. "I'm pretty sure the real killer—and probably your bank robber—is a former Ranger. Tanneman Rose. A bad one. Escaped from jail before he could be taken to prison. Been killing everyone who put him behind bars."

"Tanneman Rose, eh? Jolly wot." Bridgeport eyed the younger lawman. "Somehow, I take it, Aaron doesn't agree. A sticky wicket that."

"He will."

"Blimey."

Around and behind them, small groups of townspeople were quietly headed toward the hanging tree, ever drawn by the sight of the ugly violence, and now a grieving woman.

"You going to be able to arrest all of that mob?" Carlow glanced around at the curious crowd moving in the same direction.

A freight wagon cranked past them, its driver either unaware of the lynching or not caring. Both lawmen stepped to the side to let it pass. Parallel to their advance, the morning stagecoach groaned to a stop beside the Wells Fargo office. One passenger leaned out of the coach to glimpse the tragedy, then advised the others inside.

Bridgeport returned to Carlow's question. "My two deputies and I will do our duty. Strickland is a lawful town, wot."

"Most of these folks are going to want you looking for their money," Carlow said. "Not arresting some of their own—for what they think was justice."

Glancing at the young Ranger, Bridgeport frowned again. "Well, if it's not Waulken, where do we bloody look? Maybe it is the good Rangers that need to 'elp us now."

Carlow didn't respond for several steps. Finally he said, "After I check on Thunder and wire the captain, I'll be riding out. To find the man who tried to kill him—and who murdered Mirabile. To find Tanneman Rose."

"Following horse tracks that'll join hundreds? Where's that get you, lad?"

"Like I said, it's a direction."

Bridgeport thought about saying he was going to wire Ranger headquarters for a change in the young man's orders, but didn't. He wondered if the young man at his side would be effective without his famed older partner. Looking back, he saw the wolflike beast trailing them. What kind of man traveled with such an animal? Maybe Bridgeport had underestimated the youthful lawman. He chuckled to himself. The animal was probably keeping people from getting closer, or from bothering him with questions, mostly about the bank's money, that he couldn't answer.

The idea of having to arrest certain townsmen for the lynching was settling into his mind. Really settling. Some of the town's top businessmen had been involved. His first step would be to see Judge DeVere and get warrants for the multiple arrests. Eight names he could remember for certain. There were more, however. The arrests would trigger more names, of that he was certain. He thought there had been fourteen in the mob. Fourteen.

The matter was going to get more complicated. Bridgeport wasn't certain what judge would come to town to handle the case; Judge Cline was, of course, dead. He didn't think the governor had yet appointed a new one for the district. Or a district attorney, for that matter. None of that was going to bring back Alben Waulken—or the town's money. He would be criticized for his misplaced attention. Maybe lose his job. Maybe he should leave the mess well enough alone. Some candy would be nice, Bridgeport thought. Chocolate drops, perhaps.

"Mrs. Waulken, Marshal Bridgeport and I want to apologize for this awful tragedy," Carlow said softly to the distraught Margareitte Waulken, removing his hat as the two lawmen reached her.

"*Nein. Ist* too late." She looked up, her face stained with tears.

"Ma'am, the city will be paying for the burial and services," Bridgeport said, taking off his own hat. "And a fine tombstone. Granite, it will be."

She stared at him.

"Bloody run over, we were," Bridgeport mumbled and looked down at the hat held in both hands. "Didn't 'ave a chance against so many."

She continued to stare at him. Only her lower lip moved, quavering.

His shoulders twitching nervously, the marshal told her about the cowboy coming in and telling of Waulken's whereabouts during the bank robbery. He pointed out that it had happened after the lynch mob had taken the German farmer away.

It didn't look like she was going to speak, but finally she said, "Var *ist der* big Ranger?"

Carlow answered first. "He is wounded, ma'am. In the hospital. Hit bad. Sharps carbine from across the street. Lost a lot of blood. I haven't caught the shooter. Yet. I'm sure he's the man who set up . . . your husband."

She grimaced and shook her head before slowly standing. Carlow hurried to help her up.

"*Danke.*" She looked hard into Carlow's eyes. "So vat *ist* your thinking now? About *mein* husband."

"He was an innocent man, set up to look guilty. I know who did it. I will find him and bring him to justice. I promise."

She lowered her eyes. "Does *nicht* matter now. My Alben *ist* gone."

Fiddling with his hat, Carlow studied her agonized face. "Marshal Bridgeport will be arresting those involved in this."

"Vill *du* be helping with *der* arrests?"

Breath pushed its way through Carlow's closed jaw. His short night of sleep felt even shorter, and he repeated himself. "I'm going after the man who shot . . . Ranger Kileen. He's the one who . . ."

"*Der* Marshal vill need your strength," she interrupted. There was something different in her eyes.

The young Ranger didn't know how to respond. He looked down at his leggings, then his boots, then away. After all, it had been his actions—and Kileen's—that had contributed to Waulken's arrest.

"You're right, Mrs. Waulken." Carlow was surprised at his own words. "If the marshal wants my help, he has it."

His eyebrows saluting, the British lawman wrapped an arm around Carlow's shoulder. "Jolly wot! 'Twould be proud to 'ave you with me, son." A wide smile popped onto his face.

Down the street came Deputy Payne, a short, stocky man with a soiled apron and two Chinese men in Oriental workwear. Bridgeport quickly introduced the short man as Wilson Gibbs. The undertaker mumbled something that Carlow took to be an introduction of his helpers. He nodded to both and they returned the greeting with deep bows. Margareitte declined Bridgeport's offer of breakfast, but accepted his invitation to stay at Delvin's boardinghouse for women. Carlow said he would catch up with the local lawmen after wiring Captain McNelly and then visiting Kileen.

It surprised him when Margareitte told him, in parting, that she would be praying for Kileen. He thanked her and left as Bridgeport solemnly escorted the German widow away. As ordered, Deputy Payne stayed with the undertaker and his helpers.

From the shadows of a nearby building, a man watched and wrote in his small notebook.

Chapter Twenty-five

A wire was waiting for Carlow when he entered the cramped telegraph office wedged into the corner of the town's lumber store. The wire was from Captain McNelly. That didn't surprise him. It was typical of his leadership.

The message did. McNelly had been as suspicious of the reported escape death of Tanneman Rose as Carlow had become.

While the telegraph operator watched silently, Carlow read the lengthy telegram.

> ALERT TO KILEEN AND CARLOW . . .
> STOP . . . BELIEVE TANNEMAN ROSE ALIVE
> AND RESPONSIBLE FOR KILLINGS IN
> SAN ANTONIO . . . STOP . . . FOLLOW-UP
> ON DEATH REPORT REVEALS LIKELY
> ESCAPE . . . STOP . . . FACE OF MAN
> IDENTIFIED AS TANNEMAN BURNED
> AWAY . . . STOP . . . FELL IN CAMPFIRE . . . NO
> RECOGNITION POSSIBLE . . . STOP . . . ONLY
> HIS NECKLACE FOR PROOF . . . LOOKS LIKE
> CAREFUL SETUP . . . STOP . . . BELIEVE DEAD
> GUARD BRIBED THEN KILLED . . . REAL
> DEAD PERSON LIKELY FARMER WHO
> DISAPPEARED SAME NIGHT . . . STOP . . . DO

NOT BELIEVE THERE IS A GANG . . . STOP . . .
ARRESTED MAN FOR MURDERS OF JUDGE
AND OTHERS LIKELY INNOCENT . . .
STOP . . . WATCH YOURSELVES . . . STOP . . .
ADVISE OF SITUATION . . . STOP . . . MCNELLY.

"That's the longest one I've gotten since them Injuns killed Custer. Way up north," the operator observed. He wanted to ask about the wire, but knew he shouldn't.

Carlow looked at him, saying nothing.

"Is everything all right, R-Ranger? I-I heard the b-big Ranger got shot. He gonna make it?" the operator asked. He wasn't sure why he was frightened, but he was. Something in the young Ranger's eyes.

"Ah . . . sorry, I wasn't paying attention, sir," Carlow finally said. "What did you say?"

"It was n-nothing. Just made a comment about the day. That's all."

Carlow wrote out the message he wanted sent to McNelly, placed a coin on the table and left for the hospital.

Chapter Twenty-six

Bright shards of late-morning light cut through the tiny hospital room where Kileen lay. Originally a fine home built by a wealthy lumberman, the building hadn't changed much since wounded soldiers, on both sides, had been treated within its walls during the War of Northern Aggression. The smell was unmistakable—an odor of death, medicine and stale air. Carlow hated it. It reminded him of his near-death wounds two years earlier, when his best friend had died in that terrible gunfight in Webster.

Carlow studied his uncle, looking for signs that the big man was, indeed, sleeping and not dead. Kileen's breathing was shallow and the agile Ranger slipped beside him to check his pulse. It was there. The young Ranger shut his eyes and prayed silently.

The big man stirred; his eyelids fluttered and he was awake.

"Hi, Unc. How are they treating you?" Carlow said, as confidently as he could muster.

"Holy mither of Mary . . . me be . . . hurting, son. But shot before meself has been," Kileen muttered, barely more than a whisper. "What be happening . . . to our prisoner?"

Carlow explained and the older Ranger shut his eyes for a moment and groaned. Carlow told about the cowboy witness and the big man's shoulders rose and fell.

"Bridgeport asked me to help him arrest the lynch mob," Carlow said reluctantly. "Actually Mrs. Waulken did the first asking."

"Good, me son. Good. This ye . . . should be doin'. We were a party to his arrest, aye, we were," Kileen said. "Afterward, ye can wire . . . the good Captain. Tell hisself what has happened . . . and ask for . . . some more Rangers . . . to go after the . . . Rose Gang."

It wasn't the time to tell him about McNelly's wire. Or that the captain was certain Tanneman Rose had escaped and was behind these murders. That could come later. The news would only worry his uncle.

"May I help you, *señor*?"

The question startled Carlow and he looked up to see a woman with bright brown eyes and an easy smile. Her black hair was bound by a nurse's cap and her figure was covered in a light gray dress and white apron.

She was Mexican. She was beautiful.

Jerking off his hat, Carlow explained his presence, his words jolted by her stunning appearance. His hair brushed against heavy shoulders.

"I, ah, I'm Time Carlow. This is . . . my uncle. We're, ah, Rangers."

"Mariah, me nephew this be," Kileen weakly waved his hand in Carlow's direction.

"He ees spoke of you, *Señor* Carlow," she said. "I am Mariah Sanguel. I am his nurse."

All Carlow could think of was the lusty Angel Balta. He wondered if the same thought had occurred to his uncle. A quick glance at Kileen answered that question. It had.

She walked over to the foot of the bed, gazed at

Kileen and said, "You ees sleep now. That ees *bueno*." She looked up at Carlow. "Many *hombres* no strong enough to live from thees." She smiled again. "*Señor* Kileen weel live."

Carlow felt his uncle's head. It was clammy, yet sweaty.

"Lucky me be, son. 'Tis a fact ye have to be admittin'."

"Ze bullet went through. Eet hit no bone," Mariah offered. "No close to hees heart."

Looking up, Carlow asked, "Has the doctor seen him?" He decided that sounded like he was questioning her judgement and added, "I mean . . ."

"Dr. Morrison has treated heem—and give us orders. After he sleep, we weel give him water—and some broth." She pointed toward a table where two medicine bottles stood sentry. "Theen, he weel have some more medicine. *Si*."

"Get some sleep, Thunder. I'll be back to check on you."

Carlow turned away and saw Kileen's coat lying on the nearby chair. He reached into the pocket, retrieved the badge and pinned it on Kileen's bed, adjacent to his pillow. He had never seen his uncle wounded badly. From Carlow's lips came a blessing in Irish that he had learned from his mother—and his uncle.

"Aye. The Waulken lady, ye be sure she be doin' all right. A fine lady she be," Kileen said and added, "Me lad, a dream me be havin'. Tanneman Rose be ridin' through it."

Carlow nodded and stepped away. As he left, Mariah touched his arm. "You must tell me, *Señor* Carlow, *por favor*. When he come in, he asks if three persons have made ze bed and tells us not to put hees hat on ze bed—and not to put hees boots under it. And we had to move thees bed so eet faces the west, not the north. Do you know why he wants thees so?"

Her eyes examined Carlow's face and he felt dirty. Involuntarily, he brushed his coat with his hands, then chuckled. "Well, my uncle, he's kinda superstitious. Ah, he thinks it's bad luck to put a hat on a bed—or boots under it." He shook his head. "An' a bed that faces north, well, it'll bring nightmares. If three people make a bed, it means someone is going to die within the year. I think that's how it goes. I don't always get his superstitions straight. There are a bunch of them."

"Oh, I see. I have an aunt who ees so. Et ees most . . . ah, funny." She reached out and touched his sore left cheek. "You ees been hurt."

"It's all right. Looks worse than it feels."

"You must have ze doctor look at thees."

Not wanting to leave, but knowing he should, Carlow told her the marshal and his deputies were waiting for him, and he must go.

"I'll be back. After supper," Carlow said. "Will you be here?" The crimson at his neck was growing.

She bit her lower lip and ran her fingers along the raised cast-iron foot of the empty bed they were passing. "I weel be here. 'Til midnight et ees."

"Good. Thank you for all you're doing for . . . my uncle," Carlow said. "I look forward to seeing you again."

She smiled, said she must check on her other patients and walked in the other direction. Just before reaching the next occupied bed, she looked back.

Carlow was watching. He smiled and she returned the intimacy. Their eyes flirted.

Walking out, he passed a bed holding a young boy with his head wrapped in linen strips. The boy's mother sat beside him; her face was gray from lack of sleep and worry.

"A-are you a R-Ranger?" a small voice asked.

Carlow stopped as the question reached his tired mind. He turned and smiled. "Yes, I am. Ranger Time Carlow. What's your name?" He walked toward the bed.

The boy of eight or nine with wide blue eyes sat up, leaning on his elbows. His eyes were bright with interest. Even the boy's mother appeared energized by the youngster's sudden attention.

"I-I am D-Duval Jonas," the boy said. "I h-hurt my head. Y-yesterday."

The woman quickly explained the boy had been kicked by a horse and had actually been unconscious for three days. He had regained consciousness just a few hours ago.

"How is your friend? I saw him come in," the woman asked, softly.

"He's going to make it," Carlow said with more confidence than he felt. "And Duval? How's he doing?"

"Good, I think. Now that he's awake—and back with us. Praise the Lord." The woman bit her lip.

"That's good to hear," Carlow said, then frowned. "Well, Duval, you listen to your mother—and the doctor."

"I will, sir."

"I know you will."

They talked for a few minutes, with the boy doing most of the talking, as if feeling a need to make up for the lost time. Carlow listened intently, occasionally glancing up to see where Mariah might be. It was the first time he hadn't thought of Ellie. He knew he should be going to help Bridgeport, but he wasn't in a hurry and told himself that it was all right.

"You're going to arrest the men in that lynch mob, aren't you?" the woman finally asked.

"Yes."

She nodded approval. "Has the bank money been found?"

"No, ma'am, it hasn't," Carlow acknowledged. "Likely the man who shot Ranger Kileen has it. He tried to make it look like Mr. Waulken did it. I'm going after him, after the lynchers are arrested."

Duval leaned forward and pointed. "What kind of gun is that? I've never seen one like that!"

Patting the hand carbine, the young Ranger explained that it was a Winchester with the barrel and stock shortened.

"What's that on the stock? Is that an Indian mark?"

Carlow smiled. "Actually, it's an old Celtic symbol. Irish. For victory."

"And you have a revolver, too!" the boy exclaimed. "Isn't that a Colt?"

"Yes, it is." Carlow realized he had been stalling. "Duval, I gotta go, but I'll see you again."

"Promise?"

"Promise."

Near the entrance, Carlow saw a man talking quietly to one of the hospital's administrators. He heard the name "Kileen" and decided to see what was going on.

He vaguely recalled seeing the small, wiry man outside the hotel when they had ridden in yesterday. Like then, he had a pad of paper in his hand and took notes as the two men talked.

"Pardon me, couldn't help overhearing you mention Ranger Kileen's name," Carlow said, stepping up to both men. "You look like a newspaper man. Are you?"

Smiling slightly, the small man said, "Not quite. I write for *Harper's Bazaar*. On assignment out west, so to speak. I live in New York. Ever been there?" He glanced at the administrator, who quietly excused himself and left.

Carlow didn't answer his question. "You're interested in Ranger Kileen for what reason?"

Carlow's tired mind jumped to Kileen's secret about his real last name. He had a hunch that was what this interest was all about.

"Well, I'm not sure it's any of your business, sir."

"Look, I'm tired. That's my uncle who's lying in there, all shot up," Carlow said, his dark eyes snapping. "Don't play games with me. Why are you interested in Ranger Kileen?"

Swallowing, the reporter explained that he was certain Kileen was actually a former bare-knuckle prizefighter named Thunder Lucent from New York. He said the big man had killed a man with his fists and then disappeared. That had been years ago. His readers would be interested in the tale and the irony of the Irishman becoming a Texas Ranger.

Carlow listened, trying hard not to let his temper rise. When the reporter finished, Carlow asked, as quietly as he could manage, "What's your name?"

"Ah . . . Ronald James Pierson, sir," the reporter replied, surprised at the question.

"Well, Ronald, I'm sorry to tell you that the Ranger in there grew up in Missouri," Carlow said.

"And you know this how?"

"I'm his nephew. We lived close by, then moved to Texas," Carlow continued. "His nickname, 'Old Thunder', was given to him by his fellow Rangers because he liked to burp loudly. Sounds like an interesting coincidence to the fellow you're looking for. But just that."

"Oh. I was so sure," Pierson said, looking down at

his notes. "Maybe I'll do a story on this lynching. That was really something."

"That's your decision," Carlow said. "Just didn't want you writing something incorrect about my uncle." He looked at the man. "I wouldn't understand."

"Well, thank you. Thank you. I appreciate that." Pierson glanced at his notes, not wanting to engage with Carlow's glare. He wanted to ask how the young Ranger had gotten the bruises around his left eye, but didn't think it was a good idea.

"Sure," the young Ranger said and headed for the door.

Outside the hospital, he called to the waiting Chance and they walked toward the marshal's office. Mariah's sweetness settled into his mind, along with the boy's injury and his promise to return. That would be easy. He wanted to see Mariah again. For an instant, Ellie pushed into his mind, but she became Mariah. The reporter popped into his mind again and he decided to ask Bridgeport to reinforce his story about Kileen growing up in Missouri. The New York incident had occurred a long time ago, but still, he didn't want somebody coming for his uncle—either lawmen or relatives of the man Kileen had beaten.

As he strolled down the planked sidewalk, a heavy-set man in suspenders and baggy pants rushed from the general store.

"Ranger? May I have a word?"

Carlow stopped and turned back to face the nervous man. "Of course. How may I help you?"

Chance was barely a trot behind.

Hitching up his pants to make them settle better around his ample waist, the townsman looked left and right and whispered, "I just wanted you to know I had nothing to do with that awful lynching. Nothing." He glanced at Chance, shivered, and looked back at Carlow.

"I see. Were you there? At the jail this morning?"

"Well, yes, but I didn't want trouble," the agitated townsman said. "Just my money." His eyebrows danced with the words.

Carlow folded his arms. "I see. What did you think was going to happen? With that mob?"

The townsman scratched his head, then placed his right hand over his mouth and spoke through it. "I, ah, I don't know. Rightly. I just, ah, went along. Some friends of mine wanted me to." His hand went to his forehead and rubbed it.

"If I were you," Carlow growled, "I'd give myself up to Marshal Bridgeport. Might help."

"What do you mean?" The man's face glowed crimson.

Carlow hooked his thumbs into his gunbelt. "Well, for starters, you boys killed an innocent man, assaulted an officer of the law and beat up a woman."

"That's not quite what happened," the townsman protested. "You make it sound . . . terrible. That German stole our money. Every cent I had was in that bank!"

"I'm sorry for your loss, but Mr. Waulken didn't rob the bank."

"You arrested him," the townsman gulped, color retreating from his face. "You have all kinds of evidence. A gray horse. That fancy rifle. Even that wood mask. I heard all about it. My God! What else do you want?"

Carlow wanted to ask the man how he knew this information, but it didn't matter. He dropped his arms to his sides.

"Well, I figure you've also already heard about his alibi, mister, or you wouldn't have stopped me." His eyes locked with the man's eyes and wouldn't let go.

Waving his arms, the townsman asked in a rushed voice, "What makes you think that cowboy was telling the truth? I hear they were in it together."

Carlow cocked his head to the side. "Lynching is murder, mister. For any reason. Pure and simple. I gave you a suggestion. Do what you want." He turned to his wolf-dog. "Come on, Chance. We've got work to do."

Carlow resumed walking with Chance bounding behind him.

"Goddamn you! You should be looking for our money!"

The curse sought the Ranger's attention, but he continued on to the marshal's office. Around him the town seemed to be busying itself in a rush to forget the morning's awfulness. The combined marshal's office and jail was crowded as he joined the three other lawmen standing inside.

Entering, Carlow saw Marshal Bridgeport, the stuttering Deputy Payne and the other deputy, Joe Roth. Six empty cells lined the back walls. The marshal's desk, although heavily scratched, was quite neat. Only a few papers occupied the right corner; the rest of the desktop was empty. In the corner of the room, a black stove was working to keep a coffeepot ready. Above the stove was a framed photograph of the governor.

On the adjoining short wall was a rack of rifles and shotguns. Barred widows sported heavy wooden shutters that could be closed from the inside and braced. Two wall lamps had been recently cleaned and quietly awaited their next usage.

Roth was confident as Bridgeport introduced him to Carlow. Like the Ranger, he wore two handguns, with one carried handle forward and the other with the handle to the back.

"Glad to meet you, Ranger," Roth declared as they

shook hands. "Sounds like you boys had a rough morning." His pockmarked face broke into lines around his eyes and mouth. "Sorry I missed it. Another gun might've made the difference." He pushed back the brim of his hat. "How's your partner? Heard he took a bad one."

"He's feeling poorly, but he'll live, I reckon. Be laid up for a while, though." Carlow didn't like the man; he wasn't sure why, but he didn't like him.

Bridgeport grabbed several gumdrops from the sack on his desk and popped them into his mouth. "Arrest warrants I 'ave, for eight." He pointed to the only papers on his desk. "There were more, but that's all I can recall." He rattled off the eight names.

Carlow wondered if the marshal was deliberately forgetting some important civic leaders—or friends—who had been part of the lynching. There had definitely been more than eight men there.

"Would you care for a gumdrop? Have a wet? Ah, hot tea? It's fresh. Made it myself." Bridgeport motioned toward the sack, then the stove. "Wish we had some wad . . . ah, some cake . . . to go with it."

"No, thanks. How do you want to handle this?" Carlow said.

"I took the liberty to wire Ranger 'eadquarters, told them what 'ad 'appened and received approval for you to 'elp us. It's there." He pointed to the smaller sheet of paper beside the warrants.

Carlow walked over to the desk and read the telegram, half angered at the lawman's audacity, half glad to have the authority made clear. There was no indication in the wire that McNelly had received his own report. He laid down the paper and said nothing.

Putting two more gumdrops in his mouth, the British marshal announced he wanted Carlow with him;

one of his deputies would cover the back door of whatever building was involved. The other deputy would remain at the jail to guard the men as they were arrested. Joe Roth hitched his double gun belts and volunteered to go with Bridgeport and Carlow; Payne was quite satisfied to remain behind.

Meanwhile, across town, six men spat their anger at the turn of events in a hastily called meeting above the lumber company.

"What the hell does Bridgeport think he's doing?" Ira Samuelson bellowed. "He should be out looking for our money—not arresting good and true men. We were trying to help, that's all. Just trying to help."

"We weren't the only ones." Turner Omallden, the man who had stopped Carlow earlier, added his own feelings. "That damn Irish Ranger told me I should give myself up. Can you believe that?"

The six men continued their angry accusations, then became silent as the futility of the exchange became apparent.

"Well, I'm not running. That's for damn sure," Samuelson said. "I'll sit in my office—with my shotgun—an' just wait for the bastards." He shook his head affirmatively for emphasis.

George Tyler, a tall man who owned the town's gun shop and held aspirations of becoming mayor, stood and faced the others. "There is a simple way out of this."

He paused for dramatic effect, waiting for their eager questions. His temple pounded with the eagerness he felt. Pulling on his suitcoat, he licked his lips and gave the answer they were waiting for.

"It's simple. We get the town council to fire Bridgeport—and we hire a marshal, ah, more suitable to our town's needs," Tyler said in an even voice that carried only a hint of his Eastern upbringing. "Some-one who will spend his time looking for our money."

"Makes good sense to me," Samuelson agreed. He always seemed taller than he actually was; his dominating voice was the major reason. It could take over any room, any conversation. He loved the sound of it.

Looking around, Tyler took Samuelson's expression for agreement from all of them. He loved being in control of a room. "I'll go to Dickersly and get him to have a quick town meeting. We can have this thing done by midday."

"You think Dickersly will go for that?" James Concannon asked. The small man with an impeccable manner of dressing ran an insurance, real estate and loan business. He adjusted his silk cravat so it sat well under his pinstriped vest.

"Why wouldn't he?" Tyler's eyes flashed, matching the anger in his voice.

Concannon pulled on his French-cuffed sleeves and took his time in responding. "Don't you plan on running against him in the next election? Ol' Wilford Dickersly might like the idea of you—and some of the rest of us—out of the way. Or, at least painted with judicial stain." He held up his fingers and counted the offenses against them. "Assaulting an officer of the law. Attacking an innocent woman. Destruction of public property. We broke that door something awful." He blinked his eyes and finished, "And, of course, we hanged an innocent man. That, my friends, is murder."

Taken by surprise by the argument, Tyler could only ask if the businessman had a better idea.

"No, I don't, George," Concannon answered, looking around the room. "But I think we should be prepared for him to reject the idea."

Omallden asked if it made sense to go and talk with Judge DeVere; Tyler reminded him the feisty judge had warned them not to take the law into their own hands.

"What if Bridgeport—and that Irish Ranger—come before you get that meeting put together?" The question came from a round-faced man in a bowtie. He owned the barbershop and bathhouse.

"If that happens, Davis, I suggest you go peacefully," Tyler said. "All of you. Don't make a fuss. After all, the town has a right to defend itself. And that's what we were doing. We can deal with this in court if we have to."

"Who are you going to get for the new marshal?" Omallden asked.

"What about Hires Quireling? He can handle himself," Tyler stated.

"Do you think he'd take it?" Omallden asked. "I thought he was busy working on that little ranch he just bought."

Tyler smiled. "I happen to know that he could use the money. No reason he couldn't do both."

Samuelson stood and shook his fist. "By God, you're right. I know what you're saying, Concannon, but we've got to try."

Taking the pipe from his mouth, the gruff owner of the lumber company asked, "What about the others who were in this? There were fourteen of us altogether, I think. Yeah, fourteen."

"Well, they had a chance to come to this meeting and didn't," Tyler pointed out. "I think Peter Wisson is going to run. That's what I heard."

The meeting quickly settled on the idea of getting a new marshal and began to break up. As the townsmen returned their chairs to the table on the far side of the room, Tyler added one more thought.

"It would be helpful, I think, if that cowboy understood the situation." Tyler smiled.

"He's in my saloon. Or was," the bearded saloon keeper said. "I'll talk to him."

"I'll go along with you," Samuelson said.

"Excellent," Tyler acknowledged. "I'll go see the mayor and get this nonsense behind us."

Chapter Twenty-seven

It was past noon when Bridgeport and Carlow reached the law offices of Wilford Dickersly, mayor of Strickland and a respected elder statesman of the region. Chance took his waiting position in the shade of the building. The British lawman had decided it would be politically smart to inform the town's titular head of the upcoming arrests. Actually, it had been Carlow's suggestion and Bridgeport had eagerly accepted it.

Deputy Joe Roth was accompanying James Concannon to jail; the immaculately dressed businessman had immediately coughed up the names of six other men in the lynch mob, seeking leniency for his cooperation. Bridgeport assured him it would be duly noted. After dropping off Concannon, Roth was to find Judge DeVere and get the additional warrants.

Bridgeport and Carlow stepped into the small office, which contained two walls of bookcases jammed with books, pamphlets and magazines.

"Afternoon, Marshal," Dickersly said warmly. "I understand you're shaking up our fair town and arresting some leading citizens."

Wilford Dickersly stood up behind his desk and held out his hand. His desk was packed with papers and files whose location only he seemed to understand. The mayor's shirt was rumpled, as were his pants. A too-small vest hung open. His bald head was offset by massive, mostly white sideburns and matching eyebrows. An easy smile matched his twinkling eyes. He was short, chunky and considerably older than Kileen or Bridgeport, but Carlow thought there was something about the friendly appearing man that read tough.

"Blimey, don't know about that," Bridgeport said, and shook the mayor's hand, "but we're trying to bring law and order back to this fine community, wot." He explained what they were doing, with some British military slang thrown in for emphasis.

The mayor smiled and glanced at Carlow, who grinned.

"Good day, Mayor. I'm Ranger Time Carlow." The young Ranger held out his hand.

"Oh, sure. Your Ranger partner was shot this morning," Dickersly said, shaking hands with gusto. "How is he?"

"Thanks for asking," Carlow responded. "He'll make it, I think. Going to be a while though."

"I'm very sorry this happened. Especially in our town," Dickersly said. "Please let me know if I can be of help in any way. The hospital care is, of course, a city expense."

Carlow thanked him for the generosity.

Dickersly turned his attention back to Bridgeport. "Had a visit from George Tyler." The mayor's smile waned slightly. "He wanted me to call a meeting of the council. To fire you."

"George Tyler's on my list. Eight I know for certain and 'ave warrants for their arrest. Just learned there be six more. Their warrants will be in our 'ands soon." Bridgeport waved the sheet of paper. "We not be firing into the brown, ya know."

Carlow guessed the British army expression had to do with firing at a group without having a specific target.

Fiddling with the top papers on his desk, the older leader spoke evenly without looking up. "I know, Lark. I told him there would be no such meeting. No such firing either. That you were doing what needed doing." He looked up into Bridgeport's face. "Lark, the town's going to be split on this. Money talks. While some folks will understand your approach, a lot more are going to be upset that you're arresting good townspeople, while our money goes unsought and unfound."

His voice rising slightly, Bridgeport described what had happened. The immediate arrest of Alben Waulken and the evidence found at his place. The subsequent enlightenment by a neighboring cowboy, who indicated the German farmer had been set up. Sadly, they had no clues, other than the likelihood that Kileen's sniper had probably been involved in the bank robbery.

"Can I assume no one on your list of townsmen had anything to do with the shooting of the Ranger?" Dickersly asked.

"That's correct, Mayor," Carlow answered. "The shooter was from out of town. I have an identification and plan to go after him as soon as the lynchers are arrested. There's a good likelihood he's connected to the murder of an old friend of ours, a former Ranger—as well as the bank robbery. It appears he set up Mr. Waulken. Very well, I'm sorry to say."

"May I announce that to the newspapers?"

"Sure."

"Does this . . . outlaw . . . have a name?"

Carlow chuckled. "He does. Tanneman Rose. He was a Ranger until we caught him robbing banks with his brothers. His brothers are dead now. Tanneman broke out of jail and is trying to kill all of the men who put him there."

"I see," Dickersly said. "Why didn't you suspect him right away—instead of going after Mr. Waulken?"

Slightly annoyed at the question, Carlow explained they had just learned of the jailbreak and faked death. With that, Dickersly pronounced his understanding of Waulken's arrest. Changing the subject, he suggested the lynchers be held for the circuit judge, instead of requiring Judge DeVere to have to do this distasteful job. A new judge, replacing the murdered Judge Cline, would be appointed soon. Dickersly also pointed out that finding a local jury that would convict them might be difficult.

Bridgeport agreed with both observations, but indicated if the jury didn't convict the men, he would resign.

"Don't tell anyone that, please," Dickersly said. "This town needs your strength, Lark." He turned to Carlow. "What do you think are the chances of catching this killer—this Tanneman Rose, Ranger?"

"I don't intend to stop until I do," Carlow spat.

"I believe you, son."

Carlow wanted to ask the man not to call him "son," but didn't. The mayor was a man to stand with, and his opinion of Marshal Bridgeport was beginning to change. The British lawman had tenacity.

Holding out his hand again, Dickersly said he would be informing the newspapers of the plans and that it might be helpful in the long run. An informed citizenry was an important asset, he pronounced, and asked to be kept abreast of their progress.

Hunching his shoulders, Carlow said, "Got a thought you boys might want to consider about all this."

"I'm listening."

"Blimey, me, too."

Carlow pushed his hat back on his forehead. "Well, nothing we do is going to bring Mr. Waulken back. And putting all these bastards in jail isn't going to help Mrs. Waulken either."

Dickersly leaned forward, folding his arms.

"Why not make all of them fix up the Waulken place? The barn, the house, the corral, all of it," Carlow said. "Make them tend her crops. Say for five years." He paused. "And each of them has to give her a hundred dollars."

"I like it." Dickersly nodded. "Helluva lot better than the other way."

"Mrs. Waulken would 'ave to agree," Bridgeport added. "She may want them punished, instead."

Carlow pulled on his gunbelt. "Thought of that, too. They work for her. She's in charge. Anybody who bows out, you put him in jail."

Dickersly laughed and said, "I suggest you get them rounded up first . . . before telling them."

"Makes sense. You need to talk with Mrs. Waulken first, anyway." Carlow headed for the door with Bridgeport a step behind.

They stepped out of the office and a shot rang out, splitting its way into the side of the building a few feet away. Bridgeport dove to the ground. As Carlow dove himself, he grabbed Chance and pulled the wolf-dog to him for safety.

A second shot spit into the planked sideway below them.

"Blimey, it be Ira Samuelson," Bridgeport said, drawing his pistol.

"Let me handle this, Marshal," Carlow said, and told Chance to wait.

He stood. Another shot spit into the building wall behind him.

"Get down, boy! The blooming wog'll shoot ya."

"I don't think so, or he would've already." Carlow stepped off the sidewalk into the street. "He's real brave when it's fourteen to one."

People were scattering for places of safety. A buggy with an almost out-of-control horse ran past him and toward the far end of the street. In several buildings, people were staring out their windows from behind curtains or glimpsing the action through barely opened doors.

With his hands at his sides, Carlow walked toward Ira Samuelson, who stood on the sidewalk across the street.

An agitated Samuelson yelled, "Stay where you are—or I'll kill you."

"You've already killed one innocent man today."

"I mean it." He fired another shot from his Henry carbine. The bullet thumped into the dirt street in front of Carlow.

Walking directly at him, Carlow looked into Samuelson's eyes, expecting a change in his gaze to warn him if the businessman decided to try to shoot him.

Samuelson levered his gun and brought it to his shoulder. "I mean it. I'm not going to jail. I'm not."

"Yes, you are, Mr. Samuelson. You'll have a fair trial," Carlow said evenly.

Samuelson hesitated, then fired again. This time the bullet soared past Carlow's head.

Carlow stopped. "Mr. Samuelson, you are under arrest. Drop the gun."

"No! No! I won't!" Samuelson yelled and tried to lever the gun again, but this time Carlow was next to him as the man completed the loading action.

"Give me the gun." Carlow yanked it from him, pushing the barrel down and away from both of them. The new bullet slammed into the sidewalk at their feet.

Across the street, Dickersly had joined a now-standing Bridgeport.

"That boy is pure guts," the mayor said under his breath.

"Blimey, I'd say!"

Chapter Twenty-eight

Just outside of town, Tanneman Rose reined up beside his peddler wagon and the other wagon horse. The brown horse raised its head from grazing, acknowledged the appearance of its wagon mate and returned to eating. A small stream meandered through the narrow wash and continued on to its destiny. The location was perfect for leaving the wagon; anyone riding by on the main road wouldn't see it.

An idea was forming in the former Ranger's mind, one given birth by not knowing for certain whether or not Kileen was dead. The perfectionist in him was uncomfortable leaving Strickland with that uncertainty. He didn't like leaving Time Carlow alive either. Second chances were difficult to come by. Especially when it came to killing Rangers. And especially those two.

By the time he swung down, he knew he was going back, as U.S. Deputy Marshal Jubal Winchell. Wouldn't take much to get ready, he told himself. A badge from his costume trunk could be put on later. He switched to a flat-brimmed hat, in case someone had seen him from a distance earlier. His suit was fine, but he changed the silk cravat to a blue one. The belt gun at his waist was also fine. He added a knife and its sheath to the belt.

For the first time, he realized one of his fake eyebrows had fallen off. He cursed. That should never happen. Never. Forcing himself to be calm, he decided to switch from the thick mustache to a dark goatee and fake eyeglasses, and leave his natural eyebrows as they were. It took him several minutes longer than usual, as he rechecked the fake hair around his mouth to make certain the glue was holding properly.

While he waited for the glue to dry, he checked on his spider. At first it wasn't moving, but the spider wiggled around after he shook the jar.

"Come on, Portland. You can do better than that," he said. "I'm going in to kill Kileen. Who knows? He might show up as a spider, too. A big one." He laughed long and loudly.

After switching his saddle to the second wagon horse, he decided to harness the first animal to the wagon. It would make his transformation into the peddler a littler quicker if necessary. Neither horse was the kind a lawman or an outlaw would ride. Long-legged, swift steeds were the preferred choice. He would buy another horse at the livery and explain that his regular horse had been shot from under him, coming from Fort Worth. Having an extra horse gave him options, if he needed them. It had worked before.

Before riding away, he remembered his saddle sheath was carrying the Sharps. A quick switch put a Winchester in his boot and the big gun was hidden in the wagon. He grinned. No one was as careful as he was. He touched his necklace under his shirt and chanted.

Two hours later, U.S. Deputy Marshal Jubal Winchell reined up at the Strickland Livery. He put on his badge just before stopping. There was no need to alert the town that another lawman had appeared, especially with a curious Time Carlow around.

A bald man with wide suspenders holding up his filthy pants looked up from sweeping.

"Can I he'p yuh?" Punky Elliott, the livery operator, asked, leaning on the broom. "Lawman, ain't yuh?"

Tanneman, as Winchell, swung down, shook his head and pushed his glasses back on his nose. "Lost my horse. Damn good one. Shot from under me. Coming from Fort Worth." He brushed imaginary dust from his coat. "I'm U.S. Marshal Jubal Winchell. I'm in pursuit of Bobby Joe and Lifton McDorn. Brothers. They're wanted for murder and train robbery. In Missouri." He hitched up his gunbelt. "Been after them . . . for too damn long." His voice was deep. Crusty. Authoritative. "Any strangers come into town today? Hard-looking boys. Well-armed."

"Not that came through hyar," Elliott explained. "'Course, the stage came in a while back. Strangers there. All o' them."

Tanneman shook his head. "No. They'd be riding. Good horses."

"Yeah, heard o' them boys. Did they . . . ambush yuh?"

"Yeah. Guess I was lucky," Tanneman said. "Bought this fella from a farmer nearby. Best he had."

"Yeah. Farmers ain't got need for fast hosses. Jes' so they kin pull a wagon."

Without any prompting, Elliott told him about the morning's incident and the recent bank robbery. Tanneman asked if the town's money had been secured yet. The operator spat a thick brown stream, cursed and said no, but he thought the Rangers would be helping to find it.

"Don't believe in banks," Elliott pronounced. "Keep my money in a secret place."

"Good for you." Rubbing his chin, Tanneman asked, "Rangers, you say?"

Elliott eagerly told about the two Rangers seeking the killer of a local rancher and helping to find and arrest the bank robber. He told about the lynching and the arrests that had followed. He said the big Ranger had been shot and taken to the hospital, but didn't know the Ranger's condition, except he'd heard he was still alive.

"Hmm, anybody see this shooter?" Tanneman asked, looking stern. "Sounds like something the McDorn brothers would do."

"Not that I know of. Marshal Bridgeport might know somethin'. He an' his deputies been real busy, though," Elliott answered, shaking his head. "But that other Ranger, the young one, he's goin' after the shooter."

"Good. Has he left yet?"

"No, that's his black horse. A fine one, I'll tell ya. The other Ranger's hoss ain't livery slop neither." Elliott said and rubbed his bald head. "He's a tough one, that young Ranger. Has a wolf for a pet. Can you believe that?"

"A wolf?"

"Looks like one to me." Elliott spat a thick stream of tobacco juice. "That Ranger boy bin a'helpin' Lark with the arrests o' folks who dun the lynchin'. Kinda a wild day. Ira Samuelson even did some shootin' at him an' Lark. Heard tell the Ranger jes' walked ov'r to Ira, slick as ya please. No gun in his hand or nuthin'. Tolt Ira he were under arrest an' took his gun away. Jes' like that. Somethin' to watch, I reckon." He spat again, not pleased with the texture this time. "With all that a'goin' on, reckon your two brothers could'a slipped in real easy like."

"Sounds like it."

Patting the man on the back, Tanneman said, "Say, I'm going to need a good horse. Got any to sell?"

"Sure do. Got three that'll take yuh anywhar."

"I'd like to take a look."

The livery operator disappeared into the barn and quickly returned, leading three horses: a tall bay; a black with three stockings and a lineback dun.

"How much for the bay?"

"Haff to have thirty dollars for 'im." Elliott patted the bay's neck.

As he felt in his coat pocket for money, Tanneman said, "Say, I'm pretty sure I put a bullet in one of those McDorn boys. Is there a hospital in town?"

Elliott gladly described the location.

A few minutes later, Tanneman switched his saddle and bridle to the new horse and headed for the hospital, leading his wagon horse on a rope. From the livery operator, he had learned Carlow was now with the local marshal in his office and jail. Perfect. He couldn't help smiling. How gifted he was. It was amazing. From practice he had learned well that people saw what they wanted to see. It was the gift of disguise passed on from his previous life. Only the eyes were impossible to hide—or change. They carried eternity, he felt, and were unique to each person. He glanced over at the spider jar, but decided he wouldn't be able to tell if it had Portland's eyes or not.

Right now the only people who knew him in Strickland were Kileen and Carlow. Soon that big bastard would be worm meat and the young one would follow when Tanneman got the chance.

At the marshal's office, twelve of the lynch mob had been arrested and were now being held in the jail, two to a cell. The remaining two lynch mob participants,

George Tyler and Ernest Clay, had left town. Several townspeople said they had left together.

From the farthest cell, Turner Omallden yelled, "Don't get too cocky, Lark. We're gonna be oughta here—an' you're gonna be out a job."

Jeb Tatem banged his fist against the bars of his cell. "You're going to be sorry, Bridgeport. Real sorry."

"I'm going to gather supplies, check on Thunder and then head out—after his shooter," Carlow said. "Or do you need me to go after those last two lynchers?"

"I thank you, but we can get them without Ranger 'elp," Bridgeport noted and reached into the sack on his desk for the last of the gumdrops.

Carlow declined Bridgeport's offer of the candy.

"Joe will go after them—as soon as 'e's ready, right, Joe?" Bridgeport popped two gumdrops into his mouth. "I figure they'll head for Clay's father's ranch."

"On my way." Deputy Roth walked over to the rifle rack and took down a Winchester.

"Cartridges in the lower desk drawer," Bridgeport said. "I want them both back 'ere. Alive, you 'ear?"

Roth grinned at Carlow and left.

A few minutes later, the cowboy who had provided Waulken's alibi stepped gingerly into the marshal's office. His spurs clanked on the wooden floor and he seemed unnerved by the noise. He yanked off his weathered hat and pushed his yellow hair back on his head. The sun had not touched his forehead above his hat.

"Marshal, thought I'd better come to see you," he said, nervously glancing at the men in the cells. "I was wrong about seein' Alben Waulken yesterday mornin'. I'm sorry, but it was the day before." He waved his hand to indicate the change in days. "Yeah, it were the day before." He returned his hat to his head and started to back out of the office. "Sorry I couldn't be of help."

"Aye, an' which of the fine gentlemen behind me did 'elp you come to that change of thought?" Bridgeport asked, leaning against the desk.

The cowboy looked for a moment at the cells, then back at the marshal. He didn't meet Bridgeport's gaze, staring instead at the desk itself.

"Ah, nobody told me nothin', Marshal."

"Bloody lie, wot."

Carlow folded his arms. "You know, whether Waulken was innocent or not has nothing to do with the crimes these boys are charged with."

The cowboy looked like he was going to cry. "Don't know nothin' about that, Ranger. Just wanted to set things straight as far as my seein' was concerned."

Waving his hand at the man, Bridgeport disgustedly told him to leave.

"You know, we have other evidence to prove Mr. Waulken was innocent," Carlow declared, and looked at each man in the cell. "He was set up by another man. Mr. Waulken would've been set free, if you boys hadn't been so damn eager to take the law into your own hands."

Both Bridgeport and Payne looked surprised and the cowboy wasn't certain how to respond. Finally, he regathered his courage and left without speaking.

"Why didn't you tell us that when we came to the marshal's office, Ranger?" Omallden said, standing against the cell bars.

"I did. You weren't listening. Too busy yelling threats at your marshal here."

The twelve men behind bars looked like they had been struck with whips.

"I'll see you later, Marshal," Carlow said. "I'll write

out my statement—for the court—in case I'm not back in time."

Bridgeport shook his head in agreement, sat down at his desk and asked Payne to go get some candy from the general store.

Outside, Carlow felt the tension of the past two days hit him hard. Lack of sleep was piling onto his mind. The more he thought about it, the more he decided to get some sleep before starting. Being tired was a good way to make a mistake. Kileen's horse would go along as his second mount. He reminded himself to include in his letter to the court that Waulken had been afraid of horses and couldn't have ridden to town and back on the gray horse. Or on any horse.

There was no proof, of course, but he felt it was owed to Margareitte Waulken to make that statement. He was certain she was telling the truth. He was also certain one or more of the lynchers had scared the cowboy into changing his story.

After purchasing supplies and eating some jerky, Carlow headed to the livery to leave them for tomorrow and check on his horses. Chance trailed him happily. All he had to go on what was what the dress store lady had told him. A gray three-piece suit. A red tie. A gray bowler and thick mustache. The man had headed south. It wasn't much, but it was what he had. It was the closest the Rangers had been to Mirabile's killer, he was certain of that. McNelly's wire had convinced him of what he had suspected: Tanneman Rose was alive and behind all of this madness.

"Punky, I'm going to leave these here until the morning. I'm riding out then. That all right?" Carlow said.

"Hi, Ranger, yah just missed that U.S. deputy marshal. He sure liked your hoss," Punky Elliott said from where he was throwing hay into an empty stall.

Carlow laid down his supplies in the corner and stood up. "What do you mean, Punky? A United States marshal was here?"

"Oh, sure nuff, he was. Handful o' minutes ago." The livery operator spat a stream of tobacco juice. "Came in on some farm hoss. A chestnut with two stockings. His'n had bin shot by some owlhoots he was a'chasin'. You prob'ly know who they was . . . if'n I could 'member their names." He scratched his rear end. "Seems like it were some brothers. Maybe."

Carlow slipped the bridle onto Shadow's head and felt more tired than ever. "What was his name? The lawman."

"Don' 'member that neither." Elliott spat again, evaluating the thickness of the stream. "Bought a long-legged bay off'a me. Good belly. Run forever."

With some prodding from Carlow, Elliott described the mysterious lawman as wearing a gray suit and a wide, flat-brimmed hat. He was a little taller than Elliott, and thinner. Had a goatee and wore a fancy gunbelt.

"Where was he headed? I just came from the jail," Carlow said.

"Well, he was gonna check out the hospital. Thought he'd put lead in one o' them boys he was a'chasin'," Elliott pronounced, proud of his attention to detail.

"Maybe I'll see him over there. Going to check on Thunder . . . ah, Ranger Kileen."

"Sure nuff." Elliott spat again.

The livery operator didn't notice Carlow was already running toward the hospital. He didn't like the sound of this. A federal lawman would have checked in at the marshal's office first. A courtesy, if nothing else. He was afraid of who it might really be. Tanneman Rose.

Chapter Twenty-nine

At the hospital, Tanneman reined up outside the gray building and swung down, tying both horses to the rack. Touching the brim of his hat to a passing couple, he went inside. He was pleased with himself. It was almost too easy. He would ask for the wounded Ranger and when no one was looking, Tanneman would kill him with his knife. He would be gone before the death was even discovered.

A stern nurse coming his way was the first step.

"Afternoon, ma'am. I'm United States Deputy Marshal Jubal Winchell," he said, smiling and tipping his hat. "In town after some outlaws. Wanted to see Ranger Kileen, if I might. He's an old friend."

"Of course." Her stern facade vanished in response to his smile and she indicated which bed the wounded Kileen was resting in.

He thanked her and headed that way.

Duval Jonas, the young boy with the head injury, saw him walking by and yelled out, "Hi, Ranger. Are you a friend of Time Carlow and Thunder Kileen?"

Tanneman spun in his tracks, fighting his mind for control. Such an announcement was the last thing he needed, but there was nothing he could do about it. He forced himself to smile and said, "Well, good afternoon, young man. What's your name?"

The chair scooted beside the boy's bed was empty and Tanneman guessed one of his parents had been there recently.

"I'm Duval Jonas. Ranger Carlow said he would be back to see me again."

"Well, I'm sure he will, son."

The boy pointed at the badge. "Is that a Ranger badge?"

"No, it's not. I'm United States Deputy Marshal Jubal Winchell," he pronounced. "I'm in town trailing some outlaws. Heard about Ranger Kileen and wanted to see him."

"Oh, well, I'm sure he'll be glad to see you," Duval said. "Do you want me to go with you? The nurse says I can get up now."

Trying to remain composed, Tanneman thanked the boy and said that he would prefer to go by himself. Obviously disappointed, Duval Jonas muttered his understanding and lay back on his bed. The disguised former Ranger moved away quickly, hoping for no more interruptions.

No one was in sight as he reached the foot of Kileen's bed. The big Irishman was sleeping. He looked little different from the last time Tanneman had seen him up close. That had been the day Kileen and the other Rangers had escorted him to jail. Kileen, Carlow and Mirabile. The three lawmen had changed his life forever. The sight of them was burned into his mind. They raced through his dreams.

He smiled. Mirabile—and Deconer—were gone. Now Kileen. Then Carlow and McNelly, then it was done, except for some pissant jurors and that clown marshal. Tanneman's demons would be satisfied. He touched the necklace under his shirt and mumbled. The thought of their reincarnations bothered him and he shook his head to remove the thought. He would know them, he assured himself—even if they came back as spiders or owls or horses. He would kill them again. His chuckle was louder than he wanted.

The big Ranger stirred and mumbled something in his sleep. His hands rested on his stomach above the blanket. Tanneman slipped around the bed until he was next to Kileen. A part of him wanted to wake Kileen up so he would know who was killing him, but that wasn't smart. A quick slice across Kileen's throat would end it once and for all. He withdrew the shiny blade, adjusted it in his hand for easy cutting and slid it toward Kileen's neck.

"Good-bye, Aaron, you miserable bastard," he snarled through clenched teeth.

"Hey! What are you doing? You said he was your friend!" Duval yelled.

The boy was out of bed and running toward Kileen's bed and Tanneman. "Hey! He's trying to kill him! Help! Help!"

Drawn by the boy's alarm, Mariah Sanguel appeared from behind the temporary curtain that closed off another bed. In her hands was a filled bedpan.

"Eet ees a keeller!" she screamed, then ran toward Tanneman and threw the urine in the pan at him.

He stepped back as the yellow liquid slapped against his face and chest. She followed her liquid assault with a blow to his face with the empty pan.

Kileen awoke disoriented from Tanneman's cry and saw the disguised former Ranger poised to kill him. The Irish Ranger's left fist backhanded Tanneman, driving into his groin. The Irishman's right fist followed to the same location. Both blows used all the strength he could muster. Fresh blood seeped onto his hospital gown as he fell back, exhausted.

Staggering from the awful pain in his groin, the burning in his eyes and Mariah's continued blows, Tanneman dropped his knife and grabbed for his holstered pistol in a wild attempt to finish the job he had started.

Mariah slammed the empty pan onto his gun hand as he attempted to clear the holster. He screamed in pain and his gun flopped against the bed and slid to the ground. Dropping the pan, she leaned over and grabbed the fallen revolver. Tanneman cursed and pushed her out of the way. She bounced against the bed and fell to the floor, still holding the gun.

He ran, desperate for freedom.

Bravely, Duval stepped in front of him and stated, "You're no lawman. You tried to kill Ranger Kileen."

Cursing, Tanneman slammed the boy into the foot of the closest bed and raced on.

After him came a determined Mariah with his revolver in her hands, not daring to shoot in the hospital.

Pulling himself up, the boy yelled after her, "Get him, Miss Mariah. He's not a lawman. He's a killer."

Tanneman cleared the hospital door, his mind a whirl of fear. He jumped on the bay, yanking free the reins and the lead rope of the wagon horse, and spurred the new mount away. The chestnut followed, its gallop barely keeping up with the long-legged bay.

Mariah cleared the hospital door and saw him escaping. With both hands, she cocked the gun, aimed it and fired. She missed and cocked the weapon again. But he had already disappeared down the closest alley. Gasping for breath, she ran after him, reaching the alley only to see that it was empty.

Hurrying toward the marshal's office, she saw Time Carlow running toward her from the other direction and waved the gun in the air. The young Ranger was by her side quickly.

"What's the matter, Mariah?"

"A killer . . . he try to keel . . . your friend. Beeg Thunder. He had a . . . big knife . . . and thees gun."

His face revealed the question before it came.

"Your uncle . . . he ees . . . all right," she said. "He hit . . . thees keeller . . . in the . . . ah, private area. I heet heem with a bedpan. Threw ze night's waste at heem."

"Which way did this man go?" Carlow asked.

"He rode down that alley." Her voice sagged. "He ees gone."

"How did you get his gun?"

She explained what had happened, including the boy's alarm. She described the man as best she could, including the badge on his coat lapel.

It had to be Tanneman.

Carlow spun and headed away, biting his lower lip to keep his emotions from spreading onto his face. Tanneman Rose had almost killed his beloved uncle. Then Carlow stopped.

Mariah shivered and dropped her hands to her sides. Her lips quivered. Carlow turned back and brought her to him. She whimpered, and her fear burst into his shoulder. He held her shaking body as she sobbed out the emotion.

His own tired mind whirred. Tanneman's quick return to Strickland meant he was confident. So far, he had a right to be.

Mariah's gentle hand against his chest sent the threat scurrying for the corners of his mind. She looked up into his eyes.

"I am sorry, *Señor* Carlow," she whispered. "I do not mean to cause you ze embarrassment of such public . . . display."

He chuckled and wiped the last tear working its way down her cheek. "Thank you for saving my uncle's life. And holding you makes for a wonderful day." He brushed away more dampness. "I only wish the circumstances were different. I've got to go after him."

Neither noticed two women walk past them, smiling and talking again only after moving out of earshot.

Mariah held up the gun. "Here ees gun."

She smiled softly and backed away slightly. "Oh, please be so careful . . . please. Come back to . . . us." Mariah shivered and dropped her hands to her sides.

"Take care of Duval—and my uncle—'til I get back," Carlow said quietly. "I'll tell the marshal what has happened. He's awfully busy right now, but he'll send over a deputy to stand guard when he can."

"*Si.*"

Chapter Thirty

Tanneman Rose cleared a shallow hill, eased his new horse into a walk and looked back at the small shapes that were Strickland. A Texas sun had taken charge of the day and was pushing everything toward cover. He looked down at his empty holster and cursed. At least he was still carrying a Winchester.

The stench of damp urine on his coat and shirt filled his nostrils. He had to assume someone would come after him. That someone would be Time Carlow. Of all the Rangers, Tanneman feared the young gunfighter the most. He was certain Carlow had been a Roman commander in a previous life.

Swinging his mount to the west, Tanneman headed for his peddler's wagon. The chestnut following struggled to keep up. If he moved quickly, he should be able to create the right picture for the young Ranger when he came. So he could kill him. Easily.

Anger swelled again as he galloped across the prairie with his wagon horse running as fast as it could. He hated Kileen and Carlow—and he hated failure. The need for perfection gnawed on him and drove him.

As soon as Tanneman reached the wagon, he removed the saddle and bridle from the bay and slapped the animal on the rear. Startled, the horse whinnied and began to run. He was certain the road itself would not reveal that he had left town with two horses. There were too many tracks of horses and wagons.

He tossed his saddle gear into the wagon and covered them with blankets, then began work to become the peddler again. His urine-stained clothes were quickly hidden in the back of the wagon, along with the empty gun belt. His goatee was replaced by the peddler's beard, and then he finished the rest of his transformation. He swore at himself again at the realization that one of the heavy eyebrows was missing. He would have to go with his own until he found more among his disguises. Now was not the time to look.

It took a few minutes, but he found another handgun, checked the loads, shoved it into his waistband and mumbled a Persian prayer, really just jibberish he had decided was from his previous life.

Quickly he harnessed the two horses and placed the reloaded Sharps behind the wagon seat, where it could be easily reached. Only then did he put on his coat, keeping his right arm inside his shirt and coat so it looked like it had been amputated. His fingers curled around the butt of the pistol.

It would be so nice to kill Time Carlow. With a snap of the reins, Tanneman headed out of the ravine, making certain his new tracks covered the bay's brief stop.

It would merely look like he was coming to town, as he had done before. How was a slow-witted peddler to know tracks were important? He chuckled.

One more chance at Kileen, that's what he wanted. One more chance. But he wouldn't press it; killing Carlow would more than make up for it. He had already decided that after killing Carlow, he would reenter Strickland as a peddler. Nighttime would be a good time to go to the hospital. This time he would silence that fool boy first. And that Mexican nurse, if she were around.

A half hour down the road, he saw Carlow advancing. The young Ranger had his hand carbine resting over his saddle; his wolf-dog moved ahead of him easily.

Tanneman took a deep breath. Would Carlow suspect him? See through his disguise? No, he reminded himself. There was no reason for the Ranger to suspect the peddler. None at all. He would see what he expected to see. Like everyone else.

Carlow watched the peddler's wagon approach. The wolf-dog growled and he told Chance to stay near him and be quiet. The beast obeyed, but kept baring his white teeth.

"I know what you're thinking, Chance. Be quiet. I get it."

Carlow reined up and held up his hand. "Afternoon, sir. I'm in pursuit of a man. Black hat. Goatee. On a bay. Did you happen to see him?"

"Wal, I sur nuff did, suh," Tanneman said in his best Missouri drawl. "He dun went by me sumthin' fierce. A while back, it were. I jes' was fixin' to head to town."

"Where was he headed?"

Tanneman's hand tightened around his hidden gun, then changed his mind. The pistol was for an emergency only. Trying to shoot through his coat was too risky. Certainly he could clear the gun, but that would take longer. Too long against someone like Carlow with his hand carbine in readiness. Tanneman wanted to kill him outright, not just wound him. An injured Time Carlow would be a nightmare.

Tanneman pointed behind him. "Reckon thataway, suh." He paused and declared, "Got sum tobaccy. Chewin' an' see-gars. Real cheap."

"Not today, thanks," Carlow said, nudged his horse into a lope and rode past.

Tanneman reached behind the seat for the Sharps. He took a deep breath. No. He needed to have a clear shot at the Ranger, not some hurried attempt. Time Carlow was known for his ability with a gun. Some said the young Ranger was better than he was.

The sharp crash told him what he had done before he saw it. The spider jar was shattered, slammed by the butt of his rifle as he retrieved it. He saw the spider move away from the wad of dried grass.

"Oh. Oh, Portland. I'm sorry. So sorry." He looked around for something else to put the spider in, but it had disappeared. His shoulders shook. "Oh well, enjoy the wagon."

He returned his attention to Carlow and climbed down from the wagon. As soon as his boots hit the ground, he knew it was too late. The young Ranger had disappeared into the wash where he had camped. Would he suspect something? Tanneman told himself that was unlikely. All anyone could tell from the wash was that a wagon had been there and that a rider had come through and ridden on. Not even an Apache could read anything more. Besides, Carlow would be in a hurry to catch up with the rider in front of him. That would make him careless.

Should Tanneman turn the wagon around and go after him? Or wait for Carlow to come out of the wash? He didn't like either idea. The Ranger would be suspicious if he rode back, even if he announced his approach with a loud question. Carlow would see the wagon before a clear shot was possible.

Go back to town! Yes, go back to town and, this time, finish off Kileen. It was a perfect idea. No one would pay any attention to him as the peddler. No one ever did. He would be gone before anyone knew what had happened. Then he would plan his next move: to kill Carlow. The young Ranger would be following that horse for hours, maybe days. Eventually the animal would turn toward Strickland, of course, but it might meander for a while after deciding it didn't need to run anymore. He laughed shrilly. Had he dreamed such a strategy? Of course he had.

Climbing back into the wagon, he shoved the rifle back among the other merchandise and wondered if he should look for the spider. Not now. He would look for Portland after he was finished with Kileen. Portland would enjoy hearing that news.

Tanneman snapped the reins and the two wagon horses responded with a trot, then a rough canter. Nightfall was gaining control of the land. The marshal's office was definitely the center of activity as his wagon rolled into town. It looked like a gathering of townsmen had spilled out onto the boardwalk. Light from the marshal's office painted their strained faces.

He chuckled to himself.

As he walked his horses through town, a woman yelled at him from the sidewalk.

"Peddler? Oh, peddler! Please stop."

He was annoyed by the distraction, but reined in his horses.

"Yes, ma'am, kin I be of service?"

The woman straightened her hat and walked away from her husband toward the wagon.

"Peddler, do you have any large pots? I can't find what I'm looking for anywhere in town."

Tanneman bit back his irritation. "No, ma'am. Dun

solt all my big pots. Sorry. Got some tobbaccy for your husban'.'"

The woman halted and shook her head. "No. I'm looking for a large pot. Can't believe I can't find it. I'll just order one from the catalog." She spun on her heels and returned to her husband without another word to Tanneman.

Relieved of the distraction, he continued across town, heading for the hospital. His hidden hand gripped and regripped the Colt resting in his waistband. He stopped the wagon at the rail and gathered a gunnysack from behind the seat. He shoved several small items into it. If he were stopped, he would explain that he was making a delivery for the young Ranger who had purchased candy for the Irishman. He shoved a towel inside the bag as an afterthought; it would help muffle the gunshots.

As he approached the hospital door, a bearded gentleman in a top hat stepped from the shadows. Tanneman hadn't noticed him before. The bearded man's suit and shirt were wrinkled. He leaned on a cane with his left hand; his right was cradled behind his back, in a courtly pose. Tanneman guessed he was the hospital administrator—or possibly a doctor. The decision was a simple one: kill the fool now or kill him when he left.

"Good evening, peddler . . . where are . . . you going? It is . . . getting late." The voice was stilted and slow. Eastern, perhaps.

The top hat's brim was just wide enough—and pulled down enough on his forehead—to shove darkness across most of the bearded man's face. Tanneman avoided his face anyway.

"Evenin' suh. I be bringin' sum sweets to the wounded Ranger inside. His young friend bought them from me—to give him. That be all right?" Tanneman said in his Missouri drawl.

"That is . . . nice. You will . . . have to find . . . your own way. Only a few . . . on duty . . . right now. Eating supper . . . you know," the man said without moving out of the shadows.

"'Course. I shouldna haff trouble," Tanneman said. "If'n I do, I'll come back an' maybe you-all kin he'p me."

"Well, I am not . . . supposed to . . . leave here," the man said. "Someone tried . . . to kill . . . the big Ranger today. In my . . . hospital, no less. Deputy just . . . went to get . . . some supper, so I am . . . standing in . . . for him." He waved his cane. "Not sure . . . what I can do, though, I haven't . . . a gun. Don't believe . . . in them . . . you know."

"Oh my! Did ya git 'im?" Tanneman waved his arm.

The man shook his head and touched his beard. "Oh no. He got . . . away. Say where . . . did you see . . . that young Ranger? He went . . . after him."

Tanneman knew he should have expected this. He pointed toward the south. "He came past my wagon. Outside o' town. Said he were a'chasin' someone—an' asked me to bring his friend this candy. Paid me cash money."

"I see."

Tanneman was anxious to go in, but knew it was smart to act like he wasn't.

"I'll jes' be a minute, suh."

"Did you forget one of your eyebrows?" The gentleman raised his cane and poked it into Tanneman's stomach. His voice was changed. Hard. Challenging. Tanneman knew that voice.

The words jolted Tanneman more than the cane. His left hand went to his face instinctively, then dropped, and he stared at the shadowy figure before him. Time Carlow! How could that be? He was riding in the other direction.

"You're under arrest, Tanneman. For the murders of Judge Cline; District Attorney Johnson; our friend, Ranger Pig Deconer; and for a fine juryman in San Antonio. Probably more. And for attempted murder of my uncle." He lowered the cane as his right arm swung forward. A short-barreled Colt in Carlow's right fist was aimed at Tanneman's midsection.

"Wha . . . suh, ya must have me mistaken for another," Tanneman blurted, trying to regain his composure. His hidden hand tightened around the Colt in his waistband.

"Wasn't sure it was you. Out on the road," Carlow said. "Had a hunch you'd come here. If I was wrong, I was going to start on the trail tomorrow. Your disguise is real good, Tanneman. Real good. Now it's over."

"Suh, I am not this Rose fella ya be expectin'."

"Unbutton your coat real slow," Carlow demanded. "I'd better see that hidden hand opened. Palm up. With nothing in it." He motioned with his gun. "After I left you, I hurried back. The boys at the theater were nice enough to lend me all this."

Orange flame erupted through Tanneman's coat. A split second behind, Carlow's Colt roared three times.

Tanneman's gun fired again. He groaned and toppled to the ground.

The young Ranger stepped next to him, yanked open his coat and pulled the gun from Tanneman's stiffening fingers. His top hat rolled off his head and bounced on the dying ex-Ranger.

"I-I'll b-be back . . . to k-kill you," Tanneman whispered and his head sank to the side. "Hillis . . .

P-Portland . . . B-Barnabas . . . where are you? I've got the mon . . ." His eyes lost their light.

Carlow staggered. It was over. He heard footsteps coming from inside the hospital. His hand was crimson where he held his side, and then he fell.

Chapter Thirty-one

Time Carlow awoke.

He was lying in a hospital bed next to Kileen. He shook his head to clear it of the cobwebs. What had happened to Tanneman Rose? Was he on the run again? Carlow looked down at his stomach; it was wrapped in fresh bandages. His clothes and gunbelt were lying on a table a few feet away. Even his discarded leggings, weathered hat and long coat, taken off for his disguise, were there. The top hat, beard and evening coat were nowhere in sight.

"Time, me son, 'tis good to see you with us again. Been almost two days," Kileen said, watching him from a prone position. His voice was weak, but definitely joyous.

Carlow blinked his eyes to clear them more. His left eye seemed as clear as the right.

Standing at the foot of Carlow's bed was Duval Jonas, so happy to see the young Ranger awake that he couldn't remain quiet any longer.

"Hi, Ranger Carlow. I'm Duval Jonas. Remember?" the boy said.

"Well, I sure do, Duval. How are you doing?"

"I'm fine, Ranger. I helped when that awful man tried to kill . . . Ranger Kileen," Duval recited and pointed at the big Irishman.

Carlow bit his lip. "I know you did, Duval. Thank you for being so brave." He looked over at Kileen. "What happened to Tanneman?"

"Doin' no more bad, me son," Kileen said softly. "He be dead. You shot him. It be over, me son." He crossed himself, shivered and decided not to say anything about the possibility of Tanneman returning.

From the far end of the hospital came a loud stomping as Marshal Bridgeport strutted down the aisle with a sack in his hand. He stopped between the beds of the two Rangers.

"Brought you blokes some candy. Toffee. Absolutely delicious," Bridgeport announced and set them on Carlow's bed, helping himself to a large chunk.

"The doctor said you were lucky. Tanneman's shots were off, probably because he was firing through that bloody coat. Hit you on the side. Just the side," the British lawman declared. "You lost a lot of blood, though." He looked over at Kileen. "You'll be up and around before this big bloke is."

"I'm all right." Carlow sat up. Dizziness reached his head and he lay back. "Well, real soon." He realized what the British marshal had said, and looked over at Kileen and said, "He said I was lucky."

The big Ranger smiled thinly. "Aye."

"Sure. Sure." Bridgeport turned toward Kileen, then back to Carlow. "Found a list in that madman's coat. A list of bloody revenge. Even had Captain McNelly's name on it." He shook his head. "Guess what we found in the peddler wagon? A bunch of wooden masks and a trunk of disguises. Wigs. Beards and the like."

He straightened his chin and announced proudly, "And the bank's money. All of it." He folded his arms and pushed up his chin. "That's not all. There's another whole trunk of the queen's gold and currency in there, too." He shook his head. "Found a big spider. Looked like Tanneman had kept it in a jar. My deputy squashed it."

"So that's where the gold be—from the other banks," Kileen said. "Me knew it weren't no gang." His smile at Carlow took a lot of his energy. "Ye should be knowin' that seein' a spider be good luck. Never be killin' a spider, though. Never. 'Tis room for ye an' he. An' never be cuttin' down its web." He shook his head for emphasis and took several breaths to help him finish the thought. "When I was but a wee lad, a lady told meself that such should not be done. Me be findin' a web in our barn . . . an' I knocked it down. One o' our horses went lame. Aye. 'Tis true."

Smiling, Bridgeport leaned against Carlow's bed. "How did you come onto this Tanneman Rose bloke being the peddler?"

"Should've guessed earlier," Carlow said. "When I saw him on the trail . . . ah, whenever it was . . . I remembered him saying something about Rangers being with you at the Waulken place, the night we arrested Mr. Waulken. There's no way he'd know we were Rangers . . . unless he knew us. But it didn't hit me until then." Carlow licked his lower lip. "Punky said the U.S. marshal was riding a chestnut with white stockings when he came to town. One of Tanneman's horses matched that description." He stopped to regain his breath. "Still . . . I wasn't sure. Him being one-armed and all. So I rode past and curled back into town. Figured on waiting to see what happened when he thought I was out of the way." He took a deep breath. "If he didn't come, I was going to start out again."

"Ah yes, and gathered some bloody props from the drama folks, it seems."

"Yeah. They were most helpful. One lady wanted to come along." He hesitated. "Thought it would help me get close without him running again."

"Too bloody close." Bridgeport glanced over at Kileen and nodded. "There are some people waiting outside, to see you both. Mrs. Waulken, Mrs. Mirabile and her son."

"Ah, 'tis a kind thing they be doin'," Kileen said.

Bridgeport took another piece of toffee and rolled it around in his mouth. "Oh yeah, there's a reporter out there, too. From New York. Says he talked to you before, son. Wants to interview you both."

"Tell him to write about Mrs. Waulken. She'd make a good story," Carlow snapped.

Bridgeport slapped his hand down on the bed, shrugged his shoulders and grinned at such a reaction, and said, "Blimey, I almost forgot. Everyone likes your idea about the lynchers helping out. Even Mrs. Waulken. I think she bloody well is looking forward to managing the lot of them."

Carlow tried to sit up again, this time moving slowly. "Where's Chance?"

Bridgeport explained the wolf-dog and Carlow's horse, as well as Kileen's, were fine and in the stable.

After finishing her duties across the room, Mariah hurried toward them, realizing Carlow was awake. She moved past Bridgeport, close to Carlow's bed, and smiled at him.

"Oh, *Señor* Ranger Carlow. You are awake!"

Bridgeport looked at Kileen and winked.

Another commotion at the far end of the hospital drew their attention. A thin man with a long goatee, looking more like a Presbyterian minister than a legendary lawman, strode confidently down the aisle. He ignored the demands of the head nurse charging behind him, waving her arms. His clothes were of the trail and he looked weary, but determined as always.

"Thunder, that's the captain coming."

Kileen shut his eyes for a moment, then squinted at the advancing figure.

"Sweet mither of Mary."

The head nurse finally stopped and wheeled around when Carlow waved.

Captain McNelly strode to their beds, shaking his head. "What is this? Two of my best Rangers sleeping on the job." His laugh was deep. "We came as soon as we heard." His voice rang through the gray building, making everyone come to attention. "Marshal Bridgeport here was kind enough to wire me with the report. Concise. Well written. I like that." He nodded toward the British lawman, who smiled.

McNelly stepped next to Kileen's bed and held out his left hand in greeting, realizing the big Irishman would be unable to shake hands conventionally with his wounded right arm.

Kileen grabbed it with his own left paw. "Be good to be seein' ye, Captain."

"Good work, Rangers. Tanneman Rose led us on quite a chase—and took the lives of some fine men," McNelly pronounced, looking around the room as he spoke. "Everyone thought it was a gang—and that he was dead. Except you two."

Kileen looked over at his nephew. "Captain, me love. It be Ranger Carlow thinkin' it be Tanneman by hisself. Not meself."

"Yes, I know. He sent me a wire to check out his death. That's when I realized we had been fooled."

Kileen's eyes widened and he stared at Carlow, who only grinned.

Folding his arms, McNelly continued, "The banks

will be notified of your recovery. The law in San Antonio has already been told of the situation and an innocent man has been freed. I'm sorry we were too late to save the German." He frowned. "Thunder, you know the rules. You're off the payroll—until you're ready to ride again."

"Aye. 'Twill be soon."

"I know it will." McNelly's face didn't match his positive response. His mouth a narrow line, he turned toward Carlow and held out his right hand.

The young Ranger gripped it and his gaze met McNelly's steady stare.

"How soon can you ride? We can't wait for Thunder," the intense captain said. "I want to resume our drive to the border. Stop the rustling along there." His right arm moved horizontally in front of him to demonstrate their movement. "We'll cross the Rio Grande if we have to. This has to end."

Carlow straightened his shoulders. "I'm ready now, Captain. It's just a flesh wound."

Her dark eyes flashing anger, Mariah declared, "You are not ready, Ranger Carlow. You haff been hurt *mucho*." Her glare took in McNelly, who actually appeared flustered for a moment.

McNelly shook his head and glanced at Bridgeport, then Kileen. "You heard the young lady. A few more days then."

"Ees better."

"Good." The captain smiled. "There's a bunch of hard-nosed Rangers outside. They've got bets down on how soon these boys'll be back. May they come in?"

"*Si*." She put her hand on Carlow's shoulder and he held it there.

KENT CONWELL

"A great read. Be prepared for adventure."
—*Roundup* on *Chimney of Gold*

As the moon rises, the night riders come out, sweeping over ranches in the valley, bringing fear and intimidation. Someone wants the owners to sell—badly—but like a few other holdouts, Ben Elliott has sworn not to give up his land for any price. So the night riders have upped the stakes. Once they were content to rustle cattle, but now they've moved up to killing livestock…and murdering men. There's only so much a decent man can take. Ben Elliott has reached that point. It's time for him to fight back. It's time for the nights of terror to become…

Days of Vengeance

ISBN 13: 978-0-8439-6226-0

To order a book or to request a catalog call:
1-800-481-9191
Our books are also available at your local bookstore, or you can check out our Web site **www.dorchesterpub.com** where you can look up your favorite authors, read excerpts, glance at our discussion forum, and check out our digital content. Many of our books are now available as e-books!

Based on the immortal hero from the bestselling
Riders of the Purple Sage!

ZANE GREY'S™ LASSITER

BROTHER GUN

JACK SLADE

Lassiter, the solitary hero from Zane Grey's *Riders of the Purple Sage*, became one of the greatest Western legends of all time. Now America's favorite roughrider is back in further adventures filled with gun-slinging action and rawhide-tough characters.

BLOOD BROTHER

Lassiter owed Miguel Aleman for saving his life. To repay the favor, he swears to protect Miguel's troublesome son Juanito. He never thought he'd have to make good on his oath so soon, though. When Juanito kills a horse trader in a drunken brawl, he faces the gallows—unless Lassiter can save him. But the only option Lassiter has is to break the law himself...which might very well leave him swinging right along with his blood brother.

ISBN 13: 978-0-8439-6238-3

To order a book or to request a catalog call:
1-800-481-9191
Our books are also available at your local bookstore, or you can check out our Web site **www.dorchesterpub.com** where you can look up your favorite authors, read excerpts, glance at our discussion forum, and check out our digital content. Many of our books are now available as e-books!

The Classic Film Collection

The Searchers by Alan LeMay

Hailed as one of the greatest American films, *The Searchers,* directed by John Ford and starring John Wayne, has had a direct influence on the works of Martin Scorsese, Steven Spielberg, and many others. Its gorgeous cinematic scope and deeply nuanced characters have proven timeless. And now available for the first time in decades is the powerful novel that inspired this iconic movie. (Coming February 2009!)

Destry Rides Again by Max Brand

Made in 1939, the Golden Year of Hollywood, *Destry Rides Again* helped launch Jimmy Stewart's career and made Marlene Dietrich an American icon. Now available for the first time in decades is the novel that inspired this much-loved movie. (Coming March 2009!)

The Man from Laramie by T. T. Flynn

In its original publication, *The Man from Laramie* had more than half a million copies in print. Shortly thereafter, it became one of the most recognized of the Anthony Mann/Jimmy Stewart collaborations, known for darker films with morally complex characters. Now the novel upon which this classic movie was based is once again available—for the first time in more than fifty years. (Coming April 2009!)

The Unforgiven by Alan LeMay

In this epic American novel, which served as the basis for the classic film directed by John Huston and starring Burt Lancaster and Audrey Hepburn, a family is torn apart when an old enemy starts a vicious rumor that sets the range aflame. Don't miss the powerful novel that inspired the film the *Motion Picture Herald* calls "an absorbing and compelling drama of epic proportions." (Coming May 2009!)

To order a book or to request a catalog call:
1-800-481-9191
Books are also available at your local bookstore, or you can check out our Web site **www.dorchesterpub.com**.

Paul Bagdon

Spur Award-Nominated Author of
Deserter and *Bronc Man*

Pound Taylor had been wandering the desert for days, his saddlebags stuffed with stolen money from an army paymaster's wagon, when he came upon Gila Bend. It was a wide-open town without law of any kind, haven to gunslingers, drifters and gamblers. Pound might just be the answer to a desperate circuit judge's prayers. He'll grant Pound a complete pardon on two conditions. All Pound has to do is become the lawman in Gila Bend. . . and stay alive for a year.

OUTLAW LAWMAN

ISBN 13: 978-0-8439-6015-0

To order a book or to request a catalog call:
1-800-481-9191
Our books are also available at your local bookstore, or you can check out our Web site **www.dorchesterpub.com** where you can look up your favorite authors, read excerpts, glance at our discussion forum, and check out our digital content. Many of our books are now available as e-books!

LOUIS L'AMOUR

For millions of readers, the name Louis L'Amour is synonymous with the excitement of the Old West. But for too long, many of these tales have only been available in revised, altered versions, often very different from their original form. Here, collected together in paperback for the first time, are four of L'Amour's finest stories, all carefully restored to their initial magazine publication versions.

BIG MEDICINE

This collection includes L'Amour's wonderful short novel *Showdown on the Hogback*, an unforgettable story of ranchers uniting to fight back against the company that's trying to drive them off their land. "Big Medicine" pits a lone prospector against a band of nine Apaches. In "Trail to Pie Town," a man has to get out of town fast after a gunfight leaves his opponent dead on a saloon floor. And the title character in "McQueen of the Tumbling K" is out for revenge after gunmen ambush him and leave him to die.

ISBN 13: 978-0-8439-6068-6

To order a book or to request a catalog call:
1-800-481-9191
This book is also available at your local bookstore, or you can check out our Web site **www.dorchesterpub.com** where you can look up your favorite authors, read excerpts, or glance at our discussion forum to see what people have to say about your favorite books.

ROBERT J. CONLEY

FIRST TIME IN PRINT!

NO NEED FOR A GUNFIGHTER

"One of the most underrated and overlooked writers of our time, as well as the most skilled."
—Don Coldsmith, Author of the Spanish Bit Saga

BARJACK VS...EVERYBODY!

The town of Asininity didn't think they needed a tough-as-nails former gunfighter for a lawman anymore, so they tried—as nicely as they could—to fire Barjack. But Barjack likes the job, and he's not about to move on. With the dirt he knows about some pretty influential folks, there's no way he's leaving until he's damn good and ready. So it looks like it's the town versus the marshal in a fight to the finish... and neither side is going to play by the rules!

Conley is "in the ranks of N. Scott Momaday, Louise Erdrich, James Welch or W. P. Kinsella."
—*The Fort Worth Star-Telegram*

ISBN 13: 978-0-8439-6077-8

To order a book or to request a catalog call:
1-800-481-9191
This book is also available at your local bookstore, or you can check out our Web site **www.dorchesterpub.com** where you can look up your favorite authors, read excerpts, or glance at our discussion forum to see what people have to say about your favorite books.

COVERING THE OLD WEST
FROM COVER TO COVER.

Since 1953 we have been helping preserve the American West
with great original photos, true stories, new facts,
old facts and current events.

True West Magazine
We Make the Old West Addictive.

TrueWestMagazine.com
1-888-687-1881

✄ ☐ **YES!**

Sign me up for the Leisure Western Book Club and send my FREE BOOKS! If I choose to stay in the club, I will pay only $14.00* each month, a savings of $9.96!

NAME: _____

ADDRESS: _____

TELEPHONE: _____

EMAIL: _____

☐ I want to pay by credit card.

☐ **VISA**   ☐ **MasterCard**   ☐ **DISCOVER**

ACCOUNT #: _____

EXPIRATION DATE: _____

SIGNATURE: _____

Mail this page along with $2.00 shipping and handling to:
Leisure Western Book Club
PO Box 6640
Wayne, PA 19087
Or fax (must include credit card information) to:
610-995-9274
You can also sign up online at **www.dorchesterpub.com**.
*Plus $2.00 for shipping. Offer open to residents of the U.S. and Canada only.
Canadian residents please call 1-800-481-9191 for pricing information.
If under 18, a parent or guardian must sign. Terms, prices and conditions subject to change. Subscription subject to acceptance. Dorchester Publishing reserves the right to reject any order or cancel any subscription.

GET 4 FREE BOOKS!

You can have the best Westerns delivered to your door for less than what you'd pay in a bookstore or online. Sign up for one of our book clubs today, and we'll send you 4 FREE* BOOKS, worth $23.96, just for trying it out...with no obligation to buy, ever!

Authors include classic writers such as
LOUIS L'AMOUR, MAX BRAND, ZANE GREY
and more; plus new authors such as
**COTTON SMITH, JOHNNY D. BOGGS,
DAVID THOMPSON** and others.

As a book club member you also receive the following special benefits:
- 30% off all orders!
- Exclusive access to special discounts!
- Convenient home delivery and 10 days to return any books you don't want to keep.

Visit **www.dorchesterpub.com**
or call
1-800-481-9191

There is no minimum number of books to buy, and you may cancel membership at any time.
*Please include $2.00 for shipping and handling.